Claiming Their Royal Mate:

THE COLLECTION

Claiming Their Royal Mate:

THE COLLECTION

Andie Devaux

Edited by Smashing Edits

Cover design by Fiona Jayde

First Edition March 2015

Join the author's newsletter for exclusive deals and freebies.

PART ONE

Chapter One

*H*oly crap. How had she accumulated so many clothes that no longer fit?

Barely keeping hold of the bags full of old clothes, Daniella Clark bumped her butt into the door to push it open. Stepping into the hallway, she hit something nearly as hard as the door—something that grunted at the contact. The bags slipped from her fingers to land on the threshold. The hard body she'd run into was attached to a large man blocking her doorway, and her glare didn't seem to ruffle him at all.

The jerk was always in her way lately.

"Jeez. Way to skulk around my door. What do you want, Owen?" Daniella asked, hating the breathiness in her voice.

Her neighbor stared at her for a moment, and his nostrils flared. Something passed behind his gaze. Something that made her breath catch and tension build between her legs. But just as quickly as it appeared, it was gone. And he shrugged, arrogant mask engaged.

"I was just passing by. Not my fault you didn't look where you were going."

The man was seriously aggravating. She could hardly believe they'd been good friends the last year, ever since she'd accidentally locked herself out of her apartment. He'd been kind enough to give her a place to hang out while she'd waited for the building's superintendent to show up with the key. From then on, they'd hung out at least once a week, sometimes more, depending on her schedule. That is, up until a month ago.

"I'm getting sick of you always being in my way, Owen." She picked up the bags, needing something to look at that wasn't her ridiculously hot neighbor. Her attraction to him itself was irritating because he wasn't her type, even if he did make her weak in the knees. His face was hard, chiseled and memorable, but his features were too strong to be considered traditionally handsome—his nose too Roman and his jaw a little too wide. Not to mention he rarely smiled at her anymore, and she liked men who weren't afraid to enjoy life.

Heck, that was why she'd liked his company for so long—his easy laughter and quick wit. Over the last month, it was as if he'd turned into a different man. One who didn't smile much and who was quick to anger.

She tried not to take it personally, but the fact he'd just cut off their friendship, cold as ice, made being the bigger person difficult.

His full head of light brown hair was nice, if always a little too long—as if he were constantly two weeks late to the barber. But he was far bigger than guys she liked to date. Broad and muscled like a man who never left the gym. Although she'd never actually seen him at the gym near their Denver apartment complex, he had to work out somewhere. Men just didn't achieve that level of muscle naturally.

But despite the fact he didn't fit her usual mold, she found herself more than just a little attracted to him.

Of course, that was a hopeless cause if ever there

was one. She'd seen his dates—all two of them—since he'd moved into the building. They were both model thin, and while she was usually pretty proud of her voluptuous form, no one would ever accuse her of being waif-like.

Her attraction had started with a tremor. Just the slightest quavering of her voice when she spoke to him. Then, just when she'd started looking at him differently, he'd shut down. Stopped talking to her, started making excuses for why he couldn't hang out with her anymore. But he always seemed to be *around*. At her door when she walked out. Looking irritated to run into her in the parking lot.

"I was walking through a shared hallway. Would you prefer I jump out the window to get to my truck?" A hint of a smile touched his lips, and her breath caught.

Freaking-A. No way was a simple smile turning her on. She was really starting to dislike her neighbor. "I'd love for you to jump out a window or two. Heck, I'll even help with a little push."

And she wasn't lying. Sure, she wouldn't really push a man out a window, but something inside of her—the part that was continuously horny, lately—was also feeling pretty violent. It came out at the weirdest times, and it took every ounce of her self-control not to lash out. Probably she needed to go see her doctor about a new birth control or something. Out of whack hormones were likely the cause of her wild emotions.

Not that Owen was helping. He'd chased off two of her dates in the last month. Not by doing anything she could call him out for. No, he was too subtle for that. He'd just drop in to borrow sugar—when she'd never once seen the man bake. Or he'd say he thought he'd smelled gas coming from her apartment, and wanted to check. Then he'd glower in a way that made her dates run for the hills.

And then he started showing up at her apartment when she was feeling particularly...needy.

"Surely you wouldn't want to see me injured." His nose flared again, as if he couldn't get enough of her smell. It was seriously disturbing.

Even more disturbing was the sudden wetness between her legs and the tension coiling in her belly. She really needed to get some if a man she didn't even like could get her engine revving by *smelling* her. "I wouldn't bet on that."

"You'll be happy I'm around, Daniella. Very soon."

She tried to shove past him, but he moved out of her way before they touched, quick for such a large man. Part of her regretted the lack of contact, but the rest of her thought that part was batshit crazy.

Through narrowed eyes, Owen Shaw watched Daniella walk away. Her shapely hips swayed as she walked, and the scent surrounding her was nearly irresistible to him. As it would be to any of their kind who got within a few hundred feet of her. She had to be claimed. Soon.

If only to keep her safe.

After Daniella disappeared from his view, he hurried back to his apartment to watch her make her way to the back parking lot. He would have offered to take the bags, but she would have reacted the same way she did when he offered to do anything for her — with barely concealed irritation.

It was his own fault, for getting close to her. But it had seemed like the easiest way to watch over her until the heat took hold. And he had to admit, he liked her company. She was easy to laugh with, and utterly silly behind closed doors. Or she had been, when he'd allowed himself to spend time with her. Now, she mostly stared daggers and sniped at him. He couldn't blame her.

His own reaction to her was to blame. Her rising heat had brought on him a wave of lust, the likes of which he'd never dealt with before. Not that he hadn't been around women in heat before—although usually only ones in the beginning clutches of it since they were soon whisked away to private locations by their mates or a male willing to father children soon after. But none of those women had called to him the way Daniella did. As Erick's second, many would have gladly taken him to father their children, but he'd resisted.

He'd always wanted a real mate. And something inside of him refused to settle for having children in any other way.

Weretigers lived a somewhat cloistered life. His people lived in the Colorado Rockies, keeping their small clan out of the way of humans, and away from the city life that appealed most to their greatest threat—the vampires. But their cabins dotted a large territory, so it wasn't difficult for a pair to get away from the population when a female's heat hit. That distance kept fights for the right to claim females to a minimum, and quelled the tempers that flared in the men around them as they vied for dominance.

But getting away right now wasn't an option for him.

Resisting Daniella had been difficult when she'd simply been a beautiful woman with curves to die for, but now it was impossible.

So he did his best asshole impression—not difficult, considering his dick was hard half the time with no relief in sight, and he ached to claim her something fierce—to keep her at a safe distance.

He admired her independent spirit. And her stolid resistance to what had to be a steadily building lust for him surprised him. He didn't take the attraction personally, even though a small part of him wished he could. It was simple biology. She was coming into her first heat. And he was the only male of their kind nearby.

Humans couldn't satisfy her lust properly, and instinctually she likely knew that, but he'd kept any suitors away, anyway. As for other non-humans, none were likely to appeal to her instincts the same way as a tiger, but he watched all the same. A female were of any kind in heat was vulnerable, needy. Not to mention irresistible to any male who could smell her sweet scent.

Which was why he had to avoid her as much as possible. Why he'd had to end their friendship. But it also was why he still had to stay close enough to protect her.

She deposited the bags in her trunk and then swiped her hands on her thighs to rid herself of germs she didn't even realize couldn't hurt her. His cock swelled at the sight of her perfect ass. She had him so worked up all the time with her erotic scent that the briefest glimpse of her made him excited.

She headed back toward the building, and he watched her until she disappeared. The desire to leave his apartment, to meet her along the route to her home, to make sure she made it safely, was overwhelming. But it would be too easy to do more.

And that wasn't *his* right.

No. He'd do his duty. Protect her. Watch over her. Keep her safe. And hope to hell Erick would get here in time.

Erick should have come months before, instead of

sending Owen to watch over her. But his best friend and prime of their weretiger clan was methodical and logical; he wasn't driven by passion or even empathy. He wanted to wait until her acceptance of him wouldn't even be a question. Until she was so driven by need she would beg for him to take her.

By leaving her here in the human world, far away from where most of their clan lived, Erick avoided the risk of losing her affections to another of their kind. Her tiger would be attracted to Erick's power, of that there was no doubt. But if Erick brought her to their territory too soon and her human self fell for another, Erick would have no choice but to challenge the male.

And there were too few weretigers left as it was.

Hell, their numbers were barely sufficient to hold the territory against other shifters and vampires who sought to make them into unusual, pricy pets.

Mating wasn't necessarily permanent, but it often made both parties feel affection for the other, and attachment wasn't uncommon. It could be resisted, but many times a couple remained paired beyond the initial heat. It was a reality that Erick was counting on. Like real tigers, weretigers weren't always driven by animal instincts to live in clans or remain in couples, but their human sides did make it likely.

If nothing else, Erick hoped she would throw herself at him during her first heat. A heat he'd take advantage of by breeding her relentlessly until she carried his cub. After that, Erick would have little interest in her until she was in another heat. He made no effort to hide his goal—securing another generation of royal leaders.

Owen buried the growl in his throat at the thought.

It wasn't right, the approach Erick was taking, even if Owen could see the logic in it. Erick needed to stay with the clan, keep them together as only a royal could. So Owen would guard her. Keep her safe until it was time to call Erick. It was his duty.

But he wouldn't touch her, even if his dick never forgave him.

Chapter Two

She hurt. Ached. *Needed.*

Daniella's eyes flew open and she blinked against the darkness filling her room. She gulped air into her lungs. Had she been dreaming? She wasn't sure. Whatever the cause, it was almost impossible to breathe around the wanting.

Two days had passed since she'd literally run into Owen outside of her apartment, and she hadn't been able to get him out of her mind. Part of her felt empty, and that emptiness had grown into all-out need. But was it real? Or was she just horny and missing their friendship? It was possible she was transferring her feelings, mixing things up in her head.

She'd considered calling an ex-boyfriend. Surely one of them wouldn't mind coming by for a quickie. But the idea didn't excite her. Something inside of her insisted none of them would do. And even touching herself in the shower, slipping her own small finger inside her constantly aching sex, had only given her a moment's reprieve.

"What the hell?" she whispered, her voice a wisp of its normal strength. But the darkness around her was silent.

Screw this. She was done waiting for whatever it was that her body needed.

Owen. He was the answer to this. She had to talk to him.

She pulled herself out of bed onto shaky legs. She'd slept naked—odd for her, but she hadn't been able to stand the feel of clothing against her skin the last two nights. The soft material of the robe she pulled on teased her sensitive skin. Caressed it. She bit her lip against a moan.

A voice in the back of her mind protested. This wasn't her. She'd never leave her apartment wearing only a short, thin robe, especially not to see her frustrating jerk of a neighbor.

But that voice was only a whisper against the need raging through her body.

She struggled into the hallway and banged on his door; the sound hurt her sensitive ears. Three knocks and the door opened.

Owen stood in the doorway, his large, muscular body bare save for a pair of boxer briefs. He pulled her inside, a motion so quick she barely felt his hands grip her arms before he released her on the other side of the doorframe. Then he wasn't touching her. Instead, he peered out into the hallway, as if he thought she might not be alone.

"Are you all right? Did someone—"

"What the hell is wrong with me?" That wasn't what she'd meant to ask, dammit. There was no real reason to believe Owen would have any idea what ailed her, but her instincts screamed he knew the answer.

Or maybe she was just confused. She couldn't even manage a rational conversation at the moment. She clenched her hands into fists to keep herself from reaching out and touching him. And *oh,* how she wanted to touch the man who even now made her angry. Feel the muscles barely contained by his skin. Take in his scent, which teased the edge of her senses.

He stared at her, then took a long breath. His eyes widened. "Ah, hell, Daniella."

The simple act of him saying her name pushed her blood pressure up a notch. She licked her lips and took an involuntary step toward him before stopping herself in her tracks.

"What is wrong with me?" She ground out every word.

"It's not my place to say." He shut the door behind him, turning his back to her.

She laughed, but the sound held no amusement. She was about ready to either jump out of her skin, or shove this man who she didn't even care for to the ground so she could screw him seven ways from Sunday, and he was keeping *secrets?*

"Tell me!"

"It's—you're special. There's something that your adoptive parents never prepared you for, didn't know to prepare you for. But I'm only here to keep you safe. I can't go into any more detail." His eyes met hers, more amber than brown, and just his gaze sent a jolt of lust through her body.

"Fuck your secrets." Her sex ached so badly that it hurt. And he smelled good, so damn good. Like a twisted mix of man and cinnamon. She wasn't sure if she wanted to sleep with him or eat him. She pressed her thighs together, but the pressure only served to make her sensitive skin more inflamed.

His eyes narrowed in understanding. "Dammit. You're in full heat. Come with me."

He led her to a couch and had her sit. But she couldn't sit—pressure seemed to only make it worse. So she lay down instead. The world was surreal, and Owen's scent seemed to inundate the couch—a deep, masculine scent that teased her desire. A murmured voice caressed her ears and she realized he was on the phone.

What had he said—full heat? She had no clue what that could be. Was he calling an ambulance? She might be ill. She certainly didn't feel right, although she didn't feel sick, either. Could she have been poisoned? The pipes in the apartment building had to be old as dirt, probably filled with lead. Maybe she'd been drugged. But she hadn't left her apartment all day, so how was that possible? Time-released Ecstasy wasn't a thing, as far as she knew. It felt as though something—something outside of herself, outside of her control—was assaulting her.

"I'm going to try to help you," Owen said, his voice strained.

Daniella opened her eyes and blinked against the brightness. She hadn't noticed him approaching.

"Need you," she managed.

"I know, kitten. I can't give you that. But I can help you. Maybe make it not hurt so much. But to do that I have to touch you." His voice deepened and her sex throbbed in response. "Do you want me to help you?"

"Please," she said, her voice a whisper.

He tugged on the belt of her robe, and then slid it open with a hiss. Only vaguely did she realize she was naked in front of her annoying neighbor. Her former friend. Full breasts jutting out, her nipples were hard as rocks, as if they begged for his attention. And her core ached, electricity springing from it as if his gaze alone excited whatever it was inside of her that needed quenching.

"Goddamn, you're beautiful," he said, reverently.

He took one of her nipples into his mouth and suckled. She moaned and slid her fingers through his hair, pulling at it. Begging him silently to do more. Faster. More pressure.

He responded by moving to her other nipple and sucking harder. He bit down softly as his hand slid down to cup her sex, pressing only the slightest bit against her hard nub.

"Owen," she cried out, not even recognizing her own voice. She came immediately, a flash of colors and light crisscrossing her vision.

He growled in response and rubbed her softly with his palm, pulling small aftershocks from her.

"That won't be enough," he muttered, as if to himself. But he pulled the sides of her robe back over her, hiding her body from his view. He didn't get up from where he crouched by her on the couch, but he settled his hands on either side of her.

He was right. It wasn't enough. Already she could feel the hunger just sated building again. But she could think better. Not clearly, by any means, but any ability to think was an improvement.

"Owen, what's happening? Please, tell me." Her pride bristled at the pleading tone in her voice. But she needed to know, and now. Because the desire was already pooling between her legs and crawling along her skin.

His expression was hard, as if he would refuse her again. But when his gaze locked onto hers, his face softened. "You're not a normal woman, Daniella. When you hit maturity, your first heat began. Only sex with one of your own can sate the lust."

"One of my own? I don't understand. And what

do you mean, maturity? This only started a couple of weeks ago, and I'm well into maturity."

"It doesn't hit like clockwork, at an exact age. But generally between nineteen and twenty-two, our women start going into heat. It's not usually a problem, because we live in a community. There are men around to…take care of things, when the heat hits. But you're different, Daniella. You weren't raised with us."

"I was adopted," she murmured, mind racing. It was getting harder to think again. She squirmed, but the pressure only grew. "I'm twenty-three."

"You're a little older than normal. But like I said, it's not clockwork. It's all hormones, and hormones are unpredictable."

She squirmed a bit, unable to help herself. Why did he have to rest his hands at her sides, when she needed his touch?

A haze settled over her vision, and he cursed under his breath. Suddenly the explanation didn't seem so important. The why didn't matter. Only the need.

"Owen," she mumbled.

"I know, beautiful."

She watched him this time, as he opened her robe. The amber flecks she'd noticed before in his eyes seemed to no longer be flecks; instead, the light amber appeared to overtake his irises, so that they were almost golden.

His gaze raked over her body again, and it made her already sensitive flesh burn. Suddenly, she didn't feel limp. Didn't feel stuck to the couch. Didn't feel weak.

If she didn't move, she might crawl out of her skin.

She took his mouth with her own, and after a moment's hesitation, he kissed her back. His tongue slid against hers, softly testing at first, then with a fervor that made her cling to him. He tasted like peppermint.

She moaned into his mouth when he pulled her close. His body was cool against hers, or maybe whatever was wrong with her made her unnaturally hot.

With her legs wrapped around his waist, she could feel his erection pressed against where she needed it most. How could she ache for him this much? There was no doubt that he was attractive. He was the kind of man wet dreams were made of—tall and muscular and sexy as sin. But he irritated her with his constant presence, despite turning his nose up at their friendship, and his annoyingly standoffish nature. But none of that seemed to matter to her body.

Pushing her thoughts aside, she shimmied against him, rubbing her clit against the hard cock she could feel beneath his boxer briefs. His hands gripped her hips almost painfully hard, and she cried out in triumph.

"No!"

He tossed her and she had a moment of panic where she felt weightless, but she landed on something soft. A mattress. When had they gotten to his bedroom?

In a flash, she was back on him. Hands on his ass, pressing herself against his hardness. Seeking his delicious mouth with her own.

"None of that, kitten." But his hips arched against her, sliding his thickness against her soft skin.

She bit at him, a warning snap at his face. Something inside of her was wild, raging. And it wanted out. It wanted Owen. To hurt him or fuck him. Maybe both.

His hand dug into her hair and pulled hard. She cried out at the flash of pain.

"I can't take you. You're going to have to accept what I *can* give you."

Her body screamed at her to fight him. To take what was hers. But he pushed her onto the bed, easily controlling her flailing movements with his much larger frame.

But when his hand touched her mound softly, she stilled.

"That's it, kitten. Relax. I'll take care of you."

But instead of his mere touch bringing her to orgasm, it only made her more needy, and she ground against his hand. He gave her a swift kiss, tongue only brushing against her own, and met her gaze with his golden eyes. Then, very purposefully, he lowered his head between her legs.

His tongue touched her, flickering out against her clit, and she gasped. Over and over he teased her, running his tongue around her entrance and sucking on her most sensitive spot, before pulling back to watch her reaction.

Unlike the first time he'd made her come, he seemed to want to draw her out. Not just give her momentary relief, but also torment her along the way. Enjoying her reactions while he tortured her. He worked her with his mouth, one hand reaching up to cup her breasts, to tease her nipples.

She moaned and writhed and gasped his name, but he refused to be rushed. Drawing her out with quick licks and the barest of touches, he reached behind her to grab the nape of her neck, forcing her to hold still with his free hand while he worked.

"Owen, please!" She was hot, so hot, burning for release. Her whole body was swollen and needy and empty.

"You want to come?" he asked, voice low. But it wasn't really a question. He knew what she needed, but for some reason wanted to hear it from her lips. She made a mewling sound, the closest thing to words she could summon.

He leaned back down, and she could feel his fingers probing around her entrance, but no matter how she squirmed, he refused to penetrate her. Instead, he sucked on her clit, hard. Teeth nipped her, and she flew over the edge into oblivion.

He felt her spasm, and with her taste in his mouth, he almost said to hell with it and took her. How right it felt to have her shuddering beneath him. To have her calling his name. Like she was his.

Mine.

No. Thoughts like that would get him into trouble. He had a duty here. And his honor wouldn't allow him to give in to his own desires.

He helped her sit up on the bed, and she pulled the robe tightly around her body, tying the belt and glancing around the room, eyes wide and dazed. But she seemed to be able to focus better. Good.

"Owen?" Her voice was sleepy and sated. "Tell me more. Tell me what I am."

It wasn't his place, but he couldn't bring himself to deny her again. Not when she was already so vulnerable. Not after she'd already given him so much of herself. "You're a weretiger."

She blinked at him. "What?"

He took in a deep breath and regretted it immediately when her floral scent filled his nose, mixed with the spicy smell of her heat, and the intoxicating scent of her arousal.

"We're human—mostly. But over time, we develop tiger characteristics."

"So you're saying I'm like a werewolf or something?" Her tone was doubtful, and he could hardly blame her. This wasn't the way to show her what she was. He should have kept his mouth shut and waited until they were somewhere safe enough for a demonstration. But it was too late now, the cat—tiger—was out of the bag.

"No, not exactly. You aren't bound by the moon or anything. And most of us can't turn completely. The weakest of our kind eventually develop tiger traits— the strength or speed or claws. Most of us can turn partially at will. Only the purest bloodlines can shift into actual tigers."

"This is insane."

"Daniella—"

"You're insane." Her voice rose to a yell and she jumped off the bed to stand in front of him. Her fear was gone—he was glad to see that—but anger had replaced it. "What the hell are you even saying? Are you nuts or are you just messing with me?"

Shit. He had to show her. Something small, at least. Otherwise she might try to run. Hell, she might try to run after he showed her what he was, too. In that case, he'd have to wrestle her down.

Oh, yeah, smart. Wrestle down the woman in heat. See how that ends for you. You'll be inside her in two seconds flat, fucking her for all you're worth.

"Daniella. Look at me." He wasn't a royal—a tiger who could fully shift—but he wasn't far from it.

Concentrating on his face, he forced images of his other form—a partial tiger—into the forefront of his mind. And with it, he pushed with his mind. His flesh moved, and the sensation distracted him. He almost forgot why he was shifting until a squeak of fear brought him back to himself.

Daniella had fallen back. She sat on the edge of the bed, wide-eyed and unblinking, her mouth partially open

"You're—"

"A weretiger. Like you."

"But—your face." She stared at him, fascinated, but no horror crossed her features. Instead, she simply appeared stunned, and more than a little intrigued.

He knew what his face looked like, and her reaction sent a rush of joy through him. If she hadn't been shocked, he would have been surprised. It *wouldn't* have surprised him, though, if she'd been disgusted.

Not that he was a bad-looking weretiger. In fact, he liked to joke with his Erick that he got the best of both creatures. Cat-like features on a very human frame, and unlike most of his kind, he could shift parts of himself without shifting into his entire partial form—handy if you needed a sharp claw but no whiskers. But he couldn't turn into a full tiger.

Which was why she couldn't be his. No matter how much he wanted her.

A shudder ran through her body. She glanced away from him and clutched her arms, hugging herself.

He was by her side before he could think better of it, kneeling in front of where she sat on the bed, and when she looked up, she started.

"Oh, sorry," he said, then closed his eyes to concentrate on changing his face back to fully human.

When he opened his eyes, she stared at him, their faces only inches apart.

"That was cool." The tiniest of grins blossomed on her face. "I wasn't sure if I should run away or pet you."

He smiled at her and she licked her lips.

Damn.

"I need to make a phone call." He pushed up from the floor. Yes, a call. Before he asked her to pet him.

"Wait."

Barely trusting himself to not do something stupid, he turned to face her. She was so pretty in the delicate robe. So sexy. So vulnerable.

He could still taste her.

"This…heat. Or whatever. How do we make it go away?" she asked.

"Sex," he said, simply, but he clenched his hands at his sides to keep from reaching for her. Sex wouldn't actually bring her out of the heat, but it would give her a long reprieve. Maybe long enough to get through the heat. Maybe.

"Then why —"

"Because you aren't meant for me. You belong to my best friend."

Chapter Three

"What?" Anger rolled through her, pushing back some of the pulsating lust threatening to overwhelm her again. She jumped off his bed and stalked toward him. "What do you mean, I *belong* to your best friend? I'm my own person, Owen. No one owns me."

"There are things happening here that you don't understand."

"Explain them to me." How dare he? She was her own person. And this the twenty-first century.

"You have the ability to turn into a full tiger — or you will, with some training and practice. That's rare, Daniella. Full tigers are known as royals among our people — even though they aren't necessarily from the same bloodline. They breed with other royals. They keep our people strong." Belief filled his eyes — he believed what he said was true, that this insane tradition was somehow necessary. But there was guilt there, too.

"So, what? I'm supposed to have a litter of kittens with a stranger for the good of some people I don't even know? People I couldn't care less about at this point?" The idea of it was so humiliating, so disgusting, she could barely wrap her mind around it.

"Yes. We're not a fertile species—children are difficult to conceive, and impossible outside of the time when the female is in heat. Your first heat is the most powerful, and the most fertile time of your life. If we could give you more time—"

"This whole thing is bullshit." Give her time? As if her time was theirs to give? She paced the room, finally noticing her surroundings. Other than the bed and a small dresser tucked into one corner, the room looked uninhabited. He'd been here nearly a year, since not long after she moved in. And it looked like he could have just moved in. It was all temporary for him. Just like watching her—a temporary duty. Something in her chest twisted at the thought.

"It's the way things are done. For the good of the whole."

"Well, screw your ways." She stopped pacing, careful to stay a few feet away from him. Her voice softened, and she hated herself a little bit for asking because it probably sounded desperate, but it had to be said. "Why not you?"

"I have good control for a shifter—more powerful than most—but I can't make a full change. I'm no royal. But my best friend is. That fact makes him our prime. Our leader."

"Why is that so important? The full change thing?"

"It's not easy to explain, but it's not really about the form itself—it's about the power it represents." He paused, thinking. "Tigers don't congregate well. We aren't pack animals, like the wolves. It takes a powerful prime, a royal or—even better—a mated pair of royals to keep a clan together."

That made sense, sort of. But why did they need to keep their people together? She almost asked, but her thoughts shifted to something far more important to her, far more personal. "How do you know I'm one of you—let alone I'm a...royal, or whatever?" A small, nervous laugh escaped her. "I've never changed into anything. What makes you so sure? I mean, how can you be certain?" The pitch of her voice rose with every word. She was on the edge of a major freak out—she could feel the panic growing in her chest. Concentrating on the details helped.

"If only one of your parents was a pureblood, you could go either way—royal or partial shifter. Those pairings are rare, because tigers raised among the clan know the importance of keeping royal bloodlines pure, but they do happen rarely. Like with my parents." He cleared his throat. "When two royals breed, their children are nearly guaranteed to be royals. Both of your parents were purebloods, both royals."

Were—not are. He referred to her parents in past tense. The questions were on the tip of her tongue. She'd wondered about her birth parents off and on since she'd found out as a teenager that she'd been adopted. But the importance of it had faded as she grew older—or she thought it had.

She couldn't form the questions. Something about it felt like a trap. Like if she opened that door, he'd have her. He'd have something else to use to convince her of this madness.

"So you got the short end of the genetic stick," she said, instead.

"Yes, unlike Erick," he said. "Of course, he had two royal parents, so his lineage wasn't quite the lottery mine was."

"Well, screw your friend."

"That's the idea." He gave her a small grin, but she refused to smile at his joke.

"Oh, fuck you, Owen." She shook her head hard. "No. I'm not having sex with some stranger."

His smile disappeared. "You will, Daniella. You won't have a choice."

She stopped pacing and stared at him. "What is that supposed to mean?"

"He'll be here by morning. The heat will be back by then, in full." His tone turned almost angry and his face hardened. "You'll want him, then. You'll need him. Hell, you'll be ready to beg for it."

She flew at him and slapped him across the face with all her strength and ire. He didn't react to the slap; his head barely moved before his gaze returned to hers. But something behind his eyes took notice. And it was feral.

Inside of her, something reacted to the thing behind his eyes. Whatever it was, it wanted to attack him again. Push him. See if he was worthy.

What the fuck?

Panic rushed through her. He was right. The way she'd felt around him the last few hours…if it got worse and she was presented with a man who elicited in her the same rush of need as Owen, she'd be lost. And some part of her wanted it. The tiger part—if she could believe Owen.

No. She wasn't a tiger. And she definitely wasn't going to let hormones of any kind decide her fate.

"Fine, then, I'll leave. Unless you plan on trying to keep me here by force," she said.

A flash of something crossed his hard features. Regret? She couldn't be sure.

"Of course not. I'm not a kidnapper. But there are

dangers out there, Daniella. Frightening things that would love the chance at a vulnerable weretiger."

"Like what?"

"Vampires, for one. We're rare, and quite valued as pets. And worse things."

Her laugh was hysterical, but she was beyond caring. "Vampires. Of course. Why wouldn't there be vampires, too?"

He didn't reply, and she blinked back the tears threatening to blind her. Time was of the essence; even as her anger faded slightly, the lust inside of her surged. Soon, she wouldn't be able to think clearly.

"Fine," she said, looking away from him. She swiped at a single tear that had escaped to run down her cheek. "I thought that we had something here. Or, I did, before you quit talking to me and started treating me like some sort of pariah."

"Daniella—"

"No." He didn't get to talk. Didn't deserve the chance to placate her with his excuses—his bullshit traditions and medieval people. "If you don't care enough to claim me for yourself, then I guess your best friend will have to do. Hopefully, he's more of a man than you are. Or is that more of a tiger than you?" Hysteria lurked inside, barely under her control.

She looked up to see a mixture of shock and rage and lust crossing his features. His hands shook at his sides, and he looked like he wasn't sure if he wanted to hit her or fuck her.

"You don't know how hard this is. I do care about you. It makes this a million times more difficult. But my duty—"

"Is more important than me. What I want. More important, even, than what you want. I get it." She shook her head, pain building in her chest that had nothing to do with her so-called heat. "Stupid thing is, I wanted you before this heat thing started. And I was dumb enough to hope that you wanted me, too."

A low growl cut through the air. Before she even registered he'd moved, he was on her. His lips met hers, ferocious and demanding. He didn't ask—he took.

The heat surged in her, immediately reacting to his onslaught. No matter how angry she was with him, her body still wanted his. And deep down, she cared about Owen. Sex with someone she cared about, someone she wanted even without this stupid heat, was infinitely more appealing to her than sex with a total stranger, especially in this insane situation.

He pulled her against him, and for once his body felt as hot as her own. Skin crawling with need, she wrapped herself around him, molding her body to his, returning his kiss eagerly.

Then she was on the bed, his large body covering hers, his hands cradling her face.

"Do you have any idea how much I've wanted you?" he said, his voice gruff. "All those nights of watching old movies. The days of watching you, making sure you were safe."

"No," she said, honestly. There had been times when she thought she'd felt the weight of his gaze, only to glance at him and find he wasn't even looking at her. "The women I saw you bring home…you were good at hiding it. "

"I had to be. And those women were nothing to me, but I needed…otherwise, I might have come to you, and I couldn't risk that. But I didn't fuck them. I couldn't."

The question was on the tip of her tongue. What exactly had he done with those women? Lust shifted in her chest, colored by a sudden spike of jealousy. Her rational mind knew she shouldn't be jealous—they hadn't been a couple, or even dating. And she'd been the epitome of off limits to him.

But she didn't care. She was jealous anyway.

His hand slid up to cup her breast and lust rushed back. She hadn't even noticed her robe had opened at some point while they kissed. A shudder ran through her as he slid a rough thumb over her nipple. "There wasn't a single night you were here that I didn't have to struggle against a hard-on."

"You really wanted me that much?" she whispered, trying to maintain the thread of their conversation while her mind fragmented, seeking only the sensations his body could bring.

A low chuckle escaped him. "If you knew how many times I've thought of you. How many times I've had to jack off just to keep myself from breaking your door down and taking you."

An image flashed in her mind. Owen in the shower, stroking the long, hard cock she could feel against her thigh while thinking of her. Coming with her name on his lips.

Damn.

Her sex clenched at the thought, and she kissed him so he'd stop looking at her. So he wouldn't see how crazed the idea made her. But he pulled back, grinning.

"You like that, don't you?" Owen asked, not at all fooled. "The idea of me thinking of you. You want to know what I imagined? Your lips, stretched around my cock. Your pussy, hot and wet and waiting for me. Licking your pussy while you beg me to take you. I've got a million fantasies surrounding you, Daniella. Taking you every way possible." His lips brushed her ear, sending a tingle down her neck. "I intend to explore every one of those fantasies. And more."

The heat pulsed through her, mixing with her own desire, and she writhed against his hard, immoveable frame as his tongue plunged into her mouth.

He kissed and licked his way down the curve of her neck, and she slid her hands down his muscled back. Everywhere he touched, it felt like electricity flowed from him into her. Sparking and shooting pulses straight to her core.

"Need you, Owen." She gritted her teeth against the sensation. She felt empty. Swollen. Like she might burst if he wasn't inside of her right this instant.

But Owen wouldn't be hurried. He pulled her nipple into his mouth and sucked hard.

As the pain mixed with pleasure almost pushed her over the edge, she cried out and gripped his hair He growled and licked her other nipple. It was almost too much, everywhere but where she needed him most. She writhed beneath him, trying to ease the unbearable pressure building in her core. But he refused to touch her between her legs; instead, he took his time with her, as if they had all the time in the world.

His rough hands and soft mouth slid down the curvature of her neck, over her breasts, and across her abdomen. He kissed her mouth softly, tasting her, before returning to his barrage on the rest of her body.

Tears pricked her eyes, the need building to such a degree that her mind wasn't sure if it was pleasure or pain.

"Owen," she managed, her voice carrying all the desperation she felt.

"What do you need, kitten?"

Their gazes locked. He wasn't as unaffected as his onslaught had suggested. His irises appeared almost inhuman, and his expression was animalistic, despite his very human appearance.

"Need you. Please."

His hand went between them and her hips surged up, trying to meet it. But he was prepared for her response, and he pulled his hand back.

"None of that," he said, and the authority in his voice stilled her.

"Good," he murmured, never moving his gaze from hers. Very softly, his hand slid against her, grazing her clit softly. She moaned, almost beyond thought. And when the thick digit slid inside her, she bucked against him.

"What do you want, beautiful?"

She writhed and moaned, unable to form words.

His hand moved from where he'd teased her to grab her hair and tug. The small bit of pain sent a shot of need straight to her sex, but also brought her a bit of focus.

"Say it," he said.

What did he want her to say? She struggled to think.

"Tell me you want me to fuck you."

Part of her rebelled against the command in his tone, but her body shivered in need, and the authority in his voice only made the need worse.

"Please," she managed.

"Please what?" His voice offered none of the softness his gentle assault had just shown her body.

"Fuck me."

He growled, and the next thing she knew, he'd flipped her around, onto her hands and knees. Her robe was gone. She looked over her shoulder, and saw him shimmy out of his boxer briefs. The material was wet — from her excitement or his, she wasn't sure. His cock bobbed between his legs, hard and thick and long enough to make her knees shake.

He closed the short distance between them, his face a mask of concentration and lust. He slid a hand down her back and then gripped her hip, holding her still. She could feel him, sliding the tip of his hard dick over her entrance, and a low cry escaped her. She arched her back, trying to take him.

She let out a scream from the sudden fullness, the almost perfect rush of satisfaction that rolled over her. The orgasm hit, pounding through her from where they were joined to touch every part of her body. Distantly, she could feel him start to move.

Somewhere around the time she'd admitted wanting him before the heat hit, he'd made a decision. His honor was important, as was his promise to his best friend. His clan. But Daniella was more important. What she wanted mattered more than anything else.

And she wanted *him.*

With her pussy holding him tight, it was all he could do to stay still. To give her body a chance to get used to his hardness filling her. He wanted to kick himself for not going slower, for not easing himself into her trembling body. But her heat and the simple fact that he'd dreamed about this moment for months didn't allow for slowness.

He started to move as soon as her body quit shaking from the orgasm. God, she was beautiful. Body touched with sweat and smelling of sex and floral shampoo and woman.

His woman.

Slowly, he rolled his hips against her, moving as carefully as he could manage. He'd already pushed himself into her like a rutting bull; he needed to slow back down, make sure it was as good for her as it was for him—better. He couldn't live with himself if he hurt her.

She moaned, long and low when he moved, and he stopped.

"Are you all right?" He didn't even recognize his own voice, taut with the strain of holding himself back.

She turned her head and looked at him over her shoulder, swollen lips turned up in a small grin. "Harder."

He snarled. "I'm trying not to hurt you."

"Did I ever tell you I like it rough?" she asked, voice breathy. Words hanging in the air, she pushed back, impaling herself on him fully. His balls brushed her clit, and she moaned again.

"Damn," he ground out.

He couldn't resist her demands. Her sexiness. Her ass trying to grind against him. God, she was so wet and hot and tight.

Gripping her hips hard, he started to fuck her.

Despite her words, he moved slowly at first, building a delicious rhythm that was both the greatest pleasure and the worst torture he'd ever inflicted upon himself. He watched his cock slide in and out of her wetness, her back arched to take him as deeply as she could, and the sight was almost too much for him to take.

When her cries grew breathier and louder, and the buildup inside him became almost painful, he moved faster. Thrusting in and out of her, as he'd imagined doing since the day he'd met her. One hand gripping her hips, he slipped the other around to pinch her clit.

With a low cry, she came again. Her pussy clenched around him and her body shuddered with release. Control already slipping, he let go.

Inside his mouth, his canines grew long, brushing his bottom lip as he gritted his teeth. Had to claim her. Make her his.

He lashed out, sinking his teeth into her neck as he held her hips with both hands in a hard grip. Awareness of anything but her disappeared, and he pumped into her, fucking her as hard as he could, any reason or concern utterly lost to him. Only the need to come inside her—*his* mate—mattered. Only the sensation of filling her body mattered. Only solidifying their connection mattered.

Poison pumped through his teeth and into her neck. In his arms, her body went stiff, then soft, as the paralytic in his teeth penetrated her system, rendering her immobile. Defenseless against his onslaught.

He thrust inside her as deep as he could, and the orgasm ripped through him, and beneath him, he felt her pussy convulse around him again. His dick pulsed and jerked as her body milked him; he yanked his teeth from her body and groaned out her name. Pleasure overwhelmed him, the orgasm mixing with the feline satisfaction of knowing that she was claimed.

Mine.

Colors flashed across his vision, and after a few moments, he slowly pulled himself out of her. She let out a small noise at the movement.

Sudden realization hit him. He'd bitten her.

Shit.

But the effects were already fading. He lay down next to her on the bed and pulled her into his arms, and she half-heartedly batted at him.

"What the hell was that?" she asked, voice small and distant. Propping herself up on an elbow she studied him. Her hand moved to rest on his bite mark, and she flinched when her fingers brushed against the small wounds.

"I'm sorry," he said, gruffly. "I should have warned you. But I wasn't planning on biting you—not yet. But in the moment, I couldn't control it." He gave her a small smile. "You bring out the beast in me."

"I couldn't move, but I could still feel you, moving inside me." Her brows scrunched together adorably. "It was…different."

"Bad?"

"I—I don't know." She sighed. "Okay, I'll admit it was pretty good in the moment. But I'm not sure how I feel about it. I take it that was more weretiger BS?"

His smile widened at her words. *Weretiger BS.* Oh, how that would make Erick's blood boil. "It's something we do—feel the need to do—when we mate. Especially when a woman is in heat. Some sort of biological imperative. There is a paralyzing toxin that comes out when we bite. Keeps the female from getting away I guess."

A very unfeminine snort. "How romantic."

"Handy in a fight, though."

Boneless, she released a sigh, and rested her head on his shoulder. "Well, whatever. Add this to the list of stuff I'm going to need more info on sooner rather than later." A few short seconds later, a soft snore came from her.

With the heat temporarily sated, she would sleep now, probably for several hours. And when she woke up, he would be there. Ready to take care of her however he could. However she needed.

Complete and utter satisfaction hit him. It didn't matter what they'd have to deal with going forward, because they'd face it together.

Even if the challenge was his best friend, his prime, and up until the moment he'd laid eyes on Daniella, the most important person in the world to him.

Chapter Four

rick watched the road closely, his two best men silent in the cab with him, and squeezed the wheel. Driving wasn't something he enjoyed; it was unnatural. The truck was too slow. But his feet would have been slower.

He had driven as quickly as the truck would take him through the mountains his people ruled — despite the fact that the humans didn't even know of their existence. But when he'd emerged onto well-used roads that were policed by officers who knew nothing of the clan, he had to slow down to near the speed limit. Dealing with humans would slow him down more than the speed limit.

"Have you seen her?" Glenn asked from the passenger seat.

Erick didn't glance at him, the man who had acted as his second until Owen could return from his watch over Daniella.

"Yes."

Glenn didn't ask a follow-up question, and Erick didn't invite one. Talking about the woman he was going to mate wasn't going to happen.

The first — and only — time he'd seen her was still

fresh in his mind. No closer than twenty feet, and still his reaction had been visceral.

Luscious, her form was exactly what he preferred in women. Curvy, yet sleek, ripe for fucking. Ripe for bearing his cubs.

Owen had cursed him for leaving him behind to watch her, to wait until she couldn't resist him, but Erick couldn't let his friend's opinions bother him. To approach her any other way would require time, and wooing. Time was in short supply because he couldn't be away from the clan long. And Erick knew nothing of wooing women for anything more than a quick fuck.

No. This way was simpler. It had required patience, but Erick had always been patient when stalking his prey. The woman wasn't prey, but the same principles applied.

Owen had tried to convince him this way wouldn't get him anything lasting, but that wasn't his concern. His parents certainly hadn't been in any kind of relationship—lasting or otherwise. As far as Erick had been able to tell, they could barely stand one another. They'd done their duty. Bred him and his younger brother. Created two new royals in a time when it was rare to see more than one born in the same clan in a single generation.

Not that it mattered that there were two of them. Nicolas had left the clan when he was little more than a teenager. Only Erick was left to carry the duty of keeping his people together. Keeping them strong.

Keeping them alive.

Like his father before him, he'd do his duty. The royal he'd tracked down with the relentlessness he was known for—Daniella—would accept him into her bed, during her heat if nothing else. Once she learned of their people, came to know them, perhaps she would be proud to continue their line.

But she didn't have to like him.

Erick would enjoy taking her; his cock swelled even at the brief memory he had of her. And he would make sure she enjoyed being taken.

Moonlight peeked through the curtains when a heavy knock on the door rattled the apartment. Daniella was still tucked safely in his arms, fitting as if she'd been born to fit him.

Erick.

The clock radio next to the bed read three seventeen. The sun wouldn't rise for several hours yet. He'd gotten here faster than Owen thought possible.

Another knock sounded, and Daniella stirred in his arms. She let out a small sigh and then nuzzled his neck.

He'd have liked nothing better than to wake her, slowly and languidly. Make love to her again, but this time he'd explore her. Find all the things that brought her to the edge. Figure out what made her writhe and beg and scream.

"Have to wake up now, kitten," he murmured.

She blinked sleepily, but there was an edge behind her eyes. A nced that would only grow the longer she went without breeding.

"Your prime?" She made half-hearted air quotes around the title.

"Yes."

She pulled her robe tighter, and his resolve strengthened. The promises he had made to his prime and friend—and by extension, to his people—were important. But not as important as her. He would do anything he had to in order to protect Daniella. She was his. Just as he was undeniably hers.

But the cost to his clan could be huge. Guilt twinged in his chest. If only there was a way to keep her, yet allow for the certainty of a royal heir.

One possibility hadn't been discussed yet—but he wasn't sure bringing it up would do anything but push her further away. A possibility that wasn't at all strange to his people—not even strange to him and Erick. But Daniella had been raised with humans, and something so far outside of what she'd consider normal and reasonable wasn't something he could ask of her.

He gave her a quick kiss, hard and full of all the emotion he couldn't express any other way in the time they had.

"You are mine," he said, fiercely. "I will not give you up."

She nodded, and some of the tension left her shoulders. He gave her hand a final, reassuring squeeze and went to answer the door.

It flew open just as he stepped out of the bedroom.

Erick stepped inside, filling the room with his large frame and commanding presence. However much Owen despised how he'd tried to take Daniella, he had to admit that his friend was born to rule. Every fiber of the man's being screamed that he was to be obeyed.

Two of his best guards, Anton and Glenn, were at his heels. Owen stood his ground. From behind him, he heard Daniella stirring. Interested in seeing what the other man who wanted her looked like?

It didn't matter. She was his now. And he would risk his life to keep her.

Erick's gaze was hard when scanned the room.

Without a word, he took a long, deep breath of air through his nose.

"You have mated her," Erick said.

"Yes. She is *mine.*"

"You will fight for her."

Owen tensed. "I will."

Erick hesitated, but his hard expression didn't soften. "Human form, then."

His prime was giving him a chance. It didn't matter that Erick was a royal and Owen was not—he could have specified tiger form. Owen's partial shift form was powerful, but not as powerful as Erick's full tiger. With a short nod, Owen agreed to the terms.

Erick struck.

She fell back from the doorway as Erick flew at Owen. Panic constricted her throat. Owen could handle himself, she didn't doubt that, but his prime hadn't come alone.

But the other men just stepped back, out of the way as the men sparred.

Erick got in the first strike, but Owen danced away from the next punch. Then he darted to one side and swung at Erick while his side was open. Erick's expression didn't reveal any pain.

She almost couldn't follow their movements; they were that quick. Like the tigers Owen said shared their blood, they moved with a fierce grace.

They rarely hit one another, but the times they did were leaving their mark. Less than a minute of their eerily wordless sparring, blood and scrapes covered both of their faces, and she could only imagine what their ribs would look like when the bruises started to show. A crash when Owen landed on the coffee table. A loud thump when Owen threw Erick into his wall, leaving behind a large hole. But the only sound coming from them men was the occasional grunt when one got in a good hit. The sweet smell of sweat tinged with blood touched her nose.

How long would it go on? How long would Owen have to fight for her?

Her stomach churned at the thought. All of this was, in a weird way, her fault.

"Stop it!" she shouted.

Both men slowed, no longer striking, but not looking at her, either.

"This is so stupid. It doesn't even matter who wins."

That got their attention. Owen turned slightly to stare at her, careful to keep the other man in his peripheral vision.

"What is she talking about?" Erick ground out.

"Don't ask him, asshole. I'm standing right here." Somewhere in the back of her mind, she knew poking the tiger wasn't the best idea. The man was obviously violent, and even though he wasn't as physically imposing as Owen—he was tall, but not quite so muscular—Erick made her gut clench in fear in a way that Owen never had. Somehow she knew, instinctively, that under normal circumstances, Erick was the more dangerous of the two.

But she was feeling pretty violent herself. Whatever ancient machismo BS they were engaged in—well, she wasn't the shut up and do whatever the men tell her to type. Their fight had the seriousness of a death match, and she wasn't about to find out definitively how it would end. Not if she could do something about it.

Finally, Erick's gaze slid to her. A quick glance at the

fang marks in her neck, and then his intense eyes were locked on hers. "What are you talking about, woman?"

She didn't roll her eyes, but it was a close call. The man was ruggedly handsome, and quite honestly one of the sexiest men she'd ever seen close up—just like Owen, yet so different. He was a bit more grizzled—in a wild man sort of way—and a couple of years older. Charcoal hair brushed his neck. A Calvin Klein model would be thankful to be blessed with Erick's face. Yeah, he was pretty, however much that was worth. He was lucky for it because he'd never win any women with his charm.

"I've made my choice. I choose Owen. I don't care who wins this fight. I'm going—staying—home with him."

"This is a fight to the death," Erick told her, grimly. "You will go home with whomever wins."

"Wow. What year do you think this is? I will be with the man I choose, and it isn't you, buddy. I go home with him or nobody."

The smile he flashed her held no humor. "In another hour, the heat will hit and you will go home with any tiger who offers."

She returned his smile with every bit of coldness she could summon. And considering his attitude, it was a lot. "You might get the chance to fuck me while I'm in heat, I'll give you that. But you just wait. The first time you fall asleep or let your guard down, I will make you pay for his death. Can you still be king of the weretigers, or whatever the hell you are, gelded?"

Erick blinked. Hah! Apparently, even the big, bad prime of the tigers could be surprised.

One of the men behind him made a noise that sounded suspiciously like a laugh. But Owen refused to meet her gaze. He didn't look happy. Damn. She'd made a wrong move. How was she supposed to know what the rules were? Besides, she wasn't the type to sit around and knit while he fought their battles.

He should already know that.

"You would do no such thing. It is not honorable. That's the sort of honorless fighting vampires engage in. *We* do not." He stood proudly, as if his argument would hold water for her.

She shrugged, hoping she appeared far more nonchalant than she felt. Not that her appearance probably mattered to a guy who could smell the fear on her. "I'm not really into the honor thing. I was raised by humans, remember? I'm more about the sneaky vengeance."

"Do you allow your woman to fight your battles?" Erick said, turning his gaze to his friend.

"No. We will finish this fight." Owen glanced at her. "I will kill him for you."

"Do whatever floats your boat, buddy. But don't lay it on me. I don't need your friend's blood on your hands. And killing him isn't going to turn me on. It sounds like a good way to send me packing, actually." She frowned, and added, "After this heat thing passes, anyway."

Erick's frown deepened. "She is a most unusual female."

"She was raised among humans." Owen's posture straightened, some of the tension leaving his hard frame. "She is a warrior in her own right."

The unmistakable pride in his voice made her heart swell, even though she didn't exactly think she qualified as a warrior. "Look, whatever. Isn't there some kind of non-bloody compromise we could come to here? Because—no offense— you're…" *Extremely sexy but also super scary looking.* "…A good looking guy and all, but I don't even know you."

"You don't need to know me. Your tiger will recognize the dominance in mine."

"Sorry. Not enough for me, pal."

Erick's gaze moved to Owen, and they shared a long look. Were weretigers telepathic or something? That seemed unlikely. But an idea was being exchanged, even if it was simply being communicated silently by men who knew each other well. She was certain that whatever compromise they suggested wasn't something she was going to like.

Owen nodded at his friend, and Erick turned his attention to her. Her guts twisted tighter.

"Unlike some of our kind, I am not weak." Erick didn't look at Owen, but his meaning was clear, and if she'd actually had tiger fur, it would have bristled. "I do not require a female more often than her heat beckons. For the good of my people, I would be willing to share you with my second, claiming you only when your heat crests, and you are at your most fertile."

"What the hell? You want to use me as some sort of broodmare? Breed me like an animal?" And what was his second? Did that mean Owen was the one in charge if something happened to Erick? Because she wouldn't have minded something violent happening to the arrogant man in that moment. Like she was going to bend over and let this stranger breed her like an animal. An image of exactly that flashed in her mind, and she swallowed hard. No way. That was not turning her on. No matter what her body thought.

Something in his expression changed, but he covered the emotion so quickly she couldn't identify it. "We're not animals. But we are in danger of extinction. I will share you for the sake of my people. I'm not asking for a *relationship,*" he said, spitting out the last word as though it tasted bad. "I'm asking you to help preserve your clan."

Owen shifted on his feet behind his prime, and she turned her gaze to him, swallowing the angry words she wanted to lob at his friend. But Owen didn't look pissed, he looked…uncomfortable.

"You want me to do it!" She gaped at him. What the hell had just changed? How on earth could he even think of sharing her? Didn't he care about her at all?

"No." He approached and tried to take her hands in his, but she stepped back. "I'm sorry. I don't *want* to share you. But what he's saying his true. Our clan needs a royal line to lead it. They need the power that comes with it to stay together. Without a royal heir…"

"What?"

A darkness passed behind his gaze. "The clan will be no more. One way or another. Our generation will likely be the last without you."

This was too much. They were asking for her to sacrifice her…what? Her morals? Her freedom? For what? People she didn't know. "So find another broodmare!"

Erick laughed, but there was no humor in the sound. "If it were that easy, do you think I'd really be trying so hard to get into your bed?"

Outrage ran through her, and just a tiny thread of hurt—silly, since she didn't know this man, so why would she expect him to want her? Then his words sank in. "How rare, exactly, are we?"

"Female royals are extremely rare. So rare, clans will fight for them. And they become rarer all the time."

"Rarer all the—what the hell does that ominous shit mean?"

Owen closed the distance between them and touched her shoulder, no doubt trying to comfort her, but the simple touch ran through her body like fire.

"Shit," she muttered, wrapping her arms around herself and stepping back. No matter what her body said, she was so not in the mood for sex right now.

"The heat is rising again," Erick said. Then he moved forward, too. The men were too big, too overwhelming with both of them close-up, and her heat itched under her skin. Erick reached under her chin and tipped her head up so her eyes would meet his. "A decision must be made. You need only take my seed once, maybe twice a year—after this first heat ends."

"What do you mean? After this year?" Her concentration slipped, and she found herself leaning into his slight touch. God, the man so wasn't her type. Neither of them were. Too big. Too scary. Too everything. But in that moment, she had to stop herself from reaching for him, from crawling all over him.

"The first year or so, a female is very fertile. And the heat can remain, and arise, quickly. It makes pregnancy very likely. It's a biological necessity for our people. We are not especially fertile." His eyes were green, but he shared one trait with Owen—flecks of amber when the light hit them right. But they carried none of the kindness she saw in Owen's—only something hard and cruel. Would his eyes turn more amber when he got riled up? "Our children would be prized. Cared for. They'd want for nothing." His hand slid from her chin to cup her face.

Desire rolled under her skin, and she forced in a deep breath, unfortunately inhaling a tantalizing, masculine scent. So unique—similar to Owen, yes, but different. The temptation this man brought—she could never have imagined the lust a stranger could elicit. It must be the heat. Had to be. No way did she really want this man, this stranger.

She had to be logical about this.

"No."

His hand fell from her cheek. "You refuse me?"

"No — I mean, yes. Sorry, but this is just too weird. And I can't...I mean, I won't." The desire to give into him was difficult to breathe around. Knowing that not only did she have Owen's permission, but also his encouragement, made the idea difficult to resist. But there was too much going on. Too much weird shit in a very short amount of time.

"Very well." Erick didn't reveal anything on his stony, handsome face. Was he disappointed? Why did she care? She didn't know him or his clan. Worrying about herself was the best she could manage right now. "It was interesting, meeting you."

Her stomach twisted in a curious mixture of fear and triumph, lust and need. Disappointment. And she opened her mouth to ask him to stay, to fuck her senseless, before snapping it closed. Damn heat.

"Would you like Anton to remain with you?" Erick asked Owen.

"We'll be fine. I've sensed nothing since I got here, and we'll follow you soon." Owen gave her an apologetic shrug, then added, "Besides, we'd rather be alone."

One of the men — Anton maybe? — grunted a small laugh.

"That's not wise."

Owen's face hardened. "Give her — give us — some time. Crowding her with tigers isn't going to make this easier. One night. That's all I ask. We'll return to the territory tomorrow."

Erick looked like he wanted to argue—his body tense and his face matching Owen's stubborn glare. But, jaw tight, he gave Owen a short nod. "Fine. Tomorrow."

The warning didn't pass his lips, but she was pretty darn sure Erick would be back to get them if they didn't show. The man could insinuate more with a look than most people could get across in full sentences. A product of his upbringing? What kind of life would a rare royal live among their kind?

"Give us a minute," Erick said. When Owen hesitated, he grunted. "Do you fear I'll molest her if you let her out of your sight for a moment?"

"Abso-fucking-lutely."

A small quirk touched Erick's mouth and Owen fought a grin. Suddenly, she could see the camaraderie between them. What would her decision cost Owen? His friendship with Erick? His position within the clan?

"I swear I will not hurt her nor fuck her if you give us a moment alone," Erick deadpanned.

Owen snorted and turned to her. "You'll be okay?"

"No. I'm a delicate flower that must be protected constantly lest I wither and die." Hah! Take that. She could be just as sarcastic as these two.

At that, Owen chuckled. He gave Erick a look which seemed to say "good luck", then headed out of the apartment with the other two men. Erick waited, listening, before turning back to her.

When light green eyes caught hers, it was like being hit in the gut. She found herself suddenly breathless. Damn, the man was sexy.

"What did you want to talk about?" she said, her voice clearly nervous even to her own ears. There was no reason to be nervous—they'd won, right? But for some reason, it felt a little too easy. Too pat. Finally, it hit her why.

Erick wasn't acting like a man who'd lost.

With one long stride, he'd again closed the distance between them. She gasped at his sudden nearness, and her foot slid back as if of its own free will. But she stopped there. She wasn't running from this man—this predator.

No doubt he would chase her.

He cupped her face gently, and she fought not to lean into the soft touch. His lips moved close to hers and she braced herself for the kiss, her whole body suddenly flush again with renewed need.

If he kissed her, she didn't think she'd even try to stop him.

But his mouth slid past hers, and his cheek brushed her own. Lips against her ear, his voice was low, for her ears alone. "This isn't over. I will to have you. Soon."

He inhaled deeply—was he *sniffing* her hair?—but before she could move an inch, Erick headed for the door. It slammed shut behind him, no longer entirely closing since he'd broken the frame to get in.

Energy filled the room—Erick's energy. Even though he'd gone, his promise remained. Goosebumps prickled on her skin, and she was still rubbing them away when Owen returned.

"That was weird," she said, after a moment of silence passed between them. After she reined in her heat enough to speak without risking she'd ask Owen to go after Erick. She wasn't sure how to feel about Owen now, either. He'd been willing to share her...

Would that have really been so bad?

She shook off the random thought. It was the heat, not her. She had no desire to delve under the rock-hard surface of his clan's prime to see what was beneath. Nope.

"What did he want?"

For some reason, Erick's promise—threat?—wouldn't come to her lips. The moment between them felt private. Ridiculous. If she were going to have any private moments, they wouldn't be with Erick. "Nothing interesting."

Owen turned to her, his mouth twisted in a grim line, but his eyes danced with mischief despite the bruises and scrapes on his skin. "You don't have to tell me, but we do need to talk about what you did—stopping that fight."

Her stomach clenched and she could feel the heat rising within her. She shifted, suddenly wet and achy.

"Get in the bedroom, kitten. And we'll discuss weretiger protocols."

"I can think of better things to do in the bedroom," she said, and her voice came out breathless. Crap. She was supposed to be mad at him—scratch that, she was mad at him. But the need…the need was greater than her anger.

"Don't worry. I'm just sure you'll love your punishment for breaking at least three of our laws." He stepped close and she leaned toward him, taking in his masculine scent, which now intermingled with the slight smell of blood and sweat. "Maybe I should spank you."

It shouldn't turn her on, she knew that. But between his scent and the adrenaline coursing through her after watching him fight for her, she almost dropped to her knees and offered herself to him. Letting go would feel so good. So perfect to have him pushing inside of her, his teeth digging into her neck. Taking what was his.

It took every bit of her fraying self-control to stay on her feet.

"I'm never going to be the kind of woman who sits

by idly while you fight battles," she said. He had to know that. No matter how much she wanted him, he had to want her, love her, for who she was.

His voice was low when he spoke, and his words sent a shot of need straight between her legs.

"I wouldn't have you any other way."

Chapter Five

"You keep talking like that and you just might get laid." She grinned at him, and Owen's heart swelled in his chest. He'd been afraid she'd never forgive him after he suggested sharing her with Erick. She'd probably think even worse of him if he told her the whole truth. If he told her that she wouldn't be the first woman they'd shared, not by a long shot.

But she would be the only one who really mattered, so he was going to keep that little fact to himself.

Besides, he'd smelled the change in her scent when she'd mentioned his dates. His nose wasn't as good as a werewolf's, but her anger had been strong enough, deep enough, for him to identify it easily. Why bring up women he'd shared with Erick when it would only hurt her?

Closing the distance between them, he took a deep breath, and the smell of her—amplified and enhanced by the heat—filled his lungs. He tucked a tuft of her hair behind her ear. "We should leave this place."

"Now?" Her eyes sparkled with mischief and desire, then she frowned. "I'm still mad at you, you know."

"For being willing to share you?"

"I—" She swallowed hard, and the shine of tears

twisted his gut. "It makes me feel like you don't really want me."

"That's not it at all," he said, fiercely. The fact she could think that… "You're incredible. Beautiful and sexy and smart. Your kindness shines through even when you're mad at me."

"Then why?"

"Our people don't have the same view of matings as humans."

"So, what?" she said, fire back in her voice, even as the smell of her arousal permeated the air, bringing his cock near full attention. "You guys don't care about cheating? Because that's going to be a problem for me. A big one."

"That's not it—we're loyal to our mates. I don't know if it's the animal instinct inside of us, or some kind of difference of genetics, but among mated pairs—committed to being together, not just fucking—cheating is practically unheard of. But we don't always limit our pairings to traditional sets."

She blinked. "You're polyamorous?"

His lip twitched, but he managed not to smile at her very human way of looking at things. "That's a good way to describe it. Females are much rarer than males, and our people rarely breed with nonhumans—not for anything other than, than…" He almost said the occasional fuck, but stopped himself in time.

A single brow rose. "One night stands?"

"Yes." That was a nicer way to put it.

"But, that wasn't exactly what Erick was proposing. Didn't sound like it, anyway."

He was relieved she didn't ask why their women tended to number less than their men; he didn't need to go into the gory details with her yet. The details about

Erick would be difficult enough for a woman raised among humans to understand. "You have to understand. Erick was raised from birth to lead our people. He has always had that weight on his shoulders. His...priorities and the way he reacts to things, it's all driven by that responsibility." At her frown, he tried again. "We aren't humans. Nor are we beasts. We're something different. Our normal is your straight-up weird."

"I don't feel different." She shivered, wrapping her arms around herself. "Well, I didn't until this thing hit."

"You may not have seen it because you didn't know to look for it, but you are different." He pulled her close and she wiggled against him, obviously wanting to do far more than talk. "We'll speak of this later. For now...I can smell how much you need me." When her eyes widened and her cheeks reddened, he added, "And I need you, too." He took her wrist, and placed her hand on his fully erect cock. "Badly."

"Oh," she said. "I see." The smell of her arousal deepened, and he lost his last thread of control.

He reached for her, but her arm came out, blocking him. A growl of frustration cut out of him, but he swallowed the sound.

"Will there be more changes? In me, I mean. I'd like to know what to expect."

"Yes. But we have time. I will prepare you for them. Just not right this second."

Her brows drew together, scrunched in confusion.

"I have to have you. Now."

"Oh." Her mouth dropped open. "This heat thing... it doesn't just affect how I feel, does it?"

"No. It makes the men around you possessive. Makes them desire you. It kicks our instincts into even higher gear when we feel some sort of attachment. Getting near a mated pair when the female is in heat…well, men have lost their lives for simple misunderstandings. But it ensures our women are safe when they are at their most vulnerable."

For some reason that didn't seem to please her, and a frown creased her lips. But he wasn't eager to chat about weretiger biology anymore. She'd been given enough information to absorb in one night. And he had to taste her. Touch her. Take her.

"Can we be done talking?" His voice was a growl, but he couldn't help that. The scent of her arousal drowned him, and his cock was hard enough to break through his pants. Every instinct in his body thrummed with the desire to take.

Under his intense gaze, she softened. "God, yes."

That was all he needed to hear. Without another word, he wrapped his arms around her and kissed her.

There was nothing soft in the way Owen took possession of her mouth, the way his hands roamed over her body, touching and squeezing and rubbing. She mewled when his hand moved between her legs and cupped her mound.

Then he was lowering her to the floor, muttering that the bedroom was too far. He pushed his pants just far enough down to free his cock.

With care she no longer had the brainpower to appreciate, he slid into her. Slick with desire, her body welcomed him, offering no resistance.

"So good," he ground out against her neck. "Hot. So hot and tight." Again with care, he began moving.

Her body automatically matched his careful rhythm.

But she didn't want careful. For some reason, Erick's face flashed in her mind. His hard, almost cruel features, and the way his gaze had raked over her. Pure lust.

No, Erick wouldn't fuck her slow. He'd fuck her hard and fast, leaving her no option but to take what he'd give her. Dominant to a fault, he'd take her forcefully, just to show her who was in control. And she'd love every minute of it—she knew it, even if she could barely admit it to herself.

"Harder," she cried, her sex clenching around him as her orgasm touched the edge of her senses. She dug her fingers into his ass, demanding he take her the way she suddenly needed to be fucked.

Owen bit her neck—not hard, he took care to not puncture her skin again, but hard enough to push her over the edge. The orgasm crashed into her, even as he thrust into her with abandon.

"Owen!" His name was wrenched from her lips. He cried out, body shuddering over hers, even as she felt his cock twitching inside of her as he came.

Owen stayed above her, cradling her body with his for a long moment. Then he kissed her damp forehead softly and rolled to the side. Before she could grasp that he'd moved, he'd pulled her into the crook of his arm.

"Should I get ready to go?" He'd said they needed to go, hadn't he? Stupid, heat-fuzzied memory. The prospect of moving wasn't likely, but she'd do it if she had to. In a bit. A while. Maybe in an hour or so her limbs would respond to her commands. Maybe.

"Later," he mumbled.

She grinned against his shoulder. "Tuckered you out, did I?"

"Quiet now, woman. Resting."

A small laugh escaped her, and she managed to prop

herself up on one elbow to look at his face. Eyes closed and satisfaction radiating from every pore, he didn't look like he'd be moving anytime soon.

But a sudden surge of energy hit her, and she managed to get up to her wobbly feet. Was the worst of the heat over? She certainly felt better, more like herself—but different. She grinned, and she took a step toward the bathroom. Only to be stopped by a hand closing around her ankle. She looked down at Owen, but his eyes were still closed.

"Where you goin'?" he said, sounding half asleep.

"Shower, big guy. You take a nap in case this heat thing comes back. I'll need you at full energy."

He cracked a smile, but didn't open his eyes. Instead, he rolled over onto his side, and a small snore came from his throat.

She shoved a fist over her mouth to keep from laughing at the poor man. Not fair. He'd done most of the work, after all. Not to mention the fight with Erick. Wasn't fighting supposed to be one of the most exhausting things a person could do? Figured that would even wear out a weretiger.

She turned the shower on and stepped under the warm stream, reveling in the heat.

A weretiger. She wasn't even human, if Owen was to be believed, and she did believe him. Something inside of her had believed him even before he'd flashed his second face.

Frowning at the thought, she lathered up, pretending her breasts hadn't just pebbled at the smallest touch of her own hands. Worrying over the heat thing could wait. She was intent on thinking through the weretiger thing while she still had half a brain working for her.

She'd never felt like she had a beast living inside of

her, or anything like that. The urge to hiss at someone had never hit her, and to her recollection, she'd always been a dog person.

So why was she so sure he was telling the truth?

Maybe it was as simple as the fact that she'd never fit in. Her life had been spent trying her best to be who she thought she was supposed to be, but she'd always felt like an imposter—an impersonator.

The only parents she'd ever known were no exception. They loved her and she loved them. And for the most part, they'd never had any real issues. Bob and Carol Clark were standup people, with nine-to-five jobs. They went to church every Sunday and had urged Daniella to go to school for business or law. Her desire to pursue art had been almost unfathomable to them. They'd forced smiles and supported her decision, but it had always been obvious to all of them that she wasn't quite a perfect fit for their family.

Once, she would have readily blamed that on being adopted. But now…now she had a tiger with a crazier, but maybe more fitting, explanation.

And what a tiger.

Owen was everything she'd dreamed of—or he had been until he'd started acting like a jerk. Kind, intelligent, gorgeous. And with incredible taste in movies. Sure, he hadn't struck Daniella as her type when they'd first met because he'd been so physically imposing, but she was more than a little aware she'd resisted any kind of attraction because she thought he was so far out of her league that he might as well be a dream.

She blinked into the shower spray, a sudden dread hitting her. Firmly, she pinched her own shoulder, hard.

"Ow," she hissed softly. Okay, whew. Not a dream, then. But it was no wonder she was worried. Ending up with a man like Owen lusting after her was pretty unbelievable, but to have two men of that caliber fighting to have her…well, that just didn't happen. Heck, such things probably didn't even happen to super models all that often, let alone girls like herself.

The curtain flew open, and she screeched.

Wild-eyed, Owen stared at her. "Are you all right?"

"I'm fine! Holy crap, give a girl a heart attack, why don't you?" She threw the washcloth at his head, but he ducked and dodged it easily, sending it to splat against his bathroom wall.

"I heard you. You were in pain."

She just stared, until realization hit. Heat traveled up her neck to her face, and she turned to face the shower spray. "I'm fine."

"Did I hurt you?" The fear in his voice drew her attention back to him.

"God, no. Why would you think that?"

"I was…rough with you. And you haven't even changed, come into your power. You're nearly as weak as a human right now."

"Thanks, I guess. I'm fine." No way was she admitting she'd pinched herself to make sure she wasn't dreaming. That kind of thing could give a man a big head. "Really, Owen. I'm okay."

He searched her face for a moment before nodding. "Then please, scoot over."

"No way. You'll totally hog the water," she protested, but she scooted.

"I would never."

"On your honor?" she teased.

He nodded gravely and stepped into the shower.

It took all of thirty seconds before she realized he'd lied. But by then, she didn't care.

Chapter Six

Daylight had peeked through the curtains by the time they'd settled into bed—and Daniella suspected the sun had been out for a couple of hours already. She was dead tired, and after agreeing with Owen that sleeping in his apartment—now un-lockable, thanks to his prime—wasn't the best idea, they wandered over to her place to pass out. Even though her bed was queen-sized, Owen seemed to take up all the space. Luckily, he was more than willing to hold her—keeping her tucked against his body while they slept.

But when she woke, the bed beside her was empty. Still slightly warm to the touch, but empty. And night had fallen.

She blinked, searching the darkness for him. For half a second she thought it might have all been a strangely vivid dream, and her stomach dropped. Then she sat up to get a better view of the room, and her whole body ached with a mostly-pleasant pain. Her breasts were heavy and sore. And while she was a tiny bit sore between her legs—it had been a long time since she'd had sex, and never with a man as well-endowed as Owen—she could feel a different ache there as well.

The heat had calmed, but it wasn't gone.

"Owen," she called, keeping her voice pitched low for a reason she couldn't name. Instinct, maybe. Or heck, likely just unreasonable fear. Her world had changed, shifted in ways she still didn't understand, and it was no wonder she didn't have her feet back under her yet.

"Owen?" she tried again, shoving the covers off. She hurried to her dresser and pulled on a pair of loose, cotton shorts she used to sleep in, and a black camisole. Even the soft cotton and loose material teased her nipples, brushed her most unsatisfyingly between her legs.

She sighed. Maybe Owen would be up for another round. A nice, slow, *gentle* round. Just as soon as she found him.

Just the thought of the man who had been her friend, then her enemy, and finally her lover made her press her thighs together to try to relieve the sudden ache. He was so gentle with her, so loving. Yet, all man. All tiger—not that she was ready to consider that fact too closely quite yet.

The kitchen was quiet as well, and no lights had been turned on in the apartment. Of course, that wasn't exactly unusual given the amount of light that seeped through her curtains even when they were closed. Even now, when it was dark out, because of the streetlights surrounding the building.

Besides, for all she knew, Owen might be able to see in the dark like the cat he was. She grinned at the thought. It was hard to imagine—not that Owen didn't have a little beast in him, but she'd never have guessed the wildness lurking in him would be greater than that of any other virile, masculine man.

Erick, on the other hand…

The weretiger prime was more beast than man, if she didn't miss her guess. Something dark lurked in his eyes, and unlike Owen, he felt…different. Like he was a monster who just looked like a man.

Her sex clenched and she bit her lip. No. No way she found that attractive. It was just the heat. That's it. She just needed to find Owen and he'd take care of the heat issue, stat. And she could forget about his weirdly alluring prime.

Where the heck was he?

Maybe he'd gone to his apartment, for clothes. Or food. That was likely, since she wasn't sure she had anything edible other than ketchup in her fridge.

But wouldn't he hear her if he was only a thin apartment wall away, calling for him? Heck, he'd heard her tiny little "Ow" in the shower after she'd pinched herself. The man—weretiger—had crazy good ears.

Telling herself that the heavy pit in her stomach was silly, she squared her shoulders and opened the door to her apartment. Nothing jumped out at her when she stepped into the quiet hall, nor did anything seem amiss in Owen's apartment.

Except for the fact that he wasn't there.

"Chill out," she muttered to herself. "He wouldn't just up and leave you."

Great, now you're talking to yourself. She shook her head.

Maybe he'd gone to the store. Yes, that made sense. She had no food. He was normally stocked up, but maybe he didn't have whatever he'd want to feed a hungry woman in heat. Heck, pregnant women ate weird shit all the time. Yeah, she wasn't pregnant, but being in heat had to wreak all sorts of insanity on the hormones. Any second now, she'd want peanut butter and pickle sandwiches.

"Check on the car, dummy," she muttered again,

then cursed under her breath. Owen was really going to think she'd gone off the deep end if he left her alone for a few minutes and she was already conversing with herself.

After taking a second to grab a pair of slip-on shoes she kept by her front door, she headed for the back of the building, which was where Owen always parked his little pickup.

She rounded the corner to the side of the building where he parked his truck. The roar warned her before she could even make out the shapes beneath the streetlights.

Too late.

The three men circling Owen didn't look like anything scary at first glance. Two were nearly Owen's six foot height, though both were a bit slimmer. The other was much smaller, almost waif-like and definitely not an inch over five-six.

But it was Owen's reaction to them that made fear spike in her chest. He watched them warily, trying to keep them in his line of sight as they circled. Blood seeped from a new gash under his left eye, and he was avoiding putting weight on his right leg. She'd thought he'd been beat up after fighting Erick, but he'd looked damn good compared to how he looked now.

The other men didn't look much better. One was bleeding steadily from his nose, and the shorter one's neck had a large gash. The third she couldn't make out as well; he stood in the shadows. But the way he stood appeared off, like he favored one side.

But none of that was what halted her in her tracks. Owen's shifted face did that.

She bit back a gasp, but it was too late. The slight man turned his head to look at her. Something about the way he moved was off somehow — wrong. Almost robotic. He smiled at her, revealing long fangs, and she knew.

Vampire.

Holy crap.

"Run, Daniella!" Owen's voice cut through her shock, and she met his desperate gaze. "Run!" he commanded in a loud roar that barely came out as an understandable word. He waved an arm, a gesture for her to leave, and her eyes locked on the fur and claws that had taken the place of his human hands.

Run, he'd said. But there were three of them — what if Owen needed her help?

Owen knocked the larger vampire onto the ground with a full-body kick that didn't look humanly possible — and probably wasn't — and was reaching for the second vampire. If she stayed against his wishes and one of them grabbed her, she could ruin everything. Owen would never forgive her. Worse, Owen would never forgive himself if she got herself killed. And she didn't know how to shift, or if she could yet. How much help would one practically human woman be against vampires?

With a painful ache pressing against her chest and bile crawling its way up her throat, she ran. Adrenaline pumped through her body, making her move so fast she felt like she was flying. She ran without thinking. Without looking around. With the almost debilitating fear that she was being chased. When she couldn't run anymore, she paused to lean against a tree, daring a look back. Nothing.

Heart pounding in her ears, her vision went fuzzy, and she fell to her hands and knees, struggling to breathe around the panic.

You're not being chased. Breathe. Just breathe. Owen

can't be far behind you, and he'll totally make fun of you if running makes you pass out.

Owen wouldn't dare, she didn't think, but the thought kept her breathing, and after what felt like an hour of gasping for breath and fearfully watching for a vampire to suddenly appear behind her, she managed to calm down. Her whole body still shook, but she managed to get back to her feet.

How far had she come? The area didn't look super familiar, and judging by the direction she'd come, and what she knew of that was close by, she'd had to have run more than two miles.

Sheesh. Who knew a vampire was all it took to get her to run? Should have found one a few years ago. The pounds would have melted off.

The sun peeked over the horizon. Did sunlight kill vampires, or was that just a myth? If only she'd had more time to talk about all this with Owen, she might have actually had a chance to ask some useful questions about this hidden world she would have never guessed existed.

Of course, if she hadn't been so busy jumping him the whole time…

"Dammit, Owen," she muttered. "Did you have to wait until the last second to tell me what I am?" If he'd started this conversation with her a year ago, she'd know if it was safe to go back or not. She might have had some skills to fight. At least, she would have known what to do when faced with freaking vampires.

Yeah, berate the guy who could have just been killed protecting you. That's nice.

The world spun at the thought. No. No way. Owen was fine. If he'd needed help, he wouldn't have told her to run.

Except, of course, he would have.

Dread filled her, and she watched the way she'd come anxiously, willing Owen to appear. But he didn't.

He'd be pissed if she showed back up and he was still fighting those vampires, but if something happened to him and she could have helped, even a little…

She had to go back.

Daylight was making its way free, but Denver wasn't New York City, and cabs didn't just wander the streets—not in this part of town, especially. No pay phones, either. She'd just have to truck it back.

Her body objected, but she pushed on, making it to a half-jog, half-speedwalking pace. Ten minutes later, things started looking familiar. And less than ten minutes after that, she saw her apartment in the distance. Maybe she hadn't run as far as she'd thought.

Finding a sudden flood of energy at the sight of her building, she broke into a run, heading for the parking lot where she'd seen Owen. At the last second, she changed her mind and altered course, heading into her building instead. A five-second 9-1-1 call to say men were fighting in the parking lot, and she headed outside, clutching a butcher knife.

Police couldn't hurt, right? They'd do a damn sight better than she would against vampires, she was sure of that much. And the advantage of help was worth the potential risk of getting to the parking lot a few seconds too late, a mantra she repeated in her head as she ran.

She forced in a deep breath, then crept out the back door and made her way out to the parking lot.

Empty.

Sure, there were cars there, but no people. Definitely no vampires that she could see. But also, no Owen.

Dammit. She looked anxiously at his truck, but it

was still where he always parked it. A sour feeling in her stomach and panic making her breath come fast, she walked through the whole area, not seeing anything out of place, save for some dark streaking on the asphalt — blood — that no doubt had come from the fight.

Tears burned behind her eyelids and she furiously blinked them back. No time to cry now. Had to find Owen.

Maybe he'd gotten away, was looking for her even as she searched for him?

But somehow, she knew that wasn't true. Her gut, tight with worry and fear, said Owen wasn't okay.

Making another sweep of the area where they'd fought, she kept her butcher knife tightly in her grip at her side. Hopelessness trying to strangle her in its grip, she got down onto her hands and knees, looking under nearby cars, swallowing the sobs that threatened to break free.

She couldn't cry right now. Then she'd be even more useless to Owen.

Morning sunlight reflected off of something under a nearby Ford compact, and after a glance behind her to ensure she was still alone, she wiggled under the car to grab it. A cell phone.

Owen's cell phone — or the same model, at least.

Bile crawled up her throat. The phone's screen was crushed, and the body of it was in only slightly better shape. It hadn't been dropped, it had been smashed. Under someone's boot, she would guess.

Gripping the phone so hard that it bit into her hand, she stared at the broken screen.

What the hell was she supposed to do now?

PART TWO

Chapter One

He was thinking about her again.

Unwanted thoughts didn't normally bother him. His natural state was one of great clarity and purpose. Of existing solely in the moment when necessary, and of thinking through and making quick decisions when required. Dwelling was a weakness he'd never indulged in.

Until now.

Rejected. The sensation was strange—like a bitter flavor on his tongue. Useless. Just like lying in his bed and thinking of the woman who'd given him his first taste.

Daniella.

Unlike the bitter rejection she'd left him with, her name tasted sweet. Her skin would taste sweet, as well. As would the rest of her. That taste was one he intended to sample. Soon.

No matter that she'd chosen another. Owen had all but given her permission to take Erick into her bed, into her body. And she wanted him—her body, if not her mind. Once they were back with the clan, she would bend to his wishes.

The buzz of the cell phone roused him, and Erick

ANDIE DEVAUX

answered the call, despite his lingering irritation at the man on the other side of the line.

"Yes." If Owen had called to beg his forgiveness, Erick wasn't sure he could give it. Walking away from the lush woman Owen had claimed had been the most difficult thing he'd ever done—even knowing he'd only bowed out of the battle for her affections, not the war. The scent of her had overwhelmed him, and the smell of Owen on her skin hadn't dissuaded his lust one bit. It brought to mind other memories of other times they'd shared humans.

Did Daniella know about their favorite game? He doubted it. Owen had clearly not seen fit to mention it—Daniella was human, after all. Humans had curious views about sex and found odd things distasteful. And while Daniella might think Erick an asshole, he wasn't quite enough of one to bring their shared sex lives up in front of Daniella without cause.

"E-Erick?" The small, hesitant, and decidedly female voice on the other end of the line wasn't what he'd expected.

"Yes," he said again.

"It's—it's Daniella."

Fear soaked her voice, but Erick didn't know the first thing about comfort. And barraging her with questions would only delay her speaking. So he waited.

"I got his SIM card. The phone was broken but the card still worked," she said, as if he cared how she'd gotten his number.

"Tell me what's going on, Daniella."

A moment of hesitation. "He's gone, Erick. Someone—some things—took him, I think."

Erick surged to his feet, and inside his mouth his canines elongated.

"I need…I need your help. I don't know what to do. God, I shouldn't have—I should have stayed with him. I—" Her voice cracked.

"Where are you?"

The truck jostled her, hitting a bump in the road, and Daniella looked around in a panic. Confusion touched her for a second, but no danger surrounded them—only a bumpy, gravel road. Owen was gone. Taken.

And she'd done nothing to stop it.

"Where are we?" she asked, glancing at the large man on the bench seat next to her. They were seated in the back. Another man—one she hadn't met before—was driving.

"I told you we were taking you somewhere safe," Erick said.

She stared at Owen's best friend and the leader of the clan of tiger shifters she'd never known existed—let alone that she was a member of their race—before turning to look out the window.

The city of Denver was gone, and she could only see rocky forest around them. "We're in the mountains!"

"Yes."

She turned to glare at the annoyingly calm prime. "What the ever-loving fuck, Erick?"

Something that might have been a smile hinted around his lips. "Yes?"

"You answer me in one word again and I'll figure out a way to hurt you." His mouth twitched again. Definitely a smile, the ass. "Why are we out here?"

"Somewhere safe doesn't include anywhere in the

city. We aren't far outside of Denver right now. You just can't see the city on this part of the road."

"We should be in the city, looking for Owen."

"You're exhausted. Dirty. A little smelly." His nose wrinkled and she gasped in outrage. "I need to get you somewhere safe. Preferably somewhere with a shower."

"You try running miles in flip-flops and see how good you smell by the end of it," she grumbled. "And, hello? Vampires ring a bell? They have Owen. That's a tiny bit more important than my BO."

The slight amusement in his expression disappeared, and he finally turned his head to look at her. His eyes, bright green and almost unnatural looking, gazed at her without emotion. "Do you think I'm not looking for him?"

Her breath caught, and her pulse kicked into high gear at his attention. She forced out words through gritted teeth. "I think you're riding in a truck—running away and taking me with you."

Eyes narrowing, he leaned in close. She tried to scooch back, but there was nowhere left to wiggle away to in the truck. "I have my best trackers on him. And if it weren't for you, I'd be there with them. But the fact of the matter is, you're more important than he is to the clan, so I will see you safe. Then I will hunt my brother."

"You—wait, you're brother?" Despite the fact that they were both amazing specimens of all things male—and, she suspected, all things tiger—Owen and Erick didn't look at all alike. Owen was lighter, both in expression and in coloring. He had light brown hair and eyes—eyes that turned amber when he was excited. Erick was dark, dark hair and olive skin—only his green eyes didn't whisper darkness. They both towered over her, both well over six feet tall. But Owen was slightly bulkier. Yet Erick was more intimidating.

"Not in blood," he muttered, turning back to stare out the window. Voice low, he added, "But he is my brother."

"Brothas from anotha motha," she joked, and his head jerked back to glare at her. "Sorry." She waved her hands up, surrendering. "I make inappropriate jokes at terrible times. One of my many character flaws."

His brows flexed, but the brief look of confusion faded when something outside caught his eye. "Almost there."

The driver turned the truck onto a gravel road, and she shifted in her seat. She heaved a deep breath, and caught his scent.

Spicy and dark, the smell reminded her of wild things and sex. She paused, her pulse jumping and a painful ache beginning between her legs.

"Crap," she muttered. Of course the heat wasn't gone. That would be too damn convenient, wouldn't it? Tears pricked her eyes, and she blinked rapidly to clear them. She wasn't going to cry in front of Erick, and definitely not in front of the other man, a stranger, who drove them.

Owen was gone. Kidnapped. Possibly worse. And her asshole betrayer of a body was still raring to go. It felt like treachery.

Erick's head turned, slowly, and when his gaze reached her his nostrils flared.

She shifted again, placing her hands in her lap. As if she could block the scent of her body's desire with her hands.

"Drive faster, Chris." He watched her until she turned to stare out her own window, unable to look at him without feeling her whole body perk in response. Even turned away, she could still feel the steady intensity of his gaze. But she held firm. After another ten minutes of awkward silence later, they'd arrived at a small house.

Still avoiding his gaze, she hopped out of the truck and searched the area around them. The house was small and very cabin-looking, keeping with the style she'd seen on many other Colorado homes. Pine trees dotted the area, many beetle-killed. It was pretty, but situated in a state with lots of pretty land, the cabin was sort of unremarkable.

"Doesn't look much like a cat-den. Or whatever."

"It's not our stronghold. It's a safe house we keep close to the city," Erick said. "Our clan lives much farther from civilization, but it would take too long to get there now."

"The place is pretty nice inside," the other man offered, speaking for the first time since she'd woken up. He was young—younger than she'd have guessed given his height from the back of the truck. Gangly, she'd put him at no more than twenty. She hoped for his sake that he'd eventually grow into his long limbs.

She gave the young man a small smile before responding to Erick. "What's so safe about it?"

He ignored her cheeky question. "I'm leaving you here with Chris and heading back to the city. A woman will be arriving shortly to help guard you, and they will transport you to our home for safekeeping."

She whirled around, anger rising to push her desire down. "You're what? No freaking way are you leaving me here, Erick. And I'm not hiding while he's still out there in God knows what kind of condition."

Stony-faced, he shook his head. "I cannot accompany you. I must seek Owen. You will be safe, I swear it."

She laughed, but the sound held no amusement.

"Seriously? You think I'm worried about my safety? I'm going with you. No way am I sitting on the sidelines like a good little girl while you look for him. I'm helping."

"Impossible."

"Fine, then. Leave me alone with your thug here and see what happens."

Chris shot a confused look at Erick, but Erick just laughed. "You wouldn't take me into your bed, and you expect me to believe you'll let this pup breed you? Your loyalty to Owen lasts only as long as you get your way, is that it?"

If possible, Chris's eyes widened further, and his gaze shifted nervously between her and his prime.

"Holy crap! That's what you think of me? I was threatening violence, not sex." She shot Chris an apologetic glance for dragging him into this. Then she straightened her posture and hoped her lying skills had improved. "But heck, now that you've brought it up, can't say I can guarantee that I won't bow before these instincts and see what the young guy can do. He's probably ten years younger than you, right? They say the young ones have the most stamina." She shot Chris a grin, and asked demurely, "Is that true?"

His mouth dropped wide open.

"Take a walk, Chris," Erick said, voice low and carefully controlled. But he didn't look away from Daniella.

Chris didn't run away, but it was a near thing. She watched him go, then looked at Erick. Beneath his hard expression was the unmistakable edge of anger.

"So, what'll it be?" she asked him. "Want to roll the dice with me and that pup—how long do you think he can resist a persistent woman in heat? Or are you taking me with you?"

His face shifted, revealing more of his rage. She swallowed hard, wondering if she hadn't just poked a tiger with a stick.

The scent of her arousal, of her heat, was overwhelming. He'd lied to her in the truck; she didn't stink—far from it. In fact, her scent was all the more tempting now that she smelled more natural and less like whatever human chemicals she used to wash her body. And her anger only made her more attractive. He wanted to take her, make her submit, then fight with her some more. It had been difficult to accept Owen's claim, but with her here in front of him, her scent laced with heavy need, and her fiery temper, his cock ached with the need to take her.

No fucking way was he leaving her alone with Chris.

She was bluffing—he knew that. But it was still a risk; a woman in her first heat could lose control without warning, without cause. Especially given her emotional state with Owen gone. And Chris was a man just coming into his own. No matter how loyal, Chris would capitulate to the luscious creature in front of him. It wasn't even a question.

"Fine." At her triumphant look, he added, "But it may be dangerous. You will do what I say, when I say it." Rebellion blossomed in her expression, but before she could argue, he added, "If you do not agree to this, I will leave you to your child-lover."

Redness crept up her neck to flush her cheeks. "Okay."

"Say it."

She waved a hand at him, dismissing his demand. "You say jump, I'll say—"

With his long stride, he closed the distance between them in a single step. She squeaked and stumbled back, and he grabbed her upper arm to hold her steady. "This isn't a joke. Lives will be at stake, and not just yours, woman."

Her breath came faster, and the air between them electrified. "O-okay. I promise. No questioning your orders." She took an unsteady step back and he released her arm. Rubbing the spot he'd touched, she looked down at the dry earth between them. "But that only goes for out there. I'm not going to let you order me around like I'm one of your stooges anywhere else."

He blinked, idly wondering what Glenn and Anton and the others would say to being called stooges. "Argue all you like. Strong emotions only fuel the heat within you."

She gaped at him, before recovering quickly. "It's a good thing you don't evoke any strong emotions in me, then."

He stepped even closer, and this time she didn't move away. Instead, she craned her neck slightly to look up at him—glare at him. The fire in her eyes and the need in her scent, he had to touch her. But he couldn't. Owen had claimed her, and if there was any chance of getting his lieutenant back, she was off-limits. At least, until she said she wasn't. He leaned in close, moving his face into the tempting area of her neck, careful not to brush against her soft-looking skin.

Her pulse beat against her skin, and he wanted to bite her. Hold that tender flesh between his teeth while he fucked her. He inhaled deeply, taking her pleasant, womanly smell deep inside.

Smart prey, she didn't run. She didn't move an inch.

He moved his mouth up to her ear, taking in more

of her scent and the pleasing way she reacted to him along the way. "You may have no emotional ties to me, woman," he murmured. "But that won't stop you from begging me to fuck you."

She seemed unable to speak for a moment. Then, voice breathy, she managed, "Fuck you."

"You will, sweet. And I'll enjoy it. But not until you beg."

Chapter Two

*H*e tried to open his eyes, panic coursing through him even though he didn't know why. Didn't know where he was. Could barely remember his own name.

Finally, his eyelids obeyed, opening just enough so he could see the ceiling above. Popcorn ceiling. But obstructed a bit by metal bars.

He yanked on his arms, but could only move them a few inches before they jerked to a stop. Chains rattled.

He might have blacked out again.

"Owen..." a feminine voice crooned. "Wake up, darling cat."

A presence above him. The source of the voice?

He forced his eyes open, and took in a stranger's face.

She clapped with delight, her whole face lighting up with a grin that seemed to brighten the room. "Oh, goody! They didn't damage you beyond repair." She hovered over him, leaning so her body was out of his chain-confined reach, but her hand slid against the skin of his jaw.

He didn't like it. No matter how beautiful the woman was—he thought she was beautiful, but her face refused to come into focus. And he couldn't seem to get his body to move. He growled. Because it was all he could manage.

A small giggle escaped her full lips. "Don't growl, kitty." Her expression shifted from guileless young woman to predator, and she slid her finger from his jaw down to his collarbone.

He swallowed — tried to — but his throat was a desert.

The woman's expression, still predatory, turned seductive, and she leaned over him like a lover, placing a quick kiss on his cheek.

He would have cringed if he hadn't been chained to the floor, and if his pride would have allowed it. But neither was true, so he remained stiff.

"You need to get some strength back, little cat. I need your help with something."

Memories flooded him. Claiming Daniella. Falling asleep next to her, unable to believe how lucky he was to have found her. Waking in the night with a gut feeling something wasn't right. Checking the parking lot and finding two vampires waiting for him. Daniella showing up in the middle of the fight. And him, desperate, telling her to run.

She ran.

He grinned at the creature leaning over him, and she arched a perfect eyebrow.

"What are you so happy about, kitty cat?"

"You didn't get her." His grin widened and his dry lips cracked. He could feel blood welling in the cracks. But he didn't give a fuck; it was the least of his discomforts. He'd take them all so long as Daniella was safe.

Her smile evaporated, the fingernail she'd rested on his collarbone dug into his skin, and something not quite sane touched her eyes before she regained her composure. "Don't worry. We'll find her, and you'll both be mine."

A dry laugh escaped him. "Good luck with that. She's out of your reach, sucker."

"Is she?"

Her confidence shook him, but only for an instant. "You know she is."

The smile returned, wide enough to reveal her fangs. Her dainty, small fangs. "You'd be surprised how hard it is to hide from me."

His blood ran cold, and true fear filled his chest. A vampire with abnormally small fangs could only mean one thing.

The stalker bent her head and licked the blood seeping from his lips.

Daniella wasn't safe at all.

Chapter Three

The drive back to Denver was even more uncomfortable than the drive up to the cabin. Erick drove this time, leaving the pup—as he called Chris—to ride in the backseat. Daniella kept her eyes focused on the road ahead, trying not to let her conflicting emotions get the best of her.

After his promise—his shitty, asshole promise that made her body inexplicably thrum with need—Erick had mostly ignored her the rest of the night. But she'd been aware of him all the same. When she stepped out of the bathroom, towel wrapped around her because she'd forgotten to bring a change of clothes in with her, she'd glimpsed him down the hall, stepping into the bedroom he was using. The master suite, of course.

He'd seemed to be at the edge of every room she went into—her paranoid, exhausted brain assigning far too much meaning to a man happening to be nearby in a small house, no doubt. And her heat, while under far better control than she'd expected, still pulsed beneath her skin, making her even more aware of him. Making her body ready itself whenever he was near. After the evening of being tortured by his proximity, her breasts were achy this morning, swollen. And her sex was so sensitive she feared a few bumps in the road would have her orgasming in front of the men if she wasn't careful.

But she'd managed to keep her hands to herself, which said a lot for her growing control, or the fading power of her heat. She wasn't sure which. She couldn't even be sure it wasn't just a lull. That predicting her own body had become difficult was maddening.

They'd eaten together with poor Chris, who'd seemed even more uncomfortable than they were. And she hadn't even been able to summon the energy to barrage Erick with questions. She had so many questions.

Good thing they were in for a decent drive.

She'd already asked Erick if his trackers had found any sign of Owen beyond her apartment building when she'd first found him in the kitchen, rising with the sun. His "no" had been clipped, and he'd swiftly swept her into the truck, so she hadn't been able to follow up.

"So if your trackers weren't able to find anything beyond my parking lot, what are you thinking? They put him in a car?"

"Yes."

"So vampires can't fly or anything like in the stories?"

"No."

She sighed. "Please, Erick. Stop being a chatterbox. I can hardly get a word in edgewise here."

A noise that sounded suspiciously like a muffled laugh came from the backseat, and Erick leveled his hard stare on the rearview mirror, but he didn't reply to her jab.

"Let's try a question that isn't yes or no, then. Where are we going, if we don't have any leads on where Owen is at?"

A small twitch of his lips. "Yes."

She smacked his shoulder. "I will beat the answers out of you if I have to." Holy crap. Mr. Big Shot Prime had made a joke and the world hadn't stopped. Had to be a day of miracles. Hopefully that bit of miraculousness would extend to Owen. Her smile slipped. Owen was trapped—maybe hurt…or worse—and here she was practically flirting with the man who'd all but promised to steal her from him.

"He's okay," Erick said.

Were her thoughts so plain for all to see? She swallowed the lump in her throat. "How do you know that?"

"He's not a royal, but he's still a powerful cat."

"A pretty cat, too," Chris offered from the backseat. "Can't hurt."

"What does *that* mean?" Nothing about Owen being pretty keeping him alive brought any good scenarios to mind.

Erick shot another stern look in the mirror. "There are two markets for our kind, generally speaking. One is people looking for muscle—and weretigers are the cream of the crop, or near enough, when it comes to pure physical strength, even among nonhumans."

"Even compared to vampires?"

"Compared to most of the bloodsuckers—stalkers excluded. Of course, that's one-on-one. Vampires aren't big on fair fights. They multiply faster than we do and like to overwhelm with numbers during fights."

"Stalker? What are they? Creepy vampires who follow you around with evil intentions?"

Erick didn't look amused. "Stalkers are stronger—stronger than royal tigers. They're rare." He shot her a serious glance. "If you ever see a vampire with short fangs—run."

"I plan to run from all vampires, thanks. Preferably before seeing their fangs." She almost asked more about the stalkers, but that wasn't info she needed right now. Right now, she needed to know that Owen was safe. "So what's the other reason?"

"To keep as pets." His jaw tightened. "Owen's cat form is attractive, which might make him more... appealing in some markets."

Before she could ask about that terrifying-sounding revelation, Chris jumped in. "See, Owen is pretty valuable on the black market. Sure, he won't get these assholes the kind of coin they'd get for Erick—and not even close to what they'd get for you—but they'll only kill him as a last resort. Vamps like money. You won't see one living off the land."

"Non-humans," Erick clarified.

Her stomach tightened, and she forced the ideas away of what Owen might do to make them willing to kill him. "So, do you think they've moved him out of Denver?"

"No," Erick said.

Despite the annoying return of single word responses, relief rushed over her. She let out a long breath. Finding Owen in Denver was going to be tough enough, but if they took him somewhere else—how would they ever find him again?

"Chances are they're still roaming the town, looking for you," Chris said, wrenching her mood right back to near-panic.

Erick's hands tightened around the steering wheel, but he didn't reach around and grab the kid. Certainly looked like he wanted to. Maybe he wasn't the iron-fisted prime that Owen thought he was.

"Looking for me? Why? Why risk Erick's people finding them?"

Chris started to answer, but Erick's hand came up—a gesture of silence—and Chris leaned back in his seat, mouth closed.

"Royal females are rare—and rare things are expensive. They would get a fortune for you. And if they find you, you will find yourself in some gilded cage on display in a master vampire's villa somewhere for the rest of your life—if you're lucky."

Her breath was gone, and she couldn't seem to fill her lungs with air. "But—but I'm a *person*." The words sounded naive, even to her own ears.

"Not to them, you're not. They're slavers—you're something to sell. And to the creature they'd sell you to…" He shook his head, expression hard. "But there's no evidence to show they know you exist. They'd have followed you if they did and left Owen behind."

"They saw me," she muttered, feeling sick. The strange way they moved. Those fangs.

"Vamps can't smell for shit—not much better than humans. And you've never changed. They might have taken you for a human. They didn't follow you or you'd have been caught."

She bristled at his immediate assumption that she wouldn't have had a chance. True, maybe. But the man could use a lesson or ten in tact. "Owen was fighting them. He might have stopped them from following me for long enough…dawn was coming."

Illogical though it was, she suddenly wished that he would comfort her, offer her reassurances. Hell, pull this truck off the side of the road and give her a friggin' hug. Owen would have—he would have known what she needed.

But he wasn't Owen.

She wrapped her arms around herself and leaned

back in the seat, staring at the beautiful scenery passing them by and feeling more alone than she had in a very long time.

He didn't know what to do, and it was uncomfortable. Daniella's obvious pain and fear pressed against his chest like some foreign weight that didn't belong to him.

"They will never touch you."

She took in a deep breath and let it out slowly. "You can't guarantee that."

"I can." Shrugging, he added, "Of course, it would be more assured if you would return to our home."

"Not gonna happen, big guy."

Finding himself in a position where he cared about another person's feelings was an oddity. The clan was always the important thing. And what was best for the clan was always the right choice. But now, rather inexplicably, his concern for Daniella cut deep.

The heat—that had to be it. Chemicals fucking with his brain, twisting his cat up inside of him. It was nature, cramming countless years of evolution down his throat.

Definitely wasn't because the rebellious little cat was already burrowing her way under his skin.

Fuck.

He was tempted to pull the truck off the road, so he could convince her to go back to their home. Where she could be safe. Where the people who counted on her could ensure that. But how could he when she didn't have the slightest clue about what she was? About her clan? He didn't know how to begin to talk to someone about what was really important when that person had an entirely different background. How did you convince a human to sacrifice her freedom for strangers?

Daniella wasn't a human. But for his purposes, she might as well be.

"You'll just have to trust me," he said quietly.

A long moment of silence. "I'm not sure if I can."

Primes didn't flinch, but he blinked at her words. "I don't play games. I don't lie. Everyone in this clan will step up to protect you, and the only way they'll get to you is over my dead body." He shot her a glance. "And, sweetheart, my body isn't that easy to kill." He shrugged. "Besides, not like you have much choice in protectors right now."

She went blissfully silent then, but he could feel her steady gaze, studying him, all the way into town.

Chapter Four

They swung by her apartment and picked up the two men who'd been with Erick the night they'd met. Erick introduced them briefly as Anton and Glenn. She attempted to engage the men in some semblance of conversation, if only to keep herself feeling sane and normal, but it didn't work out the way she'd hoped. Glenn seemed to have the personality of a brick—and talked about as much as one. And Anton was immediately more than a tad flirty—his usual state, she could guess—which Erick put a stop to with a terse command for quiet that made her bristle.

And it also made her talkative.

No one answered aside from the occasional nod, headshake, or grimace, but she talked anyway.

Finally Erick turned his hard stare her direction—not a safe way to drive. "Don't you understand how to follow orders?"

"I'm sorry, are we in mortal danger at the moment?" she asked sweetly. "Maybe you should watch where you're driving this multiple ton killing machine."

His only answer was a tick in his jaw muscle, but he did turn back to the road.

"That's what I thought. I don't follow your orders

otherwise, remember? Unless I choose to. I'm not one of your henchmen." Around her, the henchmen all seemed to be suddenly very busy at looking at everything outside of the truck.

Sure, following his orders might have been easier. Definitely smarter. And heck, a small voice inside of her was shouting that this man was her only hope of getting Owen back. Of not ending up as some sort of tiger slave to a rich vampire dude. But poking the tiger wasn't something she seemed to be able to resist, logic be damned.

"Guess I should let the vampires eat you, then." No humor laced his tone, but there was something less than serious in his deadpan. Enough that she still felt brave.

"Sounds interesting. They do make vampires look sexy in all the movies—even the scary ones." The vampires she'd seen surrounding Owen hadn't been sexy, but she wasn't going to tell him that.

"Do they?"

"Two words. Colin Farrell."

A grunt to acknowledge he'd heard her, then nothing. The man seriously needed to work on his communication style.

"Where are we going? Shouldn't we be walking around so you can smell the bushes for vampires or something?"

"Later."

She opened her mouth to ask more questions, but settled back in her seat when they parked at a warehouse. The building was old but otherwise indistinguishable from the dozens around it.

"Seriously?"

He arched a brow at her, his eyes catching the light

in a way that could make a girl lose her breath if she wasn't careful.

"We're meeting questionable people at a creepy old warehouse? Isn't that a little cliché?"

A touch of confusion clouded his expression. "Where would you rather meet the werewolves? The mall? Maybe their alpha—their leader—can meet us by the movie theater."

Werewolves. Right. Of course there were werewolves.

No doubt taking her silence as a win, a satisfied smirk touched his lips. He reached for the door handle."

"Wait. Can we talk for a minute? Alone?"

A hard glance shot to the men in the back seat, and in mere seconds they were alone. She shifted in her seat, trying to think of a way to word her question without sounding weak. The man in the truck with her didn't respect weakness—two seconds in his presence had told her that. But fuck it, she needed some reassurance or she was going to lose it—really lose it. And something told her that losing her shit in front of his men—or worse, in front of these unknown werewolves—would be worse.

"I don't have all day."

"Fuck. You don't make anything easy, do you?"

A raised eyebrow was his only response.

She licked her lips. "I need you to be one hundred percent honest with me for a minute. I need to know that Owen is going to be okay. No empty promises. No bullshit."

Silence reigned for a few seconds, and the absolute lack of emotion in his expression gave her the crazy urge to shake him, if only to get a response.

"You really care about him."

Her mouth dropped open at the silliness of the question. "Of course I do. Even if—even without this heat thing, and all the crazy that comes with it. I mean, we were friends, Erick. Really friends over the last year." She looked down at her hands clasped in her lap, at her white knuckles. "Maybe you're used to your friends being in mortal danger, but I'm certainly not."

"I didn't know."

Her gaze snapped back to his face. "You didn't know what?"

"That you'd been spending time together. Friends." A growled curse. "He fucked up any chance I had with you before you even laid eyes on me."

She blinked, stunned at the bit of emotion that leaked through his normally rock-like exterior. The anger didn't exactly make him more approachable or relatable, but it was something.

Before she could come up with a response, he continued. "Owen is fine. He will live. Worst case, he's a vampire's pet until we can track him down. But I won't allow that to happen. I will find him before they get him out of the city. And once he's recovered, I'll beat the shit out of him for denying me my mate." He opened his door and stepped out, but he didn't turn back to look at her. "For the record, I don't make promises I can't keep, and I don't do bullshit." He slammed the door.

Something loosened inside her chest, and she took a deep breath and hopped out of the truck to follow him. Erick didn't slow his pace, and she'd barely caught him by the time he reached the door where his men waited.

His reassurances shouldn't have made her feel better in light of his threat to beat Owen, but they did. If ever there was a man who didn't beat around the bush, who lacked even the smallest amount of tact, it was Erick.

Instinct told her that if he said he'd get Owen back,

he would. Not that she was ready to rest easy by any means, but she also didn't feel quite so panicky, so afraid.

Erick knocked firmly on the large warehouse door and it opened. But what peeked out wasn't what she'd expected.

A small woman with big Bambi eyes and long, blond hair roped into a braid let them in before leading them farther into the building. As a group, they were eerily silent about the whole thing. No words were exchanged, and the whole thing made her skin prickle.

The woman led them past a couple of offices and into an open area, concrete and metal, and nearly empty save a couple of motorcycles and two men. The interior of the building wasn't exactly homey, but it did look comfortable. Nicer than the older exterior had led her to expect.

"I thought we said even numbers, Erick."

Erick's gaze flickered to her before moving back to the man. "She doesn't count. Never shifted."

The man who'd spoken stepped forward into the light. Like the wolf he must be, he looked rangy—not thin, but not overly muscled like the tigers seemed to all be. Blond hair hung to brush his collar and there was a definite friendliness in his gaze that took her aback. He looked eerily similar to the blonde woman, although she was much smaller. Siblings?

"I'd say she counts." He winked at her, not seeming bothered by her presence, then offered a hand. She stepped forward and shook it automatically. A low growl cut the air beside her, and the wolf's grin widened, revealing normal-sized—if super bright—teeth.

"I'm Grayson," he said, apparently not bothered by Erick's anger.

She offered him a small smile, then stepped back. "Daniella."

"What a lovely name."

"Cut the bullshit, wolf."

Grayson stiffened at Erick's words, and a flicker of wariness touched his expression before it was smoothed away with what seemed to be his signature smile. "I see this is your normal pleasant nature, Erick. I'd hoped that we might have just met on a bad day."

Erick crossed his arms and stared. The man got a lot of mileage out of that stare.

"Fine. I see time is of the essence. Kara has informed me of your dilemma. I hate to see anyone fall prey to the bloodsuckers, but we do still have terms."

"Name them."

"Well, it's just the one term, actually." Grayson shrugged. "The treaty, of course. Sign it."

From the corner of her eye, she could see Anton and Glenn shifting their weight ever so slightly. Were they expecting an attack, or did the idea of this treaty just make them uncomfortable? She resisted the urge to move closer to Erick.

Unlike the other two, Erick's thoughts remained hidden. "No. I explained to your wolf that we will pay in cash."

Grayson's smile thinned. "Unlike some species, we don't hide away from civilization in the mountains. We exist in the real world where money can be earned pretty easily. I don't need your money. I need your signature. In blood."

"No."

Owen was out there, trapped. Probably hurt. These people could help, and Erick was going to refuse their price?

"Why?" she blurted out. Erick gave her a warning glance, but she ignored it and turned to Grayson. "What is this treaty?"

Grayson's gaze slid to hers, his eyes glowed subtly, like Owen's had when he'd been excited. When he'd shifted. But Grayson's were blue-gray.

Swallowing hard, she didn't look away.

"It's simple enough. An agreement to support each other against attacks. To respect each other's people, should they find themselves in the other's territory." He looked at Erick. "Something we already honor."

"That doesn't sound so bad."

A hint of a grin. "It's not."

She spun to face Erick. "Why won't you sign it?"

Erick bared his teeth at her, and suddenly her body was a mass of confusion. Need pooled in her belly, even as sudden rage rolled through her.

"Cooperating with outsiders isn't done."

"Owen could be out there hurt! Dead!" She choked on the word and swallowed hard. "And you won't help him out of some nonsense, xenophobic tradition."

"Listen to the little cat," Grayson said, most unhelpfully.

She turned and snarled at him, and his eyes widened. Hands spread to show he was unarmed, and he quirked a brow at her. "No offense."

Breath coming quickly, red flashed across her vision. These people could help, and Erick refused. A tiny part of her whispered that she was being unreasonable, that she wasn't helping things, but the rest of her was ready to pounce.

Someone gripped her upper arm, and she turned and lunged, trying to bite. But Erick kept her at a distance easily.

"I'll sign. Just get someone out there now."

"I'd rather you sign first," Grayson said, and Erick shot her a meaningful glance. "Fine," Grayson acquiesced. "But tomorrow—"

"You'll have it."

Erick wasted no time for handshakes or goodbyes before dragging her out of the warehouse. She fought him, her whole body on fire with rage and yearning. Outside, he pulled her into a small alley next to the building and shoved her against the metal building— not gently.

"Stop it," he growled. "Breathe."

Sharp pain shot through her head when he shook her against the wall again and she yelped. His words penetrated, and she tried to breathe through it— whatever the hell, *it* was.

Gradually, her body relaxed a bit. And the red in her vision retreated, leaving her able to clearly see Erick's hard expression, his strong arms that held her firm. And the claw marks on those arms.

"Shit," she gasped. "Did I—I'm sorry." She'd scratched him. With fingernails or claws, she wasn't sure. Her hands certainly looked normal. But fresh blood welled in the marks.

His eyes followed her gaze. "It's nothing. How do you feel?"

Confused. Needy. Hell, even with the injuries she'd caused, plain as day, she still wanted to crawl up him. Hurt him some more. See if he could take it.

She shook her head and pulled away from him—or tried to. What. The. Fuck. "I'm fine. Let me go."

"You're not fine. The heat is overtaking you." He moved in closer. "I could fuck you right now, in this dirty alley, and you'd let me do it. If that's not the heat talking, then let me know, sweetheart, because I'd be happy to mate you if that's the case."

She took a deep breath—a mistake, because his scent filled her lungs, making her whole body shake. It was the heat, but admitting it felt like losing somehow. Losing to her own body, to her own urges. She didn't like it.

"I told you, I'm fine." She tried to step away. Space was an absolute necessity all of a sudden. "Okay, maybe I got a little bit...out of control in there. But I'm good now. I'm ready to help."

"You're not in any shape to help yourself, let alone Owen."

Screw you was the response on the tip of her tongue, but she bit it back. Arguing with Erick right now seemed too close to tempting fate. If what he said was true, that her heat was exacerbated by strong emotion, then she couldn't afford to argue with him. It was hard enough not to crawl all over him anyway. The way he smelled, the way his large body hovered over hers, the way his intense gaze promised things her body craved.

No. She wasn't going there. No freaking way. Maybe if they got out there now, they might find Owen before the end of the day. He'd take care of her, see to her needs. The thought bolstered her, and she squared her shoulders. "I'll be fine."

Erick studied her, and she did her best not to fidget under his gaze. "You will stay by my side. You will not stray."

She rolled her eyes, but managed a short nod when he didn't seem willing to move until she answered. With great care, he released her arms, sliding his hands down her skin. She shivered, then turned away to cover the motion. Her body might ache and want, but that didn't mean she had to give in to the urges.

She'd resist, no matter what.

The female accompanied them to the apartment building. Kara. Grayson's little sister.

Erick's lip curled at the thought of the wolves' alpha. He'd been trying to get them to sign that treaty for the last year. Despite all his words about camaraderie and trust, he hadn't hesitated to push the second he had the advantage.

"Follow me," he told the much more sullen Daniella. Then he started circling out. The wolf would take in all the scents she could around the apartment, but the cats were double checking, making sure there wasn't another place nearby—perhaps where they'd spied upon the building in the past—that she needed to check.

"Do you think we'll find him tonight?" Daniella asked, breaking the silence after only a few minutes. The woman didn't care for quiet time, that was certain.

"Unlikely." For all her flaws, one second of her in his arms had almost broken his resolve to wait until they found Owen, got this sorted, to take her. And he couldn't blame it on the fact that she was in heat.

He'd grown up in the clan, and had rarely left a day since. Being around women in heat was a reality men faced in large groups of shifters, one that he'd dealt with for years. Hell, he'd even taken a few women who were in their heat, with the small glimmer of hope that he might father a royal child with one, even though the chances were low.

None had tempted him like Daniella.

She was exactly the opposite of what he'd wanted in a mate. What he thought he'd wanted, anyway. She was argumentative, bullheaded, independent. The woman seemed to relish the fight.

Yet he could barely resist her.

"What you mean, unlikely?"

"Kara has to find all the vampire scents in this area, memorize them, and then start hunting at the local vampire clubs for the same scents." He stepped off the sidewalk, crossing into an area that didn't look as residential. No vampires had passed here recently. Tigers might not have the same keen ability to take in and differentiate the most subtle of scents that wolves could, but his sense of smell was still far better than any human's. "Then we'll have to track them to wherever they are holed up."

"So, tomorrow, then?" Nerves made her voice quaver, unsure. He knew what it was on her mind. If they didn't find Owen tonight, then she'd have to spend another night alone at the cabin, resisting him. And he'd have to spend another night resisting her.

Somehow.

Fighting the urge to breed was unfamiliar to him, uncomfortable. He was the prime of his clan. A position that brought a hell of a lot of responsibility for him to bear, but one that didn't usually require him to go without companionship. If anything, females tended to throw themselves at him in a way that satisfied the beast's need to rut. But never did they require anything more complex from him. He didn't woo, he didn't seduce. He took. And they thanked him for it.

Simple. Neat. Not like the mess he found himself in now.

Something inside of him resisted simply taking what he wanted from Daniella. It would be easy enough, with her heat so set upon her. But it wouldn't be lasting.

Erick shook his head. He didn't give a fuck about lasting—his close quarters with Daniella, his best friend's kidnapping by bloodsuckers, was just messing with his head.

"Hello." Daniella drew out the word and waved at him. "I asked you a question."

"Perhaps tomorrow," he said, grudgingly. He didn't tell her the whole truth, that if they didn't find Owen soon, they might not find him at all. Not in Denver.

Closer than brothers, he and Owen had grown up together. Owen hadn't faced the same confinement Erick had—he'd occasionally gone beyond their lands once he'd hit his teen years. It was the only time in his life that Erick had truly been envious of another man.

Until Daniella.

"We should check over there." Daniella pointed to a large park across the street from them—so big and old it looked like a miniature forest, an oddity in the city. When he raised his brows in question, she explained. "Owen and I used to go there and hang out sometimes on the weekend." An awkward shrug. "It's far from the apartment, but it's one of the bigger parks around here. I like to draw, and he seemed to like the outdoors."

Jealousy sparked, hot and uncomfortable in his chest. A ridiculous emotion. What Owen had with her wasn't something he wanted. A *relationship*. He had neither the time nor the patience for such things. Freedom was denied him in many ways as the prime of his pack; why would he seek to tie himself down further?

A small laugh escaped her when they got close to an old swing set. "He pushed me on these once. Too hard. I almost flew off, and—" She sniffed, and he clenched his hands at his sides to keep from reaching for her. "He promised to catch me if I did."

The uncomfortable pressure in his chest deepened into something harsher, sharper. "Let's scout around, check the rest of the area."

Her brows scrunched when he headed west. "We didn't go over there. Owen said he could smell the trash from the alleys on the other side of the park. Said it ruined the experience for him. I told him it was all in his head." Her voice caught. "Guess it wasn't, was it?"

No answer seemed necessary, so he didn't give one. Instead, he continued on the path he'd set. They reached an outcropping of dense trees, and he halted. The scent was very subtle, on the very edge of his senses. Old. But unmistakable.

Vampire.

He pulled his phone out of his pocket and hit Anton's number. Glenn was looking alone, but Anton was keeping an eye on Kara, their wolf tracker.

"What is it?" Daniella asked.

Anton answered on the first ring, and Erick gave him clipped directions to their location before hanging up.

"Head back to the swings," he told Daniella.

She crossed her arms. "I'd like an answer to my question."

"Vampire scent here. Don't want to cloud it with our scents if we can help it." He strode back toward the swings, and after a brief hesitation, he heard her follow.

"A vampire? Here?" She swallowed so hard he could hear her throat working. "I mean—could it be a coincidence?"

"Unlikely. Vampires are more common than tigers, but not common enough for this to be anything but one watching you." They reached the swings and he halted abruptly before turning to face her. With a small surprised noise, she stopped just short of him, and he spun her around.

"Hey!" she protested.

Ignoring her, he pointed back to the trees where he'd scented the vampire, and held her shoulder with his other hand. "Do you see?"

Discontinuing her half-hearted struggle, she looked up to where he pointed. "It's a perfect vantage point to watch us."

"And it's far enough away that Owen would be unlikely to scent them."

Her voice was small when she spoke again. "Does this mean what I think it means?"

"Yes. It is likely the vampires know about you, too."

Chapter Five

*T*he drive back to the cabin was a blur. Her need mingled with mortification which mingled with fear. She was afraid for Owen. She was afraid of the vampires. She was afraid of herself.

She wanted Erick.

His scent invaded the small space of the truck's cab. Raw and sexual and more than a little wild.

The heat was to blame. But even knowing that intellectually didn't make one damn bit of difference.

"We're almost there," he said through gritted teeth.

Guilt hit her in the gut. "I'm keeping you from looking for him." Fuck. She wasn't only sitting here doing everything in her power not to rip the clothes off the man next to her, she was keeping him from finding Owen.

"Everyone else is on it. Kara will be able to track the vampires based from their scents. The one you helped us find was far less degraded than the others—fewer people around to muddle it up. She got a good read. The wolves know their local haunts."

Yes. Concentrate on the hunt. Would do to keep her mind focused on anything but her aching sex. "Why do you need her? And won't the vampires expect that and lay low?"

"Wolves have a much better sense of smell than we do," he said, voice stiff. As if admitting that fact was admitting a personal weakness. "And we don't know their local haunts. Tigers don't journey into the city—unless they're packless. The suckers won't expect the wolves to be helping us."

"It's really that far out of the realm of possibility?"

"It is," he ground out. "Species don't intermingle. We don't cooperate." His hand clenched reflexively on the steering wheel. "We don't sign fucking treaties that are bound in blood."

Blood? Yikes. Yet another question to follow up on when things settled down enough that she gave a shit again about the details. "Why not? If vampires are such a threat, it only makes sense to—"

"We can't trust any of them. Not the wolves or anyone else Grayson blackmails into signing that treaty." He sighed. "It's done. I will keep my word, sign their treaty. And I will watch them."

"For what?"

"Their inevitable betrayal."

Try as she might, she couldn't think of a response to that, and she didn't even feel up to asking more questions. If nothing else, the conversation had cooled her heat. They rode the rest of the way to the cabin in silence.

"You're not going to let me go with you tomorrow, are you?"

"Your heat is uncontrolled. I can count on Anton and Glenn—even Chris, so long as you didn't have more than five minutes alone with the pup. But I don't trust Grayson's men."

Grayson's men. Did that mean he trusted Grayson? Maybe trust wasn't entirely out of reach. Or maybe she was just looking for the silver lining in the situation she'd forced on him, forced on the people—her people—that she'd never met.

"So, what? You're dropping the little woman off so you big, strong men-folk can fight the war?

"I'm staying with you." He glanced at her and the heat in his gaze nearly took her breath away. "In case you need me."

She didn't ask what he meant. Her body thrummed with the answer.

Feeling like a wimp, she ran for the bathroom the second he shifted the truck into park, then switched the shower on. Every stitch of clothing she wore seemed to tease her sensitive flesh. It needed to come off. Now.

Breath coming fast, she tore off her clothes, then stepped under the cold stream of water.

A squeak escaped her lips when the frigid water hit her skin, but she gritted her teeth and let it drench her. The cold sank into her until her body shook violently.

The heat rolled under her skin, but the cold water seemed to calm it. When she couldn't stand it anymore, she shut the water down and grabbed a towel. Shivering, she wrapped it around her shoulders and sat in the tub.

Cliché, but the cold shower had certainly cleared her mind a little. She was no longer a single breath from finding Erick and demanding he fuck her.

One more night. That's all she had to get through. She hoped.

Because she wasn't going to make it any longer.

But Erick didn't stay with her the next day, like he'd promised. And the entirety of the day was spent in the most frustrating way possible. Alone at the cabin, after

Erick had somehow wrangled a promise out of her, a promise to behave.

Behave. Bleh.

Worse, the man had a point. She couldn't very well go with him to search for Owen in her condition. The heat grew worse with every passing hour. She'd entirely avoided Erick the night before, electing to stay in her room like a prisoner. When he'd brought her dinner, she asked him to leave it at the door. And only after she heard him move away did she dare open it.

Not that it mattered. She could barely eat as it was.

Alone, without even the benefit of the distraction of the others, her heat grew worse. Her body ached, and she finally gave up the good fight and took a long, hot shower. Three orgasms later, she felt only marginally better. Exercise only seemed to rev her up more, so she gave it up and tried to concentrate on anything but the insistent thrum of need from her sex, and the way every stitch of clothing seemed to tease her sensitive skin. She finally gave up on the bra—her breasts were so sensitive they actually hurt, and confining them only made the sensation worse.

The sound of Erick's truck pulled her from her stupor, and she rushed outside to meet him on the deck. Eager only for information about Owen, she told herself.

But the young man who waved at her sheepishly as he approached wasn't Erick.

"Where's Erick?"

Chris gave her a shy smile. "Hi to you, too."

Damn. She'd lost all sense of politeness between the heat and spending her time around Erick, who she was pretty certain didn't know what the word meant.

"Sorry, Chris. Just coming out of my skin a little here."

His smile disappeared. "I'm sorry. Erick will be

along, but not until after midnight—maybe closer to morning. I'm supposed to keep you company, make sure you're okay."

After midnight? Rage rolled through her. How could he be there when she needed him to be here so badly? She was the opposite of okay.

She shook her head. No. This was what she wanted. Erick safely away from her. Erick looking for Owen. Maybe he'd find his second and bring him back by morning. The thought gave her a tiny bit of hope.

Chris took a step forward, bringing a whiff of his scent with him—and he smelled *good*. Was her sense of smell improving? Hardly a benefit at the moment.

"No." She held up her hand, and Chris stopped. "You have to go."

A frown creased his mouth. "But Erick said—"

"I don't give a fuck what Erick said. You. Have to. Go." The kid wasn't much younger than she was— maybe nineteen or twenty to her twenty-three—but he seemed younger. Too young. She wasn't going to risk it, not in her current condition.

He hesitated.

"Please," she said through gritted teeth.

Finally, he nodded. "Call if you need anything. Erick will relay it to me. I'll be a few miles down the road. There's a hotel there."

She turned away. "Thanks."

The truck started behind her, and she shook with the effort of not calling him to come back.

The rest of the day, and the night, passed in misery. The heat made her feverish, miserable, and so uncomfortable that she gave up any hope of sleep. Instead, she paced the house. Midnight hit, and she called Erick.

"Where are you?" she snarled when he answered the phone.

A pause. "Are you all right?"

"No, I'm not fucking all right. I —" Her head throbbed, and she sat heavily on the couch. Her concentration was shit. What had she been trying to say?

"I'm coming." The line went dead.

A sob caught in her throat and she swallowed it down. The cell phone dropped from her fingers to the floor, and she curled into a miserable ball on the couch.

She could get through this. She could.

Without Erick's help.

She didn't even hear Erick pull up, didn't hear him open the door, didn't hear him approach. Realization that she was no longer alone didn't hit until he touched her, the briefest brush of his fingertips against her neck.

"Erick?" Her voice was weak. Her thoughts a messed up jumble of confusion.

"I'm here," His voice shouldn't have been soothing, part of her knew that, yet it rolled over her shattered psyche like the cold water had soothed her skin.

"I —"

"I'm going to help you, Daniella."

His words both soothed and enraged her — she didn't want him, didn't trust him. Okay, maybe she wanted him — she was a red-blooded woman, after all. Or red-blooded tiger. But she didn't trust him, not yet. She barely knew the man.

"I know you didn't want this." His voice was gruff, full of some emotion she couldn't name. "But if I leave you like this you could get sick, for a lot longer time than this heat will last. And I'm not…comfortable with this. Seeing you hurting."

Still she pulled away, into herself. Away from his touch. Away from the temptation he represented.

Erick heaved a heavy sigh. "I wish we could talk about this. Can you do something for me? Something that might make this easier for both of us—or at least bearable?"

"What you want me to do?" Her voice was muffled from the couch cushions where she'd shoved her face, but he seemed to understand her just fine.

Softly, his hand ran up and down her back. "You will touch yourself. Make yourself come. I will help you. It might be enough, just enough, to bring you to your senses for a few minutes, so we can discuss this. Like adults."

Despite her garbled thoughts, his insinuation that she wasn't treating this like an adult didn't go unnoticed. Still, his suggestion was sound. And her deep need overrode any objection she might have still felt. She found her hand moving as if of its own volition toward her aching pussy.

Her sex was so sensitive that she gasped when her fingertips brushed her clit. Ever so carefully, she massaged her sex. She'd tried it, only an hour before, but she'd been unable to bring herself to orgasm.

It was among the most frustrating moments of her life.

Even now, as she felt herself grow sopping wet, the orgasm remained just out of her reach. She cried out in frustration, then felt another hand over her own. A very large hand.

Erick didn't touch any part of her body save her needy pussy. But he trapped her hand beneath his large rough fingers, using the combination of their digits to rub her clit roughly.

Her eyes flew open, and his face came into focus. His gaze locked on hers. There was a hardness there. A command.

"Come, Daniella."

She broke.

Unlike the weak, tremulous orgasms she'd been able to give herself over the last few days, this one hit her hard. Her whole body shook with pleasure, contracting around nothing. She never felt so empty yet so fulfilled in one fell swoop.

Unlike Owen, Erick didn't pull her close and offer her comforting words. Instead, after the orgasm faded, he did the same. He stepped back, out of her reach, an expression on his face that on anyone else she would have thought was regret. But she had to be mistaken; what did the great prime of the tigers have to regret?

"You have a choice here, Daniella. You can allow me to mate with you. Or I can help you bring yourself to orgasm for the rest of the night. You'll be miserable, but not so miserable as you'd be without my touch. Women have made it through heats this way, or so I have heard. It won't be pleasant, but it is a possibility."

"And if we…" She pushed herself up into a sitting position, thankful that her mind was clear—clear-ish, anyway.

"It will be better. Days will pass without you having to be bred again."

God, it was tempting. And not only because of the heat. Because of Erick.

The last few days had revealed more of his character than she thought he even knew about himself. A character that he'd just confirmed in spades. Another man might have used her weakness tonight against her. It should have surprised her that Erick didn't use the opportunity to have sex with her, but it didn't. The man had honor, morals, even if they weren't quite as easy for her to define as those of a regular human. And he obviously cared about Owen. Heck, he might just care about her a little bit.

Erick broke the silence. "Would it be so terrible, being with me?"

The urge to lash out took her, but she swallowed the insult. The heat had her on edge, even now. Only minutes after Erick had helped her come, she could feel it building again. It wouldn't be long before she was in just as much discomfort as before. "No. I don't think it would be terrible at all. It's just—"

"You're worried about betraying Owen."

"Yes." Even though he'd encouraged her...it didn't seem right. Maybe it was just her very human way of looking at things, but dammit, she didn't have any experience looking at the world through nonhuman eyes. "Did you find any sign of him?"

"Not yet. The others are continuing to scour the local vamp hangouts, places where they're known to feed and congregate."

And he'd had to leave the search to attend to her. He didn't say it, but guilt filled her throat anyway. She swallowed hard. "I'm sorry that you had to leave the search for me. But I'm not sure I can...betray him like that. Even if he did give his permission. I'm just having a hard time imagining that he'd actually be okay with it."

He cocked his head, gaze locked on her. "Owen never told you, did he? I thought he hadn't."

"Never told me what?" She rubbed her eyes then looked at him again.

"You would not be the first woman we've shared."

Mouth dry, she asked, "What? You mean—"

"I mean together. One after the other. At the same time fucking different—" He stopped, and his voice gentled. "You understand? This would not be unusual for us."

"You've shared before." Suddenly Owen's easy capitulation made sense. Jealousy sparked. "Just another day, another bitch, for you two, huh?"

Erick's expression hardened. "Do not mistake our sharing for a lack of respect. Still, none of the others mattered. You do."

Hope surged in her chest, but cold logic cooled it quickly. Erick wasn't talking about emotional considerations. He didn't love her—they were still getting to know each other. And heck, she wasn't totally sure he was capable of such squishy emotions. She mattered only because of her blood. Because she was a royal.

But…was it possible that Owen felt the same way Erick did? No. He said he cared about her, and she had to believe him. Not like he could defend himself right now.

But if what Erick said was true, Owen could hardly fault her for this. Heck, if she'd read him right when he'd proposed this, he wanted it. She thought she'd imagined his reaction, or that it was only due to his loyalty to his clan, but if what Erick said was true, then maybe he wanted her to be with Erick, too, for very different reasons.

And she'd run when he was captured. How would she help get him back if she couldn't function?

"I ran away."

"What?"

"I should have stayed, should have run back inside

and grabbed a weapon. I could have called the cops or something. But instead, I ran. I barely even hesitated." She took a haggard breath. "I ran for over a mile, Erick. And I never once looked back to make sure he was following. To see if he was okay."

"You couldn't have helped him," he said, tone matter of fact. "You would have been captured as well. And if you hadn't called me when you did, we might not even know he was gone yet."

"But if I'd run back inside—"

"The human assumption that they are safe from vampires so long as they are cowering inside their homes is wrong. Had you not gotten far enough away, they would have caught you before the sun rose, and you'd likely be someone's pet right now."

What he said was logical—she knew that. But logic didn't hold a candle to the darkness of shame.

"Do not doubt that we will find him," Erick said, his words more an order than an attempt to offer comfort.

A long moment of silence settled over them as she considered his words. But no reply seemed appropriate. Any argument she might make would sound like she doubted his abilities—and their trust was tenuous, at best.

His face was hidden in shadow, so when he spoke, she started. "I really want to fuck you, Daniella. And mark my words, if I don't get to fuck you tonight, I won't force the issue. But I *will* fuck you someday. And you'll thank me for it."

Need surged, anger along with it, and she pressed her thighs together to try to alleviate some of the sudden pressure. She should have been insulted. Irritated by his arrogance, at least. But his words were exactly what her body wanted to hear, and she was sick and tired of fighting her own urges. "Fine. But you'll use a condom. And no biting."

His lip curled into a snarl.

"If you want to do this, you'll do it my way."

"But this way—you seek to eliminate the chance of cubs." He knelt in front of her, and his hands settled on her knees. Her breath caught in her throat and deep need curled in her lower abdomen at the touch. For a moment, she couldn't speak.

"I'm not having anyone's cubs—not until I'm ready." If that ever happened. Sure, she'd wanted kids in a someday sort of way, but never could she have imagined a situation like this. The world had to stop spinning long enough for her to take a breath, think about things, before she'd be ready to seriously consider doing anything so...permanent.

His eyebrow quirked, almost flirtatiously, and her heart fluttered wildly in her chest. "Perhaps this is your way of making sure we do this again."

Heat rushed up to her face. "No! I mean—I'm not—"

Erick chuckled, a low, deep sound that sent a spark straight to her sex. "I think you like the idea."

"Of what?" She rolled her eyes, doing her best impression of nonchalance. "Sex is sex."

"Liar." He leaned forward, lips only a breath from her own. "I think you like the idea of Owen and me, taking you every which way. Together."

She'd fantasized about that very thing, before Owen disappeared. The reminder of Owen, out there probably hurt, or worse, sobered her immediately. She leaned back, away from Erick.

His eyes narrowed in understanding. "We'll find him. I promise."

A quick nod, but she didn't try to speak.

"Let's do this." Erick said, pushing away from the couch and back to his feet in a way that appeared eerily inhuman.

"So romantic," she muttered.

"I'm a romantic kind of man," he deadpanned. He held out a hand for her and pulled her to her feet. Then he leaned in and placed his hands on her waist and took a deep breath. "You smell delicious, wildcat."

A shiver ran down her spine. He smelled pretty damn good, too.

Erick slipped her shirt over her head, and she moaned as the silky pajama top — the only piece of clothing she'd been able to stand against her skin — teased her.

Even in the low lighting, she could make out his appreciative stare. "My imagination didn't do you justice."

Before she could respond, he lowered his head to her breasts. Taking them in his hands, he felt the weight of them before licking her nipple. Then he started to massage them gently, apparently mindful of their sensitive condition.

"Oh," she breathed, and she threaded her fingers in his hair. This was happening, really happening.

He stepped back and tugged her matching shorts to the ground. At the sight of her naked pussy, he growled. "No panties?"

"Must have left them in my other pajamas."

The slightest grin, but the expression was too feral to be comforting. "Good. Now get on your hands and knees."

Chapter Six

The scent of her arousal was sharp in the air. Erick knew it wasn't just his presence, nor the heat, that put her in such a state. She liked the idea of him and Owen together, taking her the way she was meant to be taken. He relished the idea of it. Of watching Owen sink between her lips, fucking her slowly while he held her hair. Of moving in behind her, to push into her pussy while his best friend filled her mouth. Of pushing his way into her tight ass, while Owen thrust into her pussy.

And Daniella would writhe with pleasure, taking all they could give her. She'd relish in it. Coming for them over and over and over as they claimed her.

But as she went to her hands and knees in front of him, his best friend slipped from his mind. There was only him and Daniella. And their respective tigers, deep inside them at a level that operated only on instinct. Erick's tiger was more than ready to take her. So was the man.

His dick was already hard as a rock in his jeans, and he grunted as he slipped the material over his hips. Danielle looked over her shoulder at him, her eyes widening at the sight.

He took his cock in a firm grip and pulled. A hiss of pleasure escaped him when her mouth dropped open. He continued to jack himself off as he moved between her legs. It felt good, but not nearly as good as her tight little pussy was going to feel.

"You want this?" He tugged harder, relishing in the sensation. Loving the fact that she watched him with plain lust while he pleasured himself.

She licked her lips and the tiger inside of him roared with need. He dropped to his knees and moved between her legs. The scent of her sopping heat called to him, urged him to fuck her, take her, claim her.

"Condom," she said desperately. She had the offending item in her hand and he frowned at it. "Please."

He bared his teeth at her, but took the small wrapped thing from her, holding it like he might hold a snake. She turned, perhaps finally understanding that condoms weren't exactly something weretigers used regularly. Plucking the little wrapper from his hand, she gave him a nervous grin.

"Let me help," she murmured.

Before he could object, she had the condom out of the wrapper and was gripping his dick in one hand while trying to work the condom over his bulbous head. Her small hands felt good, and he closed his eyes to memorize the sensation. Then she was releasing him. A flash of disappointment until he opened his eyes and took in the sight before him.

His cock stood proudly pointing at the most luscious ass he'd ever seen. On her hands and knees, she looked to be the perfect, submissive tiger. And it didn't matter that she wasn't — hell, he enjoyed their sparring. All that mattered was that she was the perfect submissive to him right now when he and his tiger both raged to take her.

Seeing him watch her, a small sultry grin touched her lips. And very purposefully, she arched her back, presenting her gorgeous, wet heat to him. Inviting him to take her. A growl caught in his throat and he grabbed her hips, holding them tight, holding her in place. The temptation to simply take her was strong, but he slid a hand between them first, and slid a long finger into her heat.

"Fuck, you're wet," he said. So good. His cock twitched and his balls tightened. He penetrated her with two fingers, fucking her with his hand. Beneath him, she arched her back more and let out a long moan.

It was too much. He pulled his finger from her and gripped her hips, then with one swift motion, he took her.

She cried out. Ecstasy hit as her tight pussy clenched around him, her body trying to make room for his thickness. With shallow thrusts, he started to fuck her.

"Oh, God. Erick —"

A growl, and he began fucking her in earnest, gripping her hips hard as he plunged all the way in before pulling nearly all the way out and thrusting in again. His name on her lips, just like it should be. She wasn't thinking about any other man right now. This might be their only night together, and she would remember it. He'd make sure of that.

He slowed his pace, then pulled out of her all the way. Her wetness reflected off the condom she'd made him wear, and he stifled the urge to rip the thing off and toss it away. The tiger in him wanted to mate her — really mate her — spend his seed inside of her womb and ensure she would carry his cub. Just barely, he resisted the urge.

"Erick, please," she gasped.

"Will you beg me for it, Daniella?" he ground out. "Do you want me to make you come?"

Her eyes were wild when she looked back at him. "Yes. Please. I need it—I need *you*."

That was all he needed to hear. He positioned the head of his cock at her entrance and pushed. Her hands reflexively grabbed at the rug as he penetrated her fully. A deep breath and he gave into his instincts and fucked her for all he was worth.

Inside his mouth, his canines grew. The rest of his teeth would follow, readying him to bite her, claim her. Mark her as his mate.

He gritted his teeth and slipped a hand down to flick her clit.

With a loud cry, she came apart around him. Her pussy clenched hard and pushed him over the edge. Sparks lit his vision as he shot his seed inside of the condom separating them. And when they both came back down to earth, he pulled her sweat-touched body to his own, and for the first time in his life, held a woman while she fell asleep in his arms.

Erick woke with a regret—not something he'd expected. As a rule, he was not prone to regrets.

He should have kissed her.

But his father's advice—advice he'd stuck to his whole adult life—was hard to shake. *Don't kiss them, son. Unless you're certain they're the last woman you want to mate.* An idea that his father would have found ludicrous. Even though they had two sons together, Erick was certain his father had not once kissed his mother.

Would Daniella have laughed if he'd confessed to her that he'd fucked his way through more women than he could remember, but that he'd never kissed a single one?

Owen had laughed, muttering something Erick didn't fully understand about a pretty woman. But it had served him well. Getting attached was something he didn't do. His focus—his loyalty—had to be always for his people.

Daniella's breath evened as she fell into a deep slumber. She needed the sleep, that much was obvious from the dark circles beneath her eyes. The heat's fault, no doubt. And his own, for not acting sooner.

But, idiot that he was, taking her when she was desperate—a desperation he could have brought her to the first day he'd found her, frightened and alone at her apartment—no longer appealed to him. The idea of it brought a bad taste to his mouth. Even taking her in the way he just had, satisfying though it was…it wasn't enough.

He shook his head and got up from the floor. He removed the offensive thing he'd been forced to wear to prevent her pregnancy with his T-shirt and tossed them both to the floor. With a quick, silent motion, he picked her up and then headed for her room. Exhausted, she didn't wake, even when he set her down beneath the covers and pulled them to her chin.

A sound from the living room touched his ears, and he strode back, plucking his phone from his pants pocket. Quickly, he pulled on his jeans and then headed outside.

"Yes," he said.

"We've got the fuckers, Erick. Tracked the scent from one of their sleazy holes to a house in Aurora. Place has a basement. I couldn't get close enough to catch the scent to confirm it's him, but Kara swears she smells cat."

Fuck. Yeah. He gripped the phone tighter. There were a few hours before the sun would rise, but he wanted to get there as quickly as possible. "Give me an hour or so to get back down there. We'll go in at first light."

"You sure that's wise? Counting you, there will only the three of us and the kid going in."

Glenn didn't say it aloud, but that was for good reason. Erick had brought more tigers down the first day Owen had disappeared in a desperate effort to cover more ground, but he'd had to send them back for the safety of the clan. The number of warriors they had — true fighters experienced in tangling with vampires — were few. And leaving the clan unprotected for long would invite vampires to attempt raids.

"It'll have to be enough," he said, decided. Any more and the clan could fall. If he and his best men were lost, the clan would suffer, but they might rebound. Especially with the lure of a royal female to bring in another royal male to lead them. Hell, Nicolas might come back and serve, if he had to. He hadn't contacted anyone since he'd left, but the clan could track him down if they had to. Such information could be bought.

The decision wasn't an easy one. But the sacrifice was one that Owen would understand. Hell, he'd probably be pissed knowing Erick was risking those he would bring.

"Hey," a sleepy voice said behind him. He turned to see Daniella. She'd donned a new set of pajamas, and the desire to rip them off so he could see her again forced him to keep his hands at his sides.

"You should be resting."

"What did they say?" she asked, ignoring his comment.

"We've found him."

Emotions crossed her expression quickly. Elation. Worry. Happiness. Fear.

"When are we leaving?" she asked, her expression

settling into the one he was most familiar with on her: determination.

"*We* aren't going anywhere."

Anger. Oh, yeah, he was familiar with that one on her, too. "No freaking way are you leaving me behind. I'm going."

"What part of the dangerous vampires thing don't you understand?"

She jutted out her chin. "What part of the I won't be left behind thing is eluding you?"

"Daniella." Frustrated, he ran a hand over his hair and tried to find a way to explain that wouldn't offend her. Nothing came to mind. "You're a liability."

Her eyes narrowed. "Maybe so. But I have the right to be there."

"No, you don't." He wasn't budging on this, on her safety.

She tapped her chin and quirked her lips in an adorable way while she thought about it. Finally, she said, "Okay, how about this. I go, but I stay far away. Surely, the wolves have somewhere I can hang with some strong dudes or something while you're fighting. You can trust me to stay out of the way. I swear."

The idea of her being anywhere close didn't thrill him, and he also didn't like the idea of her being in the care of the wolves. But Grayson had proved himself to be honorable thus far, if too friendly and pushy for Erick's taste. It was a compromise. If nothing else, this would allow him to test the alpha and his clan. See what they were made of. See if they were as loyal as they swore.

And something told him that if he didn't give her this, show her he trusted her, that something might be damaged between them. Irreparably.

"Fine."

She squealed and jumped into his arms. He held her close for a moment before she pulled her head back to look him in the eye. "Thank you."

His voice wouldn't come, and he cleared his throat. "You're welcome."

Then she kissed him. A platonic thank-you kiss. But with her soft lips against his, he couldn't resist kissing her back. If things went south, it might be his last chance. Damn his father's advice.

After a moment's hesitation, Erick deepened the kiss. His mouth pressed hard against hers, and his tongue teased her lips until they opened, letting him in. He held her closer, tighter, and she could feel his erection, hard as a rock, pressing just where she needed him most.

The way he'd taken her before was savage, like an animal. His lips had never touched hers. It had been good—exactly what she'd needed. But now she needed something else. And strangely, she thought he might, too.

The kiss was tentative, testing, and so sweet. She moaned into his mouth, and he carried her back into the house without breaking their kiss.

Erick set her on the bed and made short work of her clothing and his own jeans. His cock was already hard and ready, and she could see the slightest bit of moisture touching the tip.

"Do you have another of those infernal things with you?"

She licked her lips.

"If you continue to look at me like that, I will not be responsible for my actions," he warned.

Heat flushed her cheeks, and she reached for her purse on the nightstand.

After she handed it to him, he tossed it beside her on the bed then joined her, his much larger frame over her making her feel very small. "I hoped you'd only brought one."

"I'll bet you did." She grinned. "But a girl's gotta dream big, ya know?" She reached between them and took hold of his thick cock. A naughty grin she couldn't help but tease him with. "Look at that. Sometimes dreams come true."

He inhaled sharply, and she started to work him, enjoying having a little bit of control this time.

Gently, she pressed his chest with her free hand, and taking the hint, he backed up a bit and went to his knees.

"I'm glad you dream big," he said, but he sounded anything but nonchalant.

"Oh, yeah?" She flashed him a grin and quirked her eyebrow. He bared his teeth at her and she laughed. Then she took him in her mouth.

Erick jerked, obviously surprised. "You—"

With a quick motion, she took as much of him as she could fit into her mouth and swirled her tongue. Then, she began rocking him in and out, taking more of him each time.

"Daniella—" He swore, but didn't try to move her, nor did he attempt to direct her.

High on the power of it and drunk on his masculine scent, she worked him all the way to the back of her throat. Swallowing automatically, she got another moan from the stolid man.

She could feel his dick swelling in her mouth. A few more seconds and she would taste him. The idea made her move faster. She wanted to know his taste.

Pain arched from her scalp as Erick pulled her off his cock. Fuck her if he and Owen didn't sport some of the same annoying ways to keep her from doing as she liked.

"No. Not tonight, wildcat. But soon." His eyes glowed, green and amber. "I can't wait to see you swallow every drop I give you. Can't wait to taste your heat. Explore every inch of you." Then he was pushing her back on the bed, trapping her with his large body. The sound of a condom wrapper tearing, then he was donning it himself. Fast learner.

His mouth found hers, and he kissed her, but with none of the sweetness he'd shown before. As if he was desperate to taste her, he plunged his tongue into her mouth and ravaged her. One hand bracing to keep from smothering her, he used the other to work his cock into place. The tip slid inside, and her whole body sparked in response.

"Hell, Daniella," he said savagely, breaking the kiss. With one smooth motion, they were joined.

The sensation of being almost unbearably full drew a cry from her. Then Erick was moving, a gentle rocking that brought her to the cusp of an orgasm just as quickly as his hard fucking. He murmured something sweet, something she couldn't make out. Then kissed her again, gently, like the first kiss. His hips moved faster. One if his hands moved to tease her nipple and cup her breast.

With her scream muffled by his mouth, she could only moan and shudder when the orgasm unfurled. The quaking started in her sex, then rolled out to send her stomach and thighs spasming. From her fingers to her toes, there was no place on her body that didn't feel it. Erick finally broke their kiss to mutter her name, and then he shuddered, pumping inside of her hard, until he grew still.

He didn't pull out of her body for a while. Time passed strangely, and she was almost certain he'd allowed her to doze. Finally he stood, leaving her feeling strangely empty for his absence.

"We need to get ready to go," he said, the low rumble of his voice filling the room, almost startling after their quiet moment together. "It's time to rescue your mate."

Chapter Seven

The gray light of predawn settled over the city as they pulled into the wolves' warehouse. It still seemed weird to her that this normal-looking metal building would be some sort of stronghold, or at least meeting place, for a bunch of werewolves.

A giggle caught in her throat, and Erick sent her a questioning glance. "My life is so weird," she explained.

In response, he reached over and squeezed her shoulder. It appeared even amazing sex couldn't make the weretiger prime talkative. She couldn't blame him. The whole thing had shut her up for a while, too.

But what a night. Her head was clear, and after a nice long shower, she felt more like herself than she had since this whole mess began. Add to all that the fact that Owen would be safe and by her side soon and she was almost giddy.

The slightest niggling of worry about what would happen when they did rescue Owen had planted itself in her mind, but she knew they'd figure things out if only they could get Owen back. But no matter how much she told herself that, she couldn't shake the tiny doubt. What if Owen was really hurt? Erick seemed to think that unlikely because it would reduce his value and the vampires wouldn't want that—but what if he tried to escape, tried to get back to her, would they have hurt him then?

And what if, despite his suggestion that she do so, Owen was bothered by the fact that she had slept with Erick? She'd been sure that if it came up she'd be able to honestly tell Owen that being with Erick meant nothing to her, and they'd be able to move on. But after being with the prime—especially after the second time, when he'd been so tender with her—saying something like that would feel like a lie.

Or hell, maybe her hormones were so fucked up she didn't know the difference between animal sex and making love.

"You ready?" Erick asked, shifting the truck into gear and cutting the engine.

She offered him a nervous smile and nodded. "As ready as I'll ever be to hang out with a pack of werewolves."

Erick didn't laugh, but she hadn't expected him to. Ever since they'd stepped outside of the cabin, outside of their intimate oasis, he'd shifted into the mindset of a hunter. Of a prime seeking his second. All business. Full intensity.

If she hadn't been so nervous about the whole thing, she might've felt bad for the vampires.

Gravel crunched under their feet as they walked to the warehouse door. Erick opened it for her, allowing her to walk through first. She hid a smile, certain he wouldn't be amused by her observation that he'd finally developed a little bit of courtesy. Had someone taught him that during his day away from her? She wouldn't be surprised if one of the other men had taken him aside and shown in the basics.

Still fighting a grin, she headed for the open area they'd met Grayson in before. Erick stuck close to her side, bumping into her as they walked. The man was certainly protective of her. Might've been super annoying if it weren't for the fact she now knew vampires were real. And possibly hunting her.

Her stomach rolled at the thought.

Grayson waited for them, this time seated at a large conference table situated in one corner of the room. Did being an alpha not demand its own office, at least? Kara wasn't with him, but several other people were. Three men and another woman. The men were, to her eye, somewhat forgettable. But then she'd been served a steady diet of pretty ridiculous levels of hotness in men lately, so her judgment there was probably messed up. The woman, however, was anything but forgettable.

If petite, blond Kara was the opposite of what Daniella might have guessed a werewolf would look like, this woman was far closer to the mark, if only because of her uniqueness. Her dark hair was short and spiked all over with red tips, and her features had a distinctive Asian cast. Heavy eyeliner and lipstick accentuated features that didn't seem to need any help. But the leather jacket and pants, biker boots, and a definite violent edge to her expression, all screamed badass.

"Grayson," Erick said. A long pause that verged on uncomfortable. "Thank you for your help."

Daniella bit her lip. Imagine that. A thank you and his head hadn't even exploded. Maybe the man could grow a little.

Grayson nodded and gave them a tight-lipped smile. "Kara scented at least eight different suckers, but no way to tell how many are in there now."

Tension filled the air, so palpable she could practically

see it. Eight sounded like a lot to her—apparently to everyone else, too.

"I'll lead you there. I assume your pretty new queen will stay here?" Grayson asked. "Aiko and the others will look after her."

The weight of Erick's gaze hit her, but she didn't look at him. She'd asked to come; she was going to stay strong.

"Swear that she will be safe in your care," Erick said.

Grayson didn't hesitate. "I swear to you that she will be safe, no matter what happens to your people during this fight."

"Wait." She turned to Erick. He didn't dodge her gaze, but his jaw tensed. "The wolves aren't helping."

"No. This is our fight."

"Eight vampires against the three of you and skinny Chris?" She mentally apologized to Chris—thank goodness he wasn't here. Poor kid was going to get a complex after dealing with her all week.

"Up to eight," he pointed out, most unhelpfully.

She'd promised herself and Erick that she was going to be calm, but she was about two seconds away from losing her shit.

"What the fuck, Erick?"

"The wolves have kept their part of the bargain. We can take care of our own." His gaze shifted to Grayson, as if this conversation was over. "Thank you for your vow to care for her."

"No." She stepped between Erick and Grayson, drawing a growl from the man behind her, but her attention was focused squarely on the wolves' alpha. "You have to help them. What the hell is your treaty good for, anyway, if you guys aren't even going to help each other when you need it?"

Grayson grimaced. "Change this big can't be done in leaps. The risk —"

"Screw your risk. Your allies need to you. What are you going to do? Just hide in the shadows so the big, scary vampires don't get you? Well, I guess that says all I need to know about wolves."

"We don't need their help." Eric's voice was firm behind her, but she didn't turn around to look at him. Her fight was with the wolves, with Grayson.

The alpha wolf didn't say anything at all, but she could see his resolve wavering.

"Sometimes you have to take great risks to accomplish great things. And banding together now," she stepped back and angled herself to include Erick in the conversation, "maybe the vampires will think twice before they grab another tiger or wolf off the street."

Her gamble struck a nerve. Grayson flinched almost imperceptibly. Erick wasn't the only leader who'd lost someone to the vampires.

"Very well," Grayson said. "But I will have his word that if we are ever in need, the tigers will come to our aid as well."

Erick hesitated and she was on the verge of trying to physically shake some sense into the man when he finally responded. "Fine. You have my word."

Grayson's gaze was steady, locked on the tigers' prime. "So it is witnessed."

His words had the gravity, the feeling of something very official. But what it might mean for the tiger clan in the future wasn't her problem—not today. Today, the only thing that mattered was getting Owen back.

Erick watched the house for any sign of life, but it was quiet in the light of day. Luckily, it was also situated on a private lot that was distant from its neighbors and had a lot of coverage with overgrown trees and bushes. The spot no doubt chosen by the vampires to keep their own activities hidden from prying eyes.

The last thing they needed to deal with were the keepers—the group of protectors slash assassins who ensured that nonhumans stayed outside of the eyes of humans, and punished those who stepped too far out of line.

With all of the windows heavily shuttered from the outside, and likely covered on the inside as well, the house was perfectly set up for vampires. The top of window frames revealed the basement, but the windows themselves had been buried.

A plan had been set, and he was confident it would work if the wolves kept their end of the deal.

He headed for the back door of the large, ranch-style house, with Anton, Glenn, and Chris at his heels. In all likelihood, Owen would be confined in the basement. The suckers themselves could be anywhere inside the house.

A blink and he'd formed claws and his teeth had stretched in his mouth. The door was reinforced, but not with a royal tiger in mind. Two kicks, and it shattered, opening and revealing the interior of the house.

The suckers had probably been sleeping, but Erick knew the noise would rouse them.

"Windows?" Anton muttered.

A quick glance revealed that would be impossible. The vamps had to leave a door accessible for their own use, but the windows were secured with metal attached to the frames of the house. They could pull them down and gain the benefit of the sunlight, but it would take too long.

He shook his head and walked farther into the space, heading into the next room. Basement access would be behind a door. They just had to find the right one.

The sucker was on him, impossibly fast.

Taken by surprise, Erick flew into a wall, farther into the dark house. Noises behind him confirmed the others were fighting as well. He jumped to his feet and took in the landscape quickly. Three suckers were closing in on him. Anton and Chris grappled with two on the other side of the room. Glenn was nowhere to be seen, but crashes in the room they'd entered from made his fight apparent.

At least six vamps, then. Maybe more.

Adrenaline pumped into his system, and he grappled with the first sucker who approached. A second tried to grab him and he managed to sink his teeth into the male's flesh. The sucker cried out, and two seconds later faltered. Erick released his hold and the vampire fell to the ground.

The paralytic in their teeth was meant for mating, for keeping females from getting away at the point the male tiger's seed was ready to be released. But it worked even better on vampires. Less than a minute of paralysis for the women of their own kind, but it could knock a sucker on its ass for closer to ten if the venom came from a royal.

The vampire he grappled with tried to scratch at his face, his eyes, but Erick threw him behind him with enough force that he went through the drywall. The third hesitated and narrowed his eyes.

A scream tore Erick's gaze from the sucker. Chris went down, a small male vampire on him and another next to him who, no doubt, had helped.

Erick growled. How many vampires were there? And where were the wolves?

"Here, kitty, kitty," a low, sultry voice said. She didn't yell, but Erick's ears were sensitive—as were all cats'—and his eyes moved from Chris to take in the female vampire that walked into the room like she owned the place. Like she had nothing to fear.

She licked her lips—blood flashed on the tip of her tongue. And as she moved closer, he could make out the dark red stains that were difficult to see on her black blouse.

Shit. Glenn.

The woman grinned at him, revealing short, sharp fangs. Her bright eyes flashed red in the low light.

A stalker.

Realization hit and his stomach twisted. Five minutes had passed, and their backup was nowhere to be seen. The wolves weren't coming.

He steeled his spine. Daniella was safe. His people were safe.

And he wasn't going down without a fight.

PART THREE

Chapter One

Erick was going to die.

Somewhere in the back of his mind, his father screamed.

About duty. About protecting the clan. About his idiocy.

The unbendable man, his face and body and mind scarred from the decades he'd spent out in the world. From the years he never spoke of before he found their little clan and wrested it from its prior prime—from all accounts, a man even harsher than Erick's father— he would never have approved his son's decision to come after Owen. Faced with the same situation, Erick had no doubts as to what his father would have done—dragged Daniella to their home in the mountains the day he'd found her, with or without her consent.

And if he'd somehow landed himself in this situation—with his second kidnapped by vampires— he would have let the man die. He never would have trusted the wolves to help.

But Erick couldn't walk away. Because Owen was his friend. Hell, Owen was his *only* friend.

His lip turned into a snarl as he circled the stalker,

and she grinned, flashing the stunted teeth that marked her the most dangerous of vampires.

No, his father wouldn't have found himself in this situation, because his father didn't have any friends. And it was only through the grace of the man's inattention that Erick found himself with another person he cared about nearly as much as his clan.

The stalker smiled, and Erick closed his eyes. A brief blink to push his tiger form into the forefront of his mind. The barest of a second to change form. And when his new eyes opened, she was there. Taller than his new form, lips curled in amusement.

A snarl, then he flew at her. But she was already in motion, so quick that even he had trouble following the movement. Claws grazed the material of her shirt, and then she was behind him. He whirled around, expecting an attack. Instead, she winked.

The stalker was playing with him.

Anger spiked at the realization, and he flew at her again, gnashing his teeth and swiping his paws in a vain effort to strike the impossibly-quick moving vampire. If he could get her with his teeth, the paralytic toxin might slow her down enough for him to take her, but she was too fast.

"Silly kitty," she purred.

She was playing with him, all right. Goading him into exhausting himself. The smart thing to do would be to try to run. But they'd lose Owen. Not only Owen, he'd lose Daniella, too. Why would she stay if Owen was gone? The thoughts sent a spike of pain through his chest.

No. He wasn't running. Hell, he was pretty damn sure the stalker wouldn't let him if he tried. If he had to go down today, he'd go facing his enemy.

As if she could see his thoughts, hear his decision, the stalker's smile widened, and her stance relaxed just the slightest bit. "Good kitty."

A howl cut through the air.

The vampire jerked, and she turned her head to watch the entrance.

Erick struck.

Someone shook Owen roughly, and his teeth immediately shifted. He snapped at the sucker shaking him a second before the scent penetrated his ragged thoughts.

He blinked at the man who had woken him — who was now a couple of feet away after dodging his bite. "Erick?" he asked, voice raspy. When was the last time he'd been given water? Oh, yeah, he'd thrown that in the fucking stalker's face.

She hadn't been amused.

"I'm here. You're safe." The prime's voice was solid. Real. And the last fleeting bit of worry that he was dreaming or coerced by that damnable stalker who, no doubt, would have loved to burrow her way into his brain disappeared. Relief hit.

Then dread.

"Where is she?"

Erick grimaced. "The stalker got away. Real fucking nice trick in the daytime."

He shook his head, and a stab of pain in his temple made him scowl. "No. Daniella."

Erick's expression softened, then his guard came back up. "She's fine. Safe."

Realization hit. He could smell Daniella here. But she wasn't here. She was on Erick. His nose wasn't as good as a wolf's, but her sweet scent was so strong on the prime that she could have been in the same room—the same cell.

Erick had claimed her.

He shouldn't be jealous—it was what he wanted. Best fucking case scenario. But the idea of Erick and Daniella together while he rotted in here…

Anger-fueled heat rushed through his body, and only a hand reaching out to grip his shoulder kept him from shifting. Whatever the hell the vampires had given him to keep him in his human form had definitely worn off.

"Breathe, brother. Breathe. She's still yours. She was always yours."

He looked up in time to see a flash of something behind Erick's eyes—but he couldn't identify the emotion before it was gone.

"Breathe," Erick said again. A command from his prime.

Owen took in a deep breath, and let it out slowly. Another. Finally, the tension making every muscle in his body ready to burst in a flash of motion relented.

"Sorry," he muttered, but he wasn't sure he spoke the truth.

Erick nodded. "You've been through a lot. And the serum fucks with you—or so the wolves tell me."

"Serum?"

"The drug they give you to keep you human. To keep you weak and exhausted."

Another surge of anger at the reminder of the syringe they'd shoved into his neck every few hours. He tamped it down with another deep breath. Damn vampires. Of course they'd have something to control shifters, to keep them weak until they were sold to someone powerful enough to control them. What happened after they were sold…well, Owen was more than happy he hadn't had to find that out first hand. "How long?"

"Few days."

Fuck. No wonder Daniella had—no, he wasn't himself enough yet to think about her yet. About his mate and his prime.

"Thanks for coming for me."

Erick's smile was grim. "I'll always come for you, brother. But save your thanks for Daniella. If the plan had been left in my hands, we'd both be dead. Or worse, slaves."

Chapter Two

Daniella clutched the oh-shit handle and tried not to glare at the man driving them to the tiger clan's stronghold. Not Anton's fault that the road shook her bones and rattled her all over the back of the SUV until she wasn't sure if she was going to throw up or fall over. The dusty, uncivilized jeep path was worst than the road to the tigers' cabin. That one had been gravel, at least. This seemed to be made of dirt potholes strung together by yet more dirt.

Every bounce and she had to fight the urge to cling to Owen. To cross the one foot distance between them in the SUV. To fling herself into his arms and seek his comfort.

Selfish.

If anyone needed comforting, it was Owen. Even now, she could make out a sickly, blue and black bruise that marred the skin between his right ear and chin. She hadn't seen the rest of him, hadn't been able to catalogue any injuries other than his jaw and his lip and his knuckles, but she was certain that he was hurt even more badly beneath the old sweatshirt and ill-fitting jeans he'd no doubt borrowed from a werewolf that was a size or four too small.

But other than a quick hug and a soft smile when

she'd flung herself at him after they'd brought him back to the wolves' warehouse, he'd kept his distance. Bridging that was the only thing she could think about. Problem was, she wasn't sure how.

"I missed you," she said, voice soft. Not the first time she'd said it, but she couldn't seem to come up with anything else. An apology for sleeping with Erick had been on the tip of her tongue when she'd first seen Owen, but she hadn't been able to utter it. The words felt like a lie.

Besides, it was hard to express herself when they hadn't yet had a moment alone.

He turned to look at her, his warm brown eyes weary. "I missed you, too."

The new distance between them wasn't something she knew how to gulf. The situation was too different from anything she'd ever experienced.

The SUV hit another large pothole and he grunted. In his eyes, she saw a flash of pain that he turned back to looking out his window to hide.

She put a hand on his shoulder, and he didn't pull away. It felt like progress.

But when they finally arrived, after darkness the likes of which she'd never seen in the city closed over them, he offered her a smile—one she was certain he meant to be reassuring, but looked forced—and a promise he'd see her later. Owen paused and squeezed her hand, but his eyes never met hers.

Then he was gone. Disappearing with a tiger she didn't know. The doctor, she gathered, by his immediate barrage of medical questions at Owen. The no-longer-flirty Anton showed her to a guest cabin.

Miserable for reasons she was too tired to wrap her mind around, she laid down on the bed without even a shower, exhaustion seeping into her every pore. Maybe Owen would come to her while she slept.

Darkness soaked Daniella's cabin — darkness Erick could easily see in, yet he hesitated at her door. Owen was almost certainly with her. It felt like he was intruding, and that feeling bugged the shit out of him.

It was for the best. He had no doubt in his mind how things would proceed. Daniella would continue to bond with Owen. His second had bitten her, mated her. They had a history. Maybe even love, or some such nonsense.

What did he have with her? A moment. A flash of pleasure. A brief second of connection. Trying to force it to be anything else would drive a wedge between them. It was for the best. Erick's main concern was for his clan. And keeping things as they were was the surest way to keep them all safe, keep the clan together.

He took in a deep breath, scenting the air, and gripped Daniella's overnight bag harder. She would want it — her clothes, toiletries. He'd made a point of stopping to get it on his way up. It would be chickenshit not to deliver it now.

Disappointment touched him, but he ruthlessly pushed the emotion away. Things would go as planned. Daniella would mate Owen, and perhaps she would allow Erick to mate her during her most fertile times. Surely being here, with her people, would convince her of the necessity.

He swallowed the sudden bad taste in his mouth.

Just a look. He'd drop off the bag, then he'd go to his own cabin. His body begged for sleep. After fighting the vampires and rescuing Owen, he'd had to send Daniella and Owen home while he met with the wolves. Grayson hadn't been happy to hear that there was a stalker running free in his territory—a stalker with an obvious interest in shifters. And the wolf had made it quite clear that this discussion wasn't over. But Erick had needed to get back to his clan. Back to his mate.

No. Not *his* mate.

Mate or not, the tiger inside of him needed to see that Daniella was okay. Whatever doubts Erick had about how he would fit into Daniella's life, his tiger didn't share them. But he couldn't allow instincts to rule him, not when the cost could be so grim.

Silently, he stepped into the cabin and made his way to the bathroom, where he set the bag quietly on the floor. The door to the bedroom stood half-open, and he nudged it the rest of the way.

In a heap, Daniella slept in the middle the bed. Jeans were in a pile on the floor, but she still wore the shirt he'd last seen her in. A soft snore escaped her, and he smiled at the noise. But something was wrong. It took him a second to realize what was bothering him.

She was alone.

Where the hell was Owen? His second had been injured, but not gravely so. The vampires, obviously planning to sell the tiger to the highest bidder, had kept him in pretty good shape. He'd been a little beat up, but had suffered no real damage. And, according to the clan doctor, he hadn't been bitten.

At least, not that the doctor could tell.

Erick frowned and filed that thought for later. A discussion with Owen was in order. The clan would do what it must to keep its second safe—to keep them all safe—but Erick needed to know the truth in order to do that.

In her bed, Daniella sighed in her sleep. Erick fisted his hands at his sides and forced himself to stay where he was. The temptation to crawl into bed with her, to slip under the covers and curl into her warm, lush body, was fierce. But it wasn't his right. And he still had work to do before he could find his bed. Waking the doctor and getting a report on Owen's health face-to-face, for one.

And he needed to find out where his second was. Why he wasn't here. Guarding their—Owen's—mate.

She wasn't Erick's, but what a mate she would be. Not only did she make every cell in his body thrum with need when she was near, or even when he caught the slightest hint of her scent on the air, but she was formidable and other ways, too. Smart. Stubborn. Brave.

If she hadn't interceded, Erick had no illusions about what would've happened to him and the rest of his men. As much as he detested admitting it, the wolves had saved them—all but Glenn. No matter the terms they'd agreed to, Erick hadn't expected that— not really. And hell, if it'd been up to him, the tigers would've gone in alone.

The woman could be his match.

He shook his head. This line of thought was pointless. She had made her feelings clear—she was in love with Owen. Erick would be lucky if she allowed him in her bed again. The next time the heat struck, she would have her Owen to satisfy her.

Anger crawled up his spine at the thought. Owen had always been his one true friend. His only friend. Erick's father had made sure of that. And no matter what stupid childish jealousy or short-term fight, he'd never wished for his friend to be gone. And he didn't wish it now. But it was a near thing.

Daniella rolled over in the bed, tossing the comforter to the side as she moved, revealing the sexy line of her barely-covered ass and cotton panties. A growl escaped him, and his cock hardened at the sight.

With a heavy sigh, she sat up in the bed. Reflexes quick, he stepped back silently, so she couldn't see him behind the doorframe. He tensed, then relaxed. What the hell? Why not go in there? It was possible her feelings had changed. Or maybe the heat would still be upon her, and she wouldn't mind sharing her bed with him again. By the time it was over, he'd make sure she enjoyed every minute of it.

A hardness formed in his stomach, and his mind rebelled at the thought. No. The idea of getting into her bed only because the heat drove her had lost its appeal.

But maybe something inside her had shifted as it had in him. Sure, she and Owen shared history, a relationship. But maybe their time together had opened her mind—hell, maybe even her heart—to Erick as well.

"Owen?" Her soft voice echoed in the mostly empty guesthouse.

Something constricted in his chest. He stood stiffly, until he heard her settle back in. Until her breathing grew even. Then he left, as silently as he'd arrived.

Light seeped between her eyelids and she scrunched her face, trying to close them tighter. Had she forgotten to shut her curtains? Utter silence surrounded her. Her fan wasn't running, and she didn't hear the family upstairs stomping around as they started their day. Had she slept late?

She sat up in the bed and blinked at her surroundings.

Night had cast its shadow over the tigers' home when they'd arrived the night before, and she hadn't bothered to even turn on a light as she'd found her way to bed.

She frowned. That didn't seem right.

Was it possible her night vision was improving? Seemed like a benefit of being part cat. She really needed to find someone to explain all this to her in more detail. Who knew when she might need some actual tiger skills? Meeting the vampires face-to-face, losing Owen, had certainly proved that the dangers of this new world were very real.

The bed was cold around the spot where she'd slept. For some reason, she'd thought Owen had come to join her in the night, but it sure didn't seem like it. And knowing Erick, he was still in Denver arguing with the wolves.

A lump formed in her throat and she swallowed. A deep breath calmed her somewhat, and she hopped out of bed. Sure, things weren't happening like she'd expected them to. For some reason, she'd had a far more romantic view of what would happen if the men ever got her back to her *people*. But she couldn't exactly expect things to go perfectly, not with how they'd arrived.

Heck, Owen had just been rescued from vampires. And the tigers had lost a man—Glenn—for crying out loud. She had no right to expect to be numero uno in anyone's mind right now.

Bolstered by her internal pep talk, she showered quickly, happy to find that someone had left her hastily-packed bag from the cabin in the bathroom. It had her last clean set of clothes, and most importantly, her toothbrush.

The shower was divine, with only the slightest hint of the sulfur that inundated the ground water in the mountains. She washed away the nervous sweat and nervous energy of the day before, and by the time she turned off the water, her confidence had returned. Finding Owen—Erick, too, if he'd arrived—was her first priority.

Her stomach growled loudly and she grimaced. Okay, maybe food first, then track down the guys. Besides, chances were if she wandered around for a bit, they'd find her.

She stepped out into the bright Colorado day. The air was brisk and clean, and blue skies extended as far as she could see. Sunlight bathed her, improving her mood even more. She headed for the main cabin, a large building Anton had pointed out to her the night before.

It appeared even more unusual in the daylight. The building was very lodge-like, large and built with what looked to be an actual old-style cabin structure—big trees and all. Strangely, it looked built into the mountain behind it. At the very least, it was close enough to touch rock from a back window.

Very unusual. How long had the structure been there? It looked old—maintained and sturdy, but definitely not modern.

Forcing her shoulders square and her back straight, she walked up to the large double doors. The one on the right was propped open with a rock large enough to conk someone good on the head, if a person was actually strong enough to pick it up. Pushing her nervous worries to the back of her mind, she slipped inside.

The smell of bacon hit her first, and the scent made her mouth water. The great room in front of her wasn't exactly bustling with people, but she glimpsed a few down a long hallway. Offices? Did weretigers need offices? Picturing Erick behind a desk made her snort. The man wasn't exactly the type. But Owen…maybe.

She took another deep breath, practically tasting bacon, and followed her nose into a room to her left. Tables and chairs filled the area in a somewhat orderly fashion, and many of the seats were occupied by people eating the bacon she'd smelled, among other goodies. The cafeteria. But there was no obvious place to pick up food. A long counter which seemed to be suited to that purpose was along the back wall, but no one manned it. And, much to her stomach's disappointment, no food.

A quick scan revealed more than a dozen faces that gave her furtive, neutral glances, but none were familiar. None were terribly friendly.

Her stomach twisted and she had a sudden flashback to her first day at a new high school. Feet itching to run, she had to force herself to stay put.

She shook herself mentally and stared right back at them. No way was she running. She wasn't a kid. She was a royal fucking tiger.

Whatever the heck that really meant. Maybe nothing to these people.

One woman wasn't giving her the same quick glances as the others. And in fact, her nose was buried so far in a book that she may not have even noticed Daniella's arrival. She seemed the safest bet.

Decision made, Daniella approached her table.

"Hi," she said, hating the hesitance in her own voice.

The woman appeared to be in her early twenties, and it took her a long moment to notice Daniella's presence. Finally, she looked up from her book and blinked. She lowered the book a few inches and pushed up her glasses. "Hello."

Taking that for an invitation, Daniella sat across from her. "I'm Daniella."

"Oh!" The young woman perked up and dropped

a bookmark into her book, then set it on the table in front of her. "The royal, right? Cool beans. We heard you were coming."

It was Daniella's turn to blink. Whatever stereotype she'd had in her head, she hadn't expected the woman to be so outgoing. "That's me. I guess."

"I'm Cat." Her face scrunched. "Terrible, I know. Just horribly predicable for a tiger." She leaned forward and Daniella did the same. In a loud whisper, she confided, "It's not my full name. If you heard it, you'd understand why I go by the nickname." There was a snicker at a nearby table and Cat huffed and turned her nose up. "Anyway," she stretched the word, exaggerating each syllable. "It's nice to meet you."

Daniella fought a grin and leaned back in her seat. Maybe this place wouldn't be so bad after all. "Nice to meet you, too."

"How are you liking our little slice of heaven here?" Cat waved at nothing in particular.

"No idea yet," she replied honestly. "I've only seen my cabin, some woods that looked very wood-like, and this bacon-less cafeteria." Her stomach chose that moment to reaffirm its displeasure at that fact, and her face heated.

Cat laughed. "Hungry?"

She leaned forward, and Cat mirrored her. A surge of hope ran through her. It felt an awful lot like she'd made a new friend. Voice pitched low, she asked, "Who do you have to screw around here to get some bacon?"

Cat laughed, then the sound cut off abruptly and she sat up straight, face suddenly solemn and eyes wide. But she wasn't looking at Daniella — her gaze was locked on something behind her.

"That would be me."

Chapter Three

*I*f she'd been embarrassed before, she was mortified now. Slowly, she turned to look over her shoulder to face the man whose growly voice had cut into the first relaxed conversation she'd had in what felt like years.

"Hi." Dammit. She was smiling at him — she'd meant to glare. Erick didn't deserve a smile after sneaking up on her like that.

To her surprise, a hint of a smile greeted her, too. Then Erick turned his attention to her new friend, and before Daniella could object, Cat had grabbed her book, made an excuse about needing to get back to the library, and hurried away.

Erick sat in Cat's seat, and Daniella finally had no problem finding a glare for him. "You chased off my new friend."

He arched a brow at her, and she wished he didn't look as scrumptious as the bacon she smelled. "You made friends with our little Catnip?"

Catnip. Holy crap. No wonder she went by Cat. Poor tiger. "I did. And you chased her away."

Erick gestured at a young man walking by. The man nodded and disappeared through a doorway at the back of the cafeteria. Had Erick just made some poor random guy get them food? It was a safe bet.

"I can get my own breakfast. I just wasn't sure where to go."

"You don't have to get your own food." When she glared harder, he only shrugged. "Get your own food tomorrow. Dale's already getting it."

"When did you get in?"

"Last night."

For some reason, her stomach dropped at that. "Oh."

He frowned. "You sound disappointed."

The words were on the tip of her tongue. She wanted to ask him why he hadn't come to her. Why Owen hadn't come to her. It had been her first night in a new place — a new home — and she'd spent it alone.

But that felt a little too needy. Bordering on whiny. So she just leaned back in her chair and crossed her arms. "I just didn't expect you to get away from Grayson so quickly."

A grimace. "The wolf does like to talk. Go over *scenarios,* as he calls them. I didn't have the patience for it last night."

She very nearly rolled her eyes. As if the man ever had patience for talking.

The man Erick had beckoned — Dale, she recalled — dropped off two plates. She muttered a thank-you, then glanced around them. The cafeteria had all but cleared out. They were alone save one older woman eating in a corner, so far away she might as well have been in another room.

"You scared them all away," she mused.

Erick snorted. "No. But they all have jobs to do. There will be another group soon — shift changes keep this place busy off and on all day."

She nodded, only half paying attention. The bacon—still sizzling a bit on her plate—had caught her attention. Smacking her lips together, she ignored her fork and grabbed a piece with her fingers. The first bite was heavenly. All salt and meaty goodness that made her moan.

A strangled noise across the table drew her attention as she took her second bite of the yummy goodness that was bacon.

Erick watched her, a strangely intense expression on his face. Their gazes locked, sending a shock of energy between them, then his eyes turned to her mouth.

Need suddenly gripped her, pooling low in her belly and turning her insides molten. A need that had nothing to do with food. She licked her lips, and he growled.

"Delicious," she said, voice more than a little breathless. She was tempted to ask him to come lick her lips, too, see if he liked the taste as much as she did. But knowing him, he would do just that.

"I'll bet it is." But he wasn't looking at the bacon.

She wanted him. So badly it hurt to think she couldn't have him. So badly, it suddenly scared the shit out of her.

Erick wasn't the safe choice. It was a shitty bit of reasoning, but true. Exploring this…attraction further with him could only lead her to one end. And it would be painful. Her heat would end, and so would his interest. Until the next struck. And what would she have to deal with in the meantime? Him tolerating her presence? Watching him gallivant around with other women?

She couldn't see him being faithful. Not when he considered her little more than a broodmare. But watching him watch her so closely made her bite her lip against another moan.

"You are teasing me," he ground out. He sniffed the air, and then gripped the edge of the table, hard, as if he had to work to keep from jumping across the table to take her right there. "Please, continue your teasing. See what happens."

The heat surged inside of her. She wanted him to close the distance. To take her wherever he pleased.

Fear raced through her, adding to her heat in the most terrible way. And there was only one thing she could think to say to break the tension before she started begging him to take her.

"Wh-where's Owen?"

The simple, tentative question was like ice water to his face. He knew she could feel the sexual tension between them just as well as he could, but unlike him, she seemed afraid of it. Or, hell, maybe he was just misreading her altogether. Maybe it was as simple as her heat spiking while he happened to be the closest male to her. Maybe she didn't want him at all. Maybe, like her question suggested, what she really wanted was Owen.

He pushed up from the table abruptly, and she started.

"Enjoy your breakfast." He stepped away for the table, but she stopped him before he could get far.

"Wait! What am I supposed to—"

He didn't turn around to face her. "I need to speak with Owen, but I'm sure he'll find you later." A tiny shuffle caught his ears and he almost smiled at his problem child's tenacity. If he didn't miss his guess, Catnip waited just around the corner outside of the cafeteria. "Have a look around. I think your new friend will spring out of hiding the second I leave. Don't let her get you into trouble."

The reaction wasn't fair to her; he knew that. But what the hell else was he supposed to do? If he'd stayed, he wouldn't have been able to hide his anger. And for whatever reason, lashing out at her wasn't something he could swallow.

Figuring out his relationship—or whatever the hell it was—with Daniella could wait. Right now, his main concern was Owen. He hadn't been bitten, not that the doctor could find. Meeting with him before Erick had collapsed in his bed in the early morning hours had confirmed as much.

Granted, the doc admitted that a stalker could cover its tracks, force Owen's body to heal even faster than tigers normally did. But Owen had sworn none of the vampires had bitten him. Owen's word was something Erick would normally take at face value, but the stalker brought a new level of complexity to the situation.

Stalkers could make people forget. And who knew what else.

He had to talk to Owen.

Erick stepped into the cabin used by the doctor for any overnight patients he needed to keep close to his own cabin. Owen wasn't inside, but his scent lingered. A clang from somewhere in the back of the house caught Eric's attention, and he followed the sound to the back deck.

"I see you aren't infirm."

Owen looked up from where he was grilling a steak over charcoals, spatula in hand. "I see you aren't still stuck talking to the wolves."

"Got in last night." He didn't bother to tell Owen the why of it. He didn't confide his feelings, such as they were, in anyone. Or his reasons for doing things. Daniella had a habit of overriding that little rule of his, but that didn't mean he was changing for anyone else. "Guess Daniella filled you in about the treaty."

"A bit. Doc knew a little, too. Filled in some blanks."

"Something we should probably go over soon," Erick said.

Owen nodded, but didn't reply.

After a long silence filled by the quiet sizzle of Owen's steak, Erick spoke. "Expected to find you elsewhere."

Owen just shrugged, and Erick bit back a growl.

The temptation to cross the few feet between them and shake the answers out of his best friend, a man closer to him than his own brother had ever been, was fierce. But he didn't. Such a motion would be useless, anyway. And the last thing he needed to do was create a bigger rift between them. The clan needed them both — especially with Glenn's loss. It needed Daniella. And it was Erick's job to keep them all together. For the good of the clan. Even if it meant he had to stay at the fringes of their relationship.

"She expected you, too."

A glimmer of regret touched Owen's features. Finally, a reaction. That was something.

"How long do you plan to hide here?"

"Get off my back, Erick." He flipped the steak. "If you're here to ask me something, spit it out."

Fine. If Owen wanted him to be blunt, he could be blunt. "Were you bitten?"

"No."

"You aren't acting like yourself."

Owen whirled. "Why don't you just say what you came here to say?"

"You wouldn't necessarily remember if you had been."

Owen laughed, a quick sound that held no humor,

and turned back to the grill. "They had me for a few days, Erick. Do you think I'm so weak she'd be able to squirm her way into my brain that quickly?"

"It isn't likely, but—"

"But what?" Owen tossed the spatula next to his steak and turned to face him. He took a step forward and Erick drew himself taller, his body tensing, ready for a fight.

When Owen merely glared, Erick forced his muscles to relax. "She is important. And she wouldn't be able to protect herself against a tiger under the influence of a stalker."

His second's expression softened. "You're worried I'd hurt Daniella? I'd never—"

"Why aren't you with her, then? If you aren't the slightest bit worried?"

Owen's brows creased and he turned away. There it was. The doubt. "I wasn't bitten. But she tasted my blood."

Erick hissed.

"From a wound. Only a drop." Careful of the fire, he grabbed his steak off the grill with his fingers and tossed it onto a plate. "I know it isn't ideal. But the fucker can't control me with it. Can't find us off that tiny drop of blood." Owen set the plate on the small table next to the grill.

"She'll be able to scent you if you get close. Find you easily."

"Only in a pretty short range."

Erick cursed. "And you don't think that's a problem?"

He gave him a level stare. "Not planning on getting close enough to that fucker for it to matter much."

Dammit. Sending Owen to Denver anytime soon was out of the question. The stalker would be able to home in on him easily if he got within a few miles. Hell, maybe more. Who knew? Erick hadn't dealt with a stalker before; neither had anyone in the clan still living, as far as he knew. Something he'd have to ask around about, just to be sure.

Not that he'd planned on sending Owen out so soon after his kidnapping, but he didn't like his hands tied. What if the wolves needed their help? Erick couldn't ignore a request now, not after they'd come through. "Why didn't you tell the doctor?"

"Because it was none of his damn business."

"It's my business. The safety of this clan—"

"Is your responsibility—I know. Which is why I just told you." Owen sat down and stabbed his steak with a fork, then began sawing into it with the knife.

Erick's mind reeled, and he forced himself to calm. This wasn't anything he hadn't been expecting. And the repercussions were minor compared to what they would have been if he'd been bitten. But the idea of even the slightest danger being so close to Daniella…

"I don't like it."

"I didn't like it much, either," Owen bit back. "There's no way to prove it either way, as you said. I guess you'll just have to believe me, then. Or not." He hesitated. "Look, stalker was planning to sell me. From what I gather, her biting me could have wrecked my asking price."

Made sense. But the lack of real, reliable knowledge was irritating. "Maybe it's like our bites. Some kind of claiming."

"Could be." Owen frowned. "But we do have a problem. They know about Daniella. You and I both know that a royal female tiger is a prize that might tempt them to be bolder than usual."

Something about that didn't track. "If they knew about her, why wasn't the stalker there when they took you? A tiger that valuable—"

"They didn't know about her beforehand. Not until that night."

Realization struck. "The heat."

"Yes. With the heat on her, even the vampires could smell what she was." He gripped his fork so tightly Erick could see it bend in his hand. He stared at his steak, but didn't seem to actually see it. "If I hadn't gotten captured…"

Erick bit back an agreement. If Owen had allowed him to leave a guard the night he had come to claim Daniella—only to find out she was already Owen's—none of this would have happened. Glenn would still be alive. He wouldn't have a damned treaty that might still bite him in the ass with the wolves.

He didn't blame Owen—not exactly. The man had made a mistake and shit happened. But he just couldn't quite bring himself to comfort his second.

After a long silence, Owen shook himself, then shoved a bite of his steak in his mouth. Around the meat, he muttered, "What's done is done. Leave me, so I can eat in peace."

Erick stiffened, a reprimand on his tongue. He swallowed the harsh words. "Make sure to visit your mate. She missed you." He turned away and took a step toward the house. "She wasn't the only one."

Chapter Four

"This is where the guards train. The tigers who patrol our land and deal with any issues."

Cat gestured toward a large outdoor area that didn't look significantly different from the rest of the land surrounding the tigers' homes, save for the fact that it was mostly cleared trees, and the dirt and bit of plant life appeared to be a little more stomped on.

"Do they train often?" she asked politely, since Cat was looking at her expectantly.

"Only all the time." She rolled her eyes. "Seems like, anyway."

The training of the clan's guards seemed to be beyond the scope of what Cat considered important. Only a week before, Daniella couldn't have blamed her for it and might have felt the same way. But after what she'd seen…well, training was a good idea, no doubt. Important.

Cat continued their tour around the close cabins and the small school used for all of the tigers' children. When she started in on the curriculum, Daniella zoned out.

After bringing up Owen to shatter the heat between them, she'd immediately regretted it. And she'd stared at the doorway Erick disappeared through for far too long a moment before she realized she was probably gaping like an idiot. He hadn't come back.

She'd hurt him.

Impossible as the idea seemed, the flash of pain on his face—she hadn't imagined it. She couldn't get that brief glimpse out of her head.

Nor could she stop wondering about Owen. Worrying about Owen.

How had her life gotten so dang complicated?

"And we're back at the main house—that's what we call it, by the way. Not sure if anyone told you." Cat scrunched her nose and stared at her from behind her dark-framed glasses, almost too adorable to be a weretiger. "Did you get any of that?"

Crap. Totally caught. "Kind of," she admitted.

To her surprise, Cat shrugged. "It's a lot to take in. And I'm sure you've got more important things filling your head right now."

The curiosity was plain on the well-named Cat's face, but Daniella merely smiled. "So, you're the librarian?"

Her face lit up and she pushed her glasses up, practically vibrating out of them with an excited little hop. "Oh, yes. I'll show you that next." She paused. "You like books, right?"

Daniella got the feeling that this was the most important question Cat would ever ask her, that their friendship might just rest on her answer. Thankfully, it was an easy question. "I *love* books."

Cat squealed and clapped her hands silently, with barely restrained glee. "Let's go!"

She followed her new friend to the library—or, as Cat called it, their "poor excuse for a library"—and tried to keep her mind on her new friend. The modest collection was located in the main house, in an area that required a few turns and a couple of windy hallways to get to.

"This place is even bigger than it looks on the outside."

"It has to be. We house all the stuff you'd find in a real town here. The closest place you can find services is a human town that's quite a drive. And believe me, the offerings there are pretty sparse."

"I take it you guys don't get to Denver often."

"Hah. If only. Nope, that kind of travel is pretty restricted." A touch of bitterness touched her tone. "I get it—especially now, after hearing the rumors about Owen. But it really kind of sucks. The words inside these books and the Internet are the closest things I ever see to the real world."

"That must be hard." To never have a chance to explore the world...the idea floored her. No matter how scary vampires were, she couldn't imagine never getting out of this small cloister. That wasn't something she could agree to, and she planned to make that crystal clear to Erick.

"I wish we could expand the library a little, at least. Maybe build a separate building for it. But no one else sees it as a priority." Cat led her to a section in the back and grabbed a duster, then absentmindedly dusted while she spoke. "I've tried to get Erick to understand that half a dozen books on biology does not a section make, but he's so stubborn. 'Go look on the Internet,' he says. Like that's the same thing. There's nothing like a book. Just the way they smell!" Something akin to rapture touched Cat's expression.

Daniella laughed. "I get that." She swallowed. "But Erick's pretty set in his ways."

Cat grimaced. "We're lucky, really. I've heard stories.

The way his father was…" She shook her head, then added firmly, "We're lucky."

Daniella had to bite back her words. Confiding in Cat was so tempting. Not only did the shifter know Erick — and maybe even Owen — better than she did, but she understood the weretiger society.

But they hardly knew each other, and she could barely wrap her own mind around her feelings for the two men, let alone try to find a way to explain them to another person. And Erick struck her as an intensely private person — Owen did, too, but not so much as his prime. Until she got to know Cat better, she had to err on the side of caution.

But still, she couldn't resist a little probing. Besides, she liked the idea of having a friend here. "So, you grew up here, then? I guess you know Erick pretty well?"

A high-pitched laugh came from behind Daniella, and Cat's face reddened. Her mouth set in a firm line, and Daniella turned to see who was laughing.

The woman was a pretty, thin thing, as were the two women who stood slightly behind her. As if she hadn't interrupted a private conversation the woman spoke. "That's Catnip's greatest tragedy, isn't it? Never getting to see the 'real world'." The woman made air quotes with nails that looked far too manicured for their surroundings. "And as if *she'd* know Erick well."

The woman's insinuation was clear. Daniella tried a tight smile, hoping it didn't look like she was ready to bite. "Doesn't seem like people get out much around here."

The woman's eyes narrowed at the thinly veiled insult. Or maybe just at Daniella in general. "You must be Danielle. Our new royal — or so they say." The woman sniffed. "You barely smell like a cat to me."

The two women behind her — like poorly rendered

carbon copies—repeated the motion and murmured their agreement.

Daniella had to stifle a laugh. The second time in a single day she felt right back in high school. What were the odds? She didn't bother to correct her name. The obvious insult was too—obvious. "And you are?"

"Leann," she said proudly, as if Daniella should recognize her name. She didn't, so she shrugged.

"Nice to meet you, Leann." She didn't add "and clones" but oh, how she wanted to. "Now, if you'll excuse us." Pointedly, she turned back to face Cat.

She heard a huff behind her and then a muttered insult that she couldn't make out. Giggles, then the girls' chatter faded as they moved away.

Her new weretiger friend's ears reddened like she'd made out the words just fine. She opened her mouth to speak, and Daniella waved her off. "I don't want to know."

Cat smiled. "Probably better off. Leann's a jerk, anyway. They came in here to get a read on you. So transparent. That girl hasn't been in the library since I've managed it. Four years, and she decides to come in today?"

"Are those my rivals?" She couldn't help the question, nor could she help the jealousy sneaking in her tone. A quick glance over her shoulder revealed they were still alone, and she almost sighed in relief.

"Hardly." Her confusion must have shown, because Cat continued, "I'm not saying Leann isn't popular with the males, but she's doesn't tend to keep them long." She snorted. "Not that she tries, really. She likes to play around with whoever strikes her fancy. But I don't think she's worried about mates. She's worried about keeping her supposed position as top female in the clan."

"Supposed?"

A conspiratorial grin. "Sure. Among people who care about that sort of thing."

She laughed. "Good thing that doesn't apply to us."

"I barely notice, to be honest."

Not surprising, considering how they'd met. She would bet that Cat didn't notice a whole heck of a lot she didn't care to. "Seems strange, though. That she doesn't care to find a mate—especially during her heat. Unless…" God, did the heat inflate emotions that much? Was it possible she was feeling more strongly than she should? Could the feelings disappear when her heat abated?

No. She couldn't believe that. Certain needs might be intensified right now, but her mind was clear. Mostly.

"Unless?" Cat prompted.

Her face heated. "I just mean, since the heat is so intense—seems like it might help forge emotional connections."

"Leann would have to feel emotions for them to be heightened." Cat suddenly looked very uncomfortable. "Not that I would know."

"Haven't you—oh, jeez. I'm sorry. That's probably a totally inappropriate question."

Cat's smile looked forced. "It's really not. People are pretty open about that here. Only reason you don't see a lot of crazy sex between unmated pairs when the women are in heat is because it's too easy to get possessive. Not like wolves' possessive, but close, and—" She laughed. "Anyway, I haven't gotten my first heat yet. So I'm operating strictly on secondhand knowledge." Her smile grew wistful. "Kind of like *all* of my knowledge. Like the jerk-squad said, I don't get out much."

Daniella reached out to pat her new friend on the

shoulder. An awkward pat, but Cat seemed to appreciate the gesture. "I thought I was the only late bloomer."

She pushed up her glasses. "Nope. I'll be twenty-four in five months. Starting to wonder if…" She shook her head. "It's fine. Doc says it'll be fine."

Daniella resisted offering false promises. Her knowledge of weretigers could fill a thimble. An idea hit, and she grinned at Cat.

The woman gave her a suspicious look. "You look like you've come up with some sort of evil plan."

Danilla smirked. "Not evil. Awesome. I know someone who could use *all* of your secondhand knowledge. At least, all of weretiger—were-anything—info."

Cat grinned. "Oh, the things I have to tell you."

Daniella was still reeling from her short info session with Cat when she started walking back to her guest cabin. The other woman had only had half an hour before she'd needed to get to some sort of meeting—where presumably she would be asking for more library funds. Just the fact that weretigers had such human problems as budgets shouldn't shock her as much as some of Cat's tidbits, but it did.

Most of what she'd told her had filled in blanks rather than given her brand new info. What Erick and Owen had told her about multiple pairings had been confirmed. Threesomes and even more were pretty standard for the cats. And aside from those mated—a ritual Cat confided was sealed with a bite—the cats tended to move between sexual partners often.

But oddly, that almost only happened once males

and females were considered mature. For the females, that meant at the start of their first heat. The males were considered mature only when they could form fangs—fangs that were used to mark and claim mates. Apparently, that tended to hit a bit younger than the twenty-two or twenty-three years that women matured in, but not more than a couple of years.

She had a hard time wrapping her brain around that. What the heck did the teenagers do, if not chase each other?

But heck, maybe it was the norm for them for biological reasons. She hadn't lost her virginity until she was twenty-one—ancient, according to her best friend, Annabel. She simply hadn't been ready until then. Maybe it was because she was a tiger.

She grinned at the thought of Annabel's expression if she told her that, but then sobered. Crap. She needed to call her. Needed to call her parents again. She'd had only the briefest phone call with them since this whole thing had started. They were going to start to worry soon. And she hadn't talked to Annabel in a week. She lived in Chicago now, but they still kept in touch.

As she approached the cabin, she frowned. It wasn't dark yet—although that wasn't far off—but a light could clearly be seen through the window. Did she have the wrong cabin? She didn't think so. The door opened as she approached, and a well-built man stepped out to greet her.

Owen.

She wanted to throw herself into his arms. Kiss him. Hold him. Shake him until he told her everything was okay between them.

With a sweep of his arm, he gestured for her to enter.

She walked in, butterflies dancing in her belly. He closed the door behind them.

"I see you got the grand tour." He smiled, but his gaze danced around hers. Something shifted uncomfortably in her chest.

"Nice digs you got here," she managed. "Pretty full of assholes, like most places."

"Someone bothered you? Who?" He stepped closer. If she reached out, she could touch his chest. She flexed her hand at her side.

"Relax. I don't need a big tiger to fight my battles." A small laugh escaped her. "Not my social battles, anyway. Vampires show up and I'm happy to let you deal with that. Until I get my claws, anyway."

A sharp intake of breath and he looked away.

Concerned, she closed the gap between them. She was sick and tired of this distance. Sure, he'd been through stuff. She could empathize, even if couldn't even allow herself to think too hard about what he'd gone through, let alone ask for details. But she got the feeling that he was punishing himself for some reason, and that had to stop.

"What is it?" When he didn't respond, she reached up and gripped his upper arm. "Owen," she said, voice low, "talk to me."

He shook his head. "I wasn't strong enough to save you then. What makes you think I will be the next time?"

The bitterness in his tone almost made her take a step back, but she stood firm. "You think that's your fault?" At his answering flinch, a flash of anger hit her. "Is that why you've been avoiding me? Because you weren't stronger than three vampires who'd been watching you for God knows how long?"

"Not just that." Finally he looked at her—really

looked — and her heart almost soared out of her chest at the contact. "I've screwed all this up so badly. I should have taken you here the first night. I should have at least let Erick leave a man with us. Hell, I should have told you what you were a year ago."

Pain shot through her at the broken sound of his voice. She reached out with her free hand and cupped his face, blinking back tears that threatened to spill. "Shoulda. Coulda. Woulda." She patted his cheek in rebuke. "We all make mistakes. And I'm not convinced half the things you said were really mistakes. They were judgment calls, some better than others. But we're here now, and we have to move forward."

His mouth opened, then closed. He seemed lost in thought, and she dropped her hand from his face, but didn't let go of his arm. If he wanted away from her again, he was going to have to pry her off.

"Fuck," he muttered, finally. But his voice was stronger, more like her Owen. "I was afraid you'd blame me. Dragging you into this world, into this mess."

"As I understand it, the world was going to find me one way or another." She slid her hand down to his and gave it a squeeze. "I'm glad I found it with you."

His nostrils flared and he stepped closer, tugging her to him. She sighed and wrapped her arms around his middle. Things were going to be okay. Owen was going to be okay.

And Erick…

Thoughts of the prime had plagued her all day. She could see why he was so focused on his people, so single-minded. There was a lot of good to protect here, to build on. But was there any room in him for something other than his clan?

She wasn't sure. But she couldn't seem to stop

thinking about him. And even now, with Owen's arms wrapped around her, keeping her safe, a painful nugget pressed against her heart.

"I love you," Owen murmured into her hair.

The moment should have shocked her—he'd never said it aloud before. But it didn't surprise her. In some ways, he'd been saying it with his every action since this whole thing had started.

"I love you, too," she said, and his arms tightened around her. Then his hand slid down her back to trace small circles. Her body tightened at his touch, his nearness, his scent.

"I want you," he murmured softly.

Throat tight, she had to force out the words. "You were hurt—taken. We don't have to—"

"Shhh…I want to." His erection pressed against her stomach, hard and insistent, proving his words.

But something else weighed on her. "Erick and I—is this something we need to talk about? Something we should talk about? Especially before—"

"Not right now." He pulled back just enough to take her mouth with his own. His kisses soft, tender. Just what she needed. Her body heated, suddenly alive. He growled against her lips and pulled her closer. And the fire he'd lit inside her flared.

She wrapped her arms around his neck, pulling him closer, pulling herself closer to him. The heat inside of her flared, and she wanted to crawl up him, inside him, join with him. In this strange new place, she'd been adrift. Owen was once again her rock.

It felt so right.

A niggling in the back of her mind whispered that it could be even more right, even better. If only their prime were here, too. But she silenced that bit of doubt.

Owen needed her right now, and she needed him just as badly.

Owen's tongue swept against hers and she reached between them to cup his hard cock with her hand. He was hot and heavy, ready for her. And she was oh so ready for him.

Far too slowly, Owen undressed her. He tugged her T-shirt over her head then unclasped her bra, freeing her full breasts. He stepped back then, to admire her. Expression serious, he cupped her breasts with his hands, brushing her nipples with his thumbs.

"God, you're so fucking beautiful. A few days in that hellhole, and I almost convinced myself that you couldn't really be that beautiful. That you had to be enhanced by my imagination. That I was so fucking desperate to see you my mind was playing tricks on me. But you… God, Daniella, you're even more beautiful than I remembered." He pressed a kiss to her forehead, still cupping her breasts. "Inside and out."

She melted at his words. Her body turned to liquid, and desire pooled between her legs. But she couldn't find the words to tell him how she felt. To tell him that she found him just as beautiful as he found her. So she did the only thing she could. She showed him.

Arms finding their way around his neck again, she pulled him down for another kiss. But this time, she kissed him. She shoved every little bit of desperation she'd felt when he was gone into that kiss, every bit of fear, every bit of love. He met her stroke for stroke, his desperation seeming to match her own.

When she couldn't stand it anymore, she stepped back and reached for the button fly of his jeans. Moving desperately, quickly, because she couldn't manage to hold herself back, she undid his jeans and pushed them down to the floor, taking herself down to her knees in the process. Then she was fisting his hard cock in her hand. Looking up at him. Taking the tip into her mouth.

Owen groaned the second the tip of his cock touched her lips. The deep desire in his eyes when he looked down at her pushed her need to something almost uncontrollable. Then she was taking him in her mouth, down her throat, tasting his masculine taste. Clean and raw. He tasted like Owen.

And she loved it.

She rolled her tongue around his thick cock, and he pressed farther into her throat, thrusting hard as he lost control.

She could feel the tightening in his body, the swelling in his dick. He was about to come in her mouth. Reveling in it, she sucked harder, took him farther into her throat.

"No — you don't have to — "

She knew she didn't have to. And that's why she wanted to so badly. Wanted him to lose control the same way she did with him. Wanted to give him the same pleasure he gave her, over and over again.

This time, he didn't wrench her from his cock. Instead, a long, guttural moan escaped him, and his hips surged. He plunged into her mouth over and over. Holding onto his hips, she did her best to take all he could give her. Finally, with her name on his lips, he came hard. The sweet, salty taste of his pleasure filled her mouth and she swallowed him down.

Owen was frozen above her for a moment, lost in the wake of his own pleasure. Then he pulled himself from her mouth, and ran his fingertips lightly over her hair. "That was amazing," he whispered.

Going to his knees, he joined her on the floor. Then he kissed her softly, not seeming to mind the taste of his own pleasure on her mouth. He pushed her back, until she was lying on the rug. With great care, he removed the rest of her clothes. He touched and petted, kissed and licked what felt like every inch of her skin as he went, expression reverent. By the time they were both nude, her need had flared even higher. The slow burn pushing her to want something far more than fucking.

And Owen seemed more than pleased to give it to her.

After another long kiss, he licked and nibbled his way down to her breasts. Taking one of her nipples into his mouth, he licked and suckled it until she was moaning and writhing beneath him. Instead of touching her where she needed most, he moved to the other nipple and gave it the same attention.

"Owen, please," she managed in a breathy, needy whisper.

"Patience is a virtue." He grinned and returned to her first nipple. This time, he wasn't so gentle. He took her tender flesh between his teeth and suckled her hard. When she moaned, he bit down. Just hard enough to blur the line between pleasure and pain.

She scratched at his back, and rolled her hips against him, desperately needing him to fill her. When it seemed like she might explode if she didn't get to come soon, she reached her own hand between them and touched herself.

Owen didn't stop her. Instead, he pulled back just enough so he could see what she was doing. She paused, hesitating. With his intense gaze on her, she was suddenly just a little embarrassed.

"Keep doing that," he ordered, voice rough with his own desire. But he didn't look up at her face as he said it. His eyes remained locked on her hand, on her pussy. "Touch yourself. Make yourself come. I want to watch."

With his eyes on her, and the knowledge that he was getting turned on by what she was doing, her need flared. It felt almost wrong, almost too intimate. But the wrongness of it turned her on even more.

The temptation to close her eyes was strong, but she kept them open. She watched his reaction as he watched her. She rubbed herself harder, feeling her little nub swell beneath her fingers, the slick wetness that he'd caused making her movements easy and sure. Within moments, she could feel the orgasm at the edge of her senses. Her body tensed, then she came with a long, low moan. Her hips rocked against her fingers. And above her, Owen growled.

Then he was on top of her. Sliding inside of her, her body so slick with desire that it offered no resistance. He cursed under his breath when he penetrated her fully. For a long moment, he was still. Everything was perfect.

Then with long, sure thrusts, he made love to her. She held him close as he cradled her body with his, and they kissed each other softly. Gradually, his pace increased, and she found herself cresting again, this time with Owen inside of her, finding his own release.

The sounds alerted him to exactly what was happening, but he couldn't stop his approach. Daniella's moans were muffled by the well-insulated walls. But Erick had very good ears.

As if they were controlled by someone else, his legs continued their confident stride toward the guest house.

And when he reached the deck, he continued. Not to the door, but to the window.

A brief glance showed exactly what he'd expected. Owen and Daniella making love.

The heavy pressure he'd carried on his chest since making the decision that he would not intrude on their relationship, that he wouldn't push for anything other than the occasional visit to her bed, twisted fiercely. Almost pushing him to his knees.

Worst of all, like the fucking traitor that it was, his dick went hard as a rock.

She was comfort. She was bliss. She was fucking everything.

The only thing that could have made it more perfect was if Erick had joined them.

It was possible Owen had been too hasty in dismissing her concern. But when she'd asked if they should talk about Erick, he knew what she'd really meant. She wanted to know if they should talk about what had happened while Owen was gone.

He didn't know the details, but it was obvious from the second he'd scented his prime that he had been with Daniella. If that hadn't told him all he needed to know, Daniella's all-too-human guilt would have filled in the blanks.

He should have taken that opportunity to reassure her. To bring up the possibility of the three of them finding their way together. But he'd been selfish. Needed a little time alone with the woman he'd spent the last few days dreaming of, worrying about.

He'd needed to make love to his mate.

Even now, spooning her much smaller frame with his own while she snored softly in her sleep, after sating himself in her body twice, he still wanted her.

She'd been so tight. So wet. So ready for him. So damn responsive. The way she'd gone down on him—taking his dick in her mouth like she couldn't get enough of his taste.

Fuck.

And watching her pleasure herself in front of him, something that obviously took her a lot of trust to do, was even better. Her soft expression when the orgasm had hit was the sexiest thing he'd ever seen in his life.

Already hard, he spent half a second wondering if he should leave her alone. A soft sigh and the tiniest of wiggles in her sleep robbed him of his last thread of self-control.

He hadn't seen her in days. His *mate*. Besides, he couldn't very well let her sleep on the hard floor. And if he needed to wake her up, anyway…

Propped on one elbow so he could watch her reaction to him, he slipped his hand down to her sex, brushing her nipple along the way. It immediately pebbled at his touch and he smiled. Her body reacted to him even while she slept.

Taking care not to startle her, he slid one leg between hers to spread her legs ever so slightly. Then he cupped her pussy.

Already wet.

If possible, his dick got harder at the realization.

He found her ear lobe with this mouth and nibbled softly. Still only half awake, she let out a quiet moan.

"Wake up, sweetness."

She muttered something indecipherable at him that sounded vaguely insulting.

With a soft laugh, he adjusted her leg and slung it over his, then started working her clit. "If you wake up now, I'll make sure you don't regret it."

"Sleeping," she mumbled, but her breath came quickly, and she was moving her hips against his hand.

"Not very convincing." He nibbled her neck. "Or maybe I'm not being convincing enough?"

With that, he took his hand away from her clit— eliciting a very un-sleepy groan of disappointment from her. He reached between them and, using his legs to spread hers wide enough for his access, he plunged two fingers into her sopping pussy.

"Oh!"

"Are you awake now?" he asked, voice rough as he fucked her slowly with his fingers.

"I was sleeping, you brute," she said, breathless, grinding against his hand.

"Just trying to please my mate," he teased.

Panting, she looked up to glare at him, but the amusement in her eyes betrayed her. "Trying to please yourself is more like it."

With one quick motion, he slid down and spread her legs even wider. Then he thrust his cock into her waiting heat.

Pleasure hit, so savagely he had to remain still or come with the first clamp of her inner muscles around his penis.

She gasped at the suddenness of his penetration, then pushed her ass back into him, making him grind his teeth in an effort to calm his body.

A deep breath, then he managed, "Don't you want to pleasure your mate, woman?"

He didn't wait for a response, and she didn't seem interested in giving one. Thrusting into her hard and fast, only their positions on their sides kept him from taking her as hard as he could. Instead, the position forced him to move at an even pace. He let her leg fall, and she groaned at the new sensation, her legs pressed together no doubt adding to the pressure against her clit.

It didn't take long before he felt himself start to unravel, and he reached down to touch her little nub.

"Come with me, Daniella." He rubbed her more insistently, and when colors shattered the edge of his vision, he pinched her firmly.

A strangled cry escaped her as her body contracted around his, her inner walls tightening hard around his cock as he spilled his seed.

As they came down together, he kissed her neck softly and held her close. Deep satisfaction filled him, and he carried his mate to bed.

Chapter Five

*D*aniella woke with a start. She sat up in the bed, clutching a sheet to her breast. Next to her, Owen slept soundly. The sleep of a man who hadn't rested well in a very long time.

Her eyes searched the darkness, and it took a moment for what woke her to come into focus.

Leaning against the doorframe, Erick watched her with hooded eyes.

"Erick," she whispered, hoping Owen might continue to sleep. The man needed every bit of rest he could manage.

"I almost left without saying—I mean, I thought I should tell you goodbye."

Her pulse jumped. "Goodbye?"

"Heading to Denver for a few days. I need to work with Grayson to try to track down the stalker."

A few days? Maybe it was totally unreasonable, but for some reason, it felt like he was leaving because of her.

"Erick—"

Next to her, Owen stirred, but didn't wake.

"Tell him, when he wakes up." He took a step back, shielding his expression from her in the shadows. "I'm glad you two worked things out."

Before she could utter another word, he was gone.
And she felt like half of her heart had gone with him.

Grayson paced back and forth in the warehouse. His normal calm, charming demeanor was gone. He looked pissed, and Erick couldn't blame him.

"There has to be a way. Something we're not thinking of." Grayson finally came to a halt, only a few paces away from Erick. "You might be safe in your little mountain hideaway, but my territory falls smack dab in the middle the city—a good chunk of it, anyway. I don't have the luxury of ignoring this problem."

"Does it look like I'm ignoring it?" Erick struggled to keep his temper under control. Focusing on the clan's needs had grown more difficult. Every cell in his body demanded that he return to his territory. That he claim Daniella.

But he had to let that go. Had to let Daniella live the life she wanted to live. A life with Owen.

As if reading his thoughts, Grayson asked, "Where's your little mate? I know you probably don't want her in the city with all this going on, but she could be useful right now. If you'd extend an invitation, I could risk leaving the city for a couple of days. Go to your territory, hash this out."

"Not going to happen."

Grayson cocked his head. "Which part?"

He just crossed his arms.

"Jesus, man, what does it take to gain your trust?" Grayson asked, exasperation plain in his tone. "Did we not just swoop in and save your life, the lives of your men, days ago?" Tone half joking, he added, "What's a wolf gotta do?"

"A wolf has to do a lot."

"Fine, then, bring her here. Hell, at least bring a few people down here to help." He held up his hands. "I'm not saying we don't appreciate you coming back, but a few more tigers might be a good idea. A quick, clean hunt, take that stalker down before she has a chance to really dig in somewhere new. Before she has a chance to build up defenses we won't ever be able to penetrate."

The hell of it was, Grayson made sense. But it was hard to wrap his mind around caring about things that happened in Denver. His territory was important. His people. Did helping the wolves take down a stalker make them safer? Or did it just make them more of a target? He'd lost Glenn. He hadn't been close to the man, despite the fact that he had served as his second while Owen was gone, but he was still a loss to the clan. They couldn't afford to lose anyone else.

But leaving a stalker running around free in the city didn't seem like a great idea either. Not to mention the fact that the idea of leaving Grayson to deal with this mess himself made Erick feel like a bigger asshole than usual. Despite the fact that they'd shown up just a little too late to save Glenn, they had come in time to save the rest of them. They had saved his ass and Owen's. They'd saved the rest of his men.

"Let's say we go to your plan," he ground out. "How the hell do you propose we find her?"

Grayson frowned. "Damned if I know. Might come down to good old-fashioned legwork. Getting as many weres on the ground as we can, trying to scent her out."

"Needle in a fucking haystack."

"I'm open to suggestions." Grayson shrugged. "Not like Denver has a city master to report her to."

"Rather deal with the rogue slaver, even a stalker, than live under some vampire with delusions of royalty." Not that Denver had had a master since before Erick was born. No one strong enough had taken control. But he was damn sure it would be a shitstorm if one ever tried.

"Damn right," Grayson agreed.

"Be nice if we could get your girl back here, give us a little bait."

Erick lunged at the wolf and snarled.

"Whoa, there." Grayson danced back a step and showed his hands, as if to indicate he didn't have a weapon. As if the werewolf actually needed a weapon to be dangerous. "Just an idea. Probably wouldn't work anyway. I doubt we're under any surveillance at this point. They're probably gathering their forces to keep that stalker safe. Would be a wasted effort to bring your girl here. The stalker wouldn't even know she was in town."

Erick almost flinched. Grayson's repeated reference to Daniella as his mate probably made sense from the werewolf's point of view. He almost wanted to correct him, but that would be damned humiliating. Besides, it was none of the wolf's business.

Shit. Daniella wouldn't be good bait—not that he'd use her as bait under any circumstances—but Owen, with the slight blood bond he now shared with that stalker, would be.

A hint of a smile touched Grayson's lips, and Erick almost lunged for him again. He knew. Or as good as. "How the fuck—"

"I didn't. Not until now. Not for sure. But it figures a stalker wouldn't resist at least a little taste—even if she wasn't willing to risk reducing his value by biting him outright."

"You think I'm going to risk my second after I just got him back?"

"It doesn't have to be a risk. You bring in some tigers. I'll bring in as many wolves as I can. Make sure he's safe. We'll think it through, come up with a good plan. Bring your little mate in on it. She's good with plans."

Anger finally overran sense. Erick exploded, throwing himself at the man and pushing Grayson back a good few feet. The wolf managed to keep his footing, but it was a near thing.

Grayson raised his arms up, ready to defend himself, teeth already elongating in his mouth. "What the fuck is your problem?"

The urge to take out all of his frustration, all of his disappointment, on the wolves' alpha was so strong he could barely hold himself back. He shook himself. What the fuck was his problem? He had better control in this. He was *known* for it. Even his own people called him cold.

He took a deep breath and stepped back. "I was out of line."

Grayson raised an eyebrow but his arms dropped to his sides, and his stance relaxed. "Apology accepted."

Erick ignored the jibe. Here he was, attacking an ally. Because of what?

Because he wanted her.

Well, he was just going to have to get over it. "She's not my mate."

"Ah," Grayson said, as if that explained everything.

Fuck him. Maybe it did. "I'll stay here and help you. I'll bring in men as needed. But we're not using any of my people as bait."

Grayson opened his mouth as if to argue, then sighed and nodded. "Fair enough."

Erick held out his hand and Grayson reached out and shook it. They weren't friends, but damn him if it wasn't a start.

Daniella didn't sleep much, but she snuggled next to Owen while he slept half the morning away. Finally, her stomach refused to wait any longer, so she took a quick shower. That way, she'd at least be ready to hunt down more bacon when he woke up.

When she got back to the room, he was stretching in the bed, showing delicious muscles on his arms and chest. Seeing her towel-covered body, he grinned. "Come back to bed, sexy."

"No way. I'm starving." She threw his T-shirt at him and ignored the flush in her body at his suggestion. "And we need to talk."

"What's wrong?" He put on the shirt, then grabbed his jeans. With a lot of effort, she somehow managed not to watch him pull them up. Did the man not care about underwear?

She cleared her throat. "We had a visitor last night."

Sniffing the air, he stood. "Erick?"

"Yes." How to start? She wasn't even entirely sure of what she wanted to say—or even how she felt. No, that wasn't true. She just wasn't sure she was comfortable with her feelings.

"You talked?"

"We did."

"I can't believe I slept through that." He shook his head. "Some great protector I am."

"You've had a bit of a rough week," she deadpanned.

"What did he say?"

"He said goodbye." Her words came out in a rush. "But it wasn't just that. It was how he said it. Like, it was permanent or something. Not that I think he's leaving the clan or anything, it's just—"

Owen held his hands up. "Whoa. Slow down. Where did he go?"

"To talk to the wolves."

Confusion touched his expression. "Okay…"

"But it's not *where* he went that's important. It's how he was acting. He seemed…" She took a deep breath. "Sad, I guess."

He thought about that for a moment. "Sad. Erick?"

"Not sad like a normal person. Sad like…well, Erick." She huffed, wishing she could explain why she felt such dread at Erick's demeanor. At his simple message. "He said he was glad we worked stuff out— between us, I mean. But he didn't seem happy."

Expression falling, he sat on the bed. "I know he's my best friend—my prime—but damn. The man is such an idiot sometimes."

She blinked. "Excuse me?"

"Isn't it obvious?"

"Not to me." Any explanation she thought of seemed too farfetched, too self-indulgent.

Too hopeful.

"He cares about you. And he doesn't know what the hell to do about it." Owen rubbed his face with his hands. "Or, I don't know, maybe he's got himself convinced that you'll be happier without him. Sounds like the kind of bullshit he'd believe after the way his father raised him." Owen looked up at her. "Question is, how do you feel about him?"

"I don't know." But butterflies whirled around in her stomach, calling her a liar.

He just watched her, waiting.

It took her a moment to think, to gather her courage. Owen didn't interrupt, and she was thankful for his courtesy. God, there was so much to be thankful for when it came to her neighbor slash nemesis turned weretiger lover. And she was scared to risk that. But he expected the truth from her — trusted her with the truth. She couldn't lie to him — not even to spare his feelings. Not about something this important.

"I care about him. I-I could fall for him, okay? Fall for him like I fell for you. And I know that probably makes me selfish — to want you both. But I do." She waited.

Owen didn't hesitate. "Good."

She gaped at him. Even knowing that weretiger culture differed from the human one she'd grown up in, she'd expected anger — or at least resentment. And although Owen himself had pushed her toward at least considering Erick as a father to her future children, she'd still expected him to act like the man he usually looked like on the outside.

He watched her with raised brows. "You're surprised?"

A nod was all she could manage.

He pushed up from the bed and took her in his arms. "Silly goose. I love him, too."

A short laugh escaped her, only slightly hysterical. "So, what do we do now?"

He pulled back just enough to meet her eyes. "We get our prime back."

Chapter Six

"What the fuck are you doing here? Why is she here?" Erick felt his skin tighten, an unwanted shift shivering at the edge of his vision. The safe house—the cabin where he'd brought Daniella while they searched for Owen—simply wasn't safe. Not like their territory.

Hell, maybe he shouldn't have ignored Owen's requests to return. Shouldn't have refused Daniella's phone calls. But he hadn't been ready yet. Besides, the stalker was still on the loose, and he had to stand by his word to help Grayson.

"We're here to see you," Owen replied, his voice maddeningly calm.

"It isn't safe for you to be here." He had to know that. "That stalker tasted your blood, Owen. And you bring her here, risk her? You're supposed to protect your mate!" The safe house wasn't in Denver, but it was close to the city. Close enough to make him uncomfortable. Besides, their territory was protected. Guarded.

His gaze was steady. "I'm also supposed to protect my prime. I'm your second, after all."

"That isn't—" Erick shook himself, wanting to shake

Owen instead. "You will take her back to our territory immediately."

A small figure stepped in between them. "We're not going anywhere."

Erick didn't look at Daniella, couldn't. Why the hell had they followed him here? Instead, he continued to address Owen. "That's an order, second. You will take her back now."

His second looked suddenly uneasy, but Erick's command seemed to have no effect on Daniella.

"He will do no such thing," she said firmly.

Erick's gaze shifted, and looking at her was like a punch to the gut. She was so goddamn beautiful. So goddamn determined. So goddamn strong.

And not even the tiniest bit afraid of him.

"You asked why we were here," she said, voice soft. The tenderness in her expression forced him to look away.

"It doesn't matter. You're going home."

She took a step toward him. "Erick—"

"Give us a sec," Owen cut in. He gave Daniella a tight smile. "Please."

She glanced between the men, then nodded. "I'll be outside."

"No," Erick said. "You wait here. It's safer. We'll talk outside."

She didn't roll her eyes, but her exasperated expression said she thought he was overreacting. "Fine, whatever."

Erick led the way. The night wasn't moonless, but clouds blocked all but a cool glow. A human would be stumbling about in the low light, but they never hesitated.

"This is far enough," Owen said. "We need to talk, brother"

"Yeah, we do. We need to talk about what an idiot

you are for bringing her up here. We need to talk about the fucking chain of command."

He grimaced. "You weren't coming home. Hell, I couldn't even be sure that you were going to come home for Glenn's funeral in a couple of days."

Owen's words were like a blow to the chest. Is that what his second thought of him? "Don't be ridiculous."

"All right, that was a low blow. I know you would've come for Glenn's funeral. But what about after? Would you have stayed and talked to us? Or would you have run away again?"

"I didn't run away. Somebody has to clean up this mess you created," he said.

Owen flinched. "Maybe so. But that doesn't mean you aren't running, too."

The truth of it was, he had been running. But no way in hell was he admitting that to Owen—he could barely admit it to himself. But what the hell else was he supposed to do? Watch them be happy together and somehow not be miserable? He just wasn't that good a person.

"Daniella wants to try this—wants to try being with us. Together."

Erick snorted, ignoring the sudden warmth in his chest. "Since when?"

"Since she had a chance to think about it. Since she realized maybe you aren't the hard ass you'd like people to think."

That gave him pause. "I am a hard ass."

Owen laughed. "That you are, my friend. But for some reason, she thinks there's hope for you." He hesitated, expression darkening. "But I don't want her hurt, Erick. I'm trusting you not to hurt her here. She's trusting you too, and given all the new, crazy shit she's been exposed to lately, that's a hell of a gift."

His words shattered the grain of hope in Erick's chest. Daniella's trust was something that he took very seriously, but it wasn't something he was sure he wanted. Okay, he wanted it. But he wasn't sure he could live up to it.

"Take her home." It wasn't worth the risk. If it had just been about the risk to him, he wouldn't have hesitated, not for second. But he couldn't risk her trust. Somehow she had come to matter to him, too much. "I don't—I can't offer her what she needs. You can."

"What she needs is for you to give this a shot. What do you have to lose?"

My heart. Fuck. "Owen—"

"Are you really going to wimp out on this?" When Erick didn't reply, he cursed. "Fine, then. If you won't even try, then you don't deserve her." Owen turned and started back toward the cabin.

Erick's life suddenly felt like it was balanced on the head of a pin. One wrong move and everything he'd worked for, everything he believed in, could collapse. But to not even try… "Owen. Wait."

It took Daniella about ten seconds to get antsy. She waited in the cabin—the safe house where she'd spent her days and nights with Erick while they searched for Owen—doing her best not to hold her breath. No need to totally freak the guys out, after all. She wasn't sure they'd support her going anywhere ever again if they came back to find her passed out.

Thankfully, they weren't gone longer than a few minutes. But when they opened the door, she thought her heart might leap from her chest.

They were both silent for a moment. Surprisingly, Erick was the one who spoke.

"Are you sure you want this?" Simple and to the point. The man was nothing if not consistent.

She was hot, achy. Just the thought of the two of them during the drive to the cabin had done that. Her heat ebbed and flowed—not as strong, most of the time. But watching them side-by-side, waiting for her answer, desire on both their faces…it made her instantly wet. Instantly on fire.

The moment of silence stretched, and she managed a nod.

"Say it," Erick said. "We're not doing this if you don't want it. If you're not sure."

She swallowed the lump in her throat. "I'm sure."

His serious expression shifted—the slightest hint of a smile. "Then say it."

"What?"

"Tell us what you want." He gestured to Owen, who winked at her.

Face hot, she asked, "Why? I mean—"

The prime merely arched a brow.

"Fine," she practically growled. She squared her shoulders and faced him head-on. No way was she going to look away, no matter how embarrassing. It would only amuse him further. "I want you two. Together."

"What do you want us to do?"

She cursed, drawing bigger grins out of the men. Speaking slowly, she enunciated every word. "I want you to fuck me."

Their amusement disappeared, and they closed in on her.

Erick's gaze was hot, savage. "If we're going to do this, we're going to do it my way."

Knees shaking, she had the sudden impulse to take things down a notch, take a step back. This was all starting to feel like it was spiraling out of her control. Her stomach was in knots, but her pulse jumped, and not because of fear.

"I don't know — how do we — " She couldn't get the words out, and heat crawled up her neck.

Owen's smile was reassuring, but his gaze was heated when it met hers. "Don't worry about the details, sweet. Trust us."

Unable to find the right words, she nodded. The men approached, too big. Far too big. Especially with both of them towering over her together. They filled the room, all the dark spaces. Their scents — both clean and strong and masculine — intertwined.

And suddenly she felt empty. Needy. Worse than she had in days. But it didn't calm her nerves — not enough.

"Sh-should I get...undressed?" Why was she so nervous? She was hardly a virgin — something both of the men knew intimately. And she wanted this so badly that half of her was ready to fling herself at them and tear their clothes off.

"I think you need to relax." Owen stepped even closer, into her personal bubble. She had the irrational urge to push him back. Make him fight her. Make him fight for her.

Then he leaned in and kissed her.

Her body took over. Inside, the heat awoke, rushing through her like the day she'd first come to Owen. Insides turning to liquid, she ran her hands through his hair and pressed her breasts against him.

Another body moved against her from behind. Erick. Large frame blocking the light, she couldn't help but lean into his heat. His hands stroked her back while Owen's tongue dipped into her mouth. Then Erick's hands moved, brushing her butt, then moving up her sides.

"Fuck, she smells good," he said, voice rough.

So many hands on her. So much heat. She couldn't get enough.

Owen broke their kiss, and she gasped in a breath.

"The heat."

But it wasn't. Not just the heat. It was them. These men. Somehow she knew that even if there were no such thing as weretigers, they'd still do this to her. Make her want them so badly she could barely think around the need.

Erick hands came around to touch her breasts, and she gasped. For a moment, he held the weight of them in his hands, then he pulled her back against his solid chest.

That he could move her so easily, even just a few inches, made her even more aware of their size, their strength. Erick was already hard; his long, thick cock pressed against her back. And when she opened her eyes, she could see the outline of Owen's bulge, straining against his jeans.

"Maybe you should see if she's enjoying herself, brother," Erick ground out.

Without pausing to ask permission, Owen reached for her pants. Before she could blink, he'd gotten them off of her, leaving her feeling suddenly exposed. Her shirt still covered her breasts — breasts that Erick continued to fondle, making it difficult to think of anything else — but Owen had taken her underwear with her pants.

Instead of returning to his feet, Owen remained on his knees. Looking up at her, he slid his hand between her legs. He brushed her clit with his knuckle, and grinned when she jumped. Erick's hard body, so close to hers, kept her from going anywhere, and Owen lowered his face toward her sex.

She could feel her center growing wetter, hotter, even with only his gaze upon her.

"She's wet all right, fucking beautiful," Owen said, voice reverent.

"Maybe you should taste her."

Like he was starving for her, his mouth fell on her pussy. He licked her clit, sending a spark of pleasure through her whole body. Only Erick's strong form behind her kept her upright. He held her close while Owen dipped a finger into her wetness. His tongue followed, fucking her insistently. At some point, Erick had slipped his rough hands under her shirt, under her bra. His massage of her breasts had turned almost too rough. She cried out, overwhelmed by the sensations.

Owen pulled her knee over his shoulder. He started sucking on her clit, using two fingers to fill her. It wasn't enough. It was too much.

"Come for us, kitten. Show us how much you like this. How much you want it." Erick pinched her nipples. The pain shot pleasure straight to her sex. Combined with what Owen was doing to her, it was too much. She couldn't hang on. A loud cry on her lips, she came hard.

Owen pulled every aftershock out of her, until she could do nothing more but lean against them, allow them to take all of her weight. Erick's ministrations on her breasts became gentle. He kissed her neck softly.

As she came back to earth, Owen stood. He wiped his mouth on his sleeve and gave her roguish grin. "Good girl." He glanced behind her at Erick. "Maybe she'll learn to follow orders yet."

Erick rumbled a low laugh behind her, and she made a halfhearted attempt to smack Owen.

"She can follow orders all right, but only when she wants to," Erick said.

Daniella blinked. She'd known the man a handful of days, yet sometimes it seemed like he knew her best of all.

"Let's see if she can follow this one." Erick helped her stand on her own, yet he stayed close, close enough to make sure she was stable on her feet. Then he turned her around so she was up looking at him.

Fierce desire coated his features — he wasn't as relaxed as his teasing made it seem. "Can you follow orders, kitten?"

She arched a brow at him. "Guess you'll have to try me and see."

A touch of a grin, but there was a challenge in his eyes. "Let's do something worthwhile with that smart mouth of yours, then." He leaned close, and said, "Get on your knees."

Her jaw dropped and she snapped it shut. No way was she letting this challenge go unmet. She wanted this. Wanted them. Heck, she'd wanted both of them, together, since the night that she'd met Erick. Since the night she learned that such a thing was even a possibility. No, she hadn't been ready to admit it yet. But she'd wanted it all the same.

With a little help from the men, she got down on her quavering knees. The rug was soft, and she settled right in.

"Show him what you got," Owen teased her.

She was going to show him all right. The two men had the advantage. Advantage in numbers. Advantage in who got the first orgasm. But she was about to even the playing field.

Before her nerves could get the best of her, she had

Erick's pants around his knees. Huge, his cock stood proudly. He was at least as big as Owen. And for half a second, she wondered if she'd even be able get her mouth all the way around him—let alone all of him inside. With great care, she took him in her hand and stroked him. A bead of moisture glistened from the tip. She bit her lower lip, and glanced up at the prime.

Erick watched her, expression almost grim. But his breath came quickly. She could see the strain in his muscles as he fought to hold himself back. With his cock in her hand, she had control.

The realization gave her a boost of confidence, and with her eyes still locked on his face, she licked the moisture from the tip of his penis.

Above her, he growled. "I'm going to fuck that pretty mouth. Open up."

Her belly tightened at his rough words. Obediently, she opened her mouth.

Despite his words, his hand was gentle on her hair. And he eased the bulbous head of his cock between her lips slowly. She licked him, teased him, as he fucked her mouth with shallow thrusts. Above her, he moaned. His thrusts grew deeper. But he kept the pace slow, manageable. She began to open to more of him. His thrusts grew quicker, but no less gentle.

She could feel wetness pool between her legs, touch her thighs. As his breath came quicker, hers did, too. She moaned around his cock.

"Fuck, brother. I didn't know —"

"I know." She could hear the smirk in Owen's voice.

He looked down at her, teeth bared. "I'm going to come on that sharp tongue of yours, kitten."

Triumph rolled through her, and she cupped his balls while clinging to his hip with her free hand. He shouted, and his dick jerked in her mouth. The sweet tang of his seed touched her tongue and she swallowed him down, sucking and licking until he was fully spent.

He pulled himself from her mouth and knelt beside her. Without a word, he pulled her into his arms.

Chapter Seven

Erick pulled her close and whispered, "That was amazing. But, we're just getting started."

With those tantalizing words still ringing in her ears, she got to her feet with their help. Owen hugged her from behind, a comforting gesture. But the moment for comfort seemed to have passed for Erick. He kissed her hard while the other man held her close.

From behind her, she could feel Owen's hard erection pressing into her back. His lips teased her neck. Her breath came quickly, and she started to squirm against them.

Erick broke the kiss, and moved his mouth down to suckle on her breasts. His veneer of gentleness was gone, and the animal peeked through. Roughly, he toyed with her sensitive nipples, sending shots of heat and need straight to her pussy.

Owens hand moved down to rub her clit. Then he was plunging his fingers inside of her. She moaned and tried to move, tried to get the pressure where she needed it most. From whom, she didn't care. She only cared that someone touch her, send her over the precipice she was suddenly hanging onto again.

"Please," she moaned. "I need —"

"What do you need, baby?" Owen murmured in her ear.

Erick broke free from one of her breasts with an audible pop. "I know exactly what she needs. You need to be filled, don't you, kitten?" He took a step back and she cried out at the loss. But he ignored her and took hold of his cock. With a tight grip, he stroked, bringing himself back to full hardness.

She gasped at the erotic sight, and he eyed her knowingly. "You want this, don't you? You want us to fill you up. Fuck you hard. Take you like you need to be taken."

A whimper escaped her, and Owen pulled his fingers from her pussy to rub her clit. Pleasure arced through her at the touch, and she ground herself against him shamelessly.

"Say it," Erick demanded. "Tell us how badly you want it. Need it."

She wanted to claw him. Bite him. She lunged, but Owen's arms held her fast.

"Say it," Owen echoed his prime, his own voice strangled with need. There would be no help from him. Traitor.

"I need it." Her shyness was gone, buried under her desperate need. Before he could demand more of her, she added, "I need you to fuck me. Both of you. Please."

Erick smirked. "I love it when you beg."

She growled, and Erick closed the distance between them. "We have to get her ready," he said to Owen.

Ready? Suddenly the mechanics of what they were about to do concerned her. "What are we—I mean, how—" She cleared her throat. "Are you going to take turns or something?"

Erick leaned in and bit her earlobe. "No, kitten.

We're going to fuck you together. Since Owen got that sweet pussy of yours first, I get to be the first one to take that sexy little ass of yours."

Fear mixed with lust in her belly. "I don't—I mean, I've never—"

Erick chuckled, but when he pulled back to look her in the eyes, there was no amusement in his expression. Only deep, intense desire. His hand moved down to cup her pussy, and she bit back a moan. "You want to be ours? Then you're going to be ours. We will claim you in every way possible." His eyes flashed amber. "Don't worry, kitten. You're going to love it."

From behind her, Owen plunged his index finger into her pussy. She gasped at the sudden invasion, but he quickly pulled out. Before she could demand he do it again, she could feel his thick digit pressing against her ass.

Erick kissed her, tongue plunging, ravaging her mouth. He started to rub her clit, even as Owen worked his way into her ass. Slowly, he managed to penetrate her. Even his index finger felt too large. But with Erick playing with her clit and kissing her so passionately, the sensation wasn't unpleasant. And after he'd worked his way in, he started moving his finger, pushing it in and out of her gently. Soon, it wasn't just unpleasant—it was strangely satisfying. She began thrusting back against him even as she tried to wriggle her clit harder against Erick's clever fingers.

"So fucking tight," Owen groaned against her neck. He nipped her softly, then pulled his finger out of her. "We're going to need lube."

"Should be some in the bathroom." Erick didn't stop his ministrations on her body even as Owen moved away.

She tried very hard not to think about why they had

lube at this cabin. It was stupid to fret over. No point in getting jealous — everyone had a past. And she knew all about their history with other women. How they'd shared before. Well, she knew as much a she needed to know. As much as she wanted to. She definitely wasn't interested in the details.

Owen returned, but Erick kept her distracted from what was happening behind her with his tongue, with his fingers, and even with his teeth. It felt like he left no part of her body untouched.

She groaned when she felt Owen pressing again at her ass. This time, it was harder. He worked in two fingers instead of one. But with the help of the slippery lube, it didn't take long before she was gasping, moaning with need, arching into him while he fucked her.

She was so close to coming. But every time stars flickered at the edge of her vision, Erick seemed to sense it. He'd move away from her clit, fuck her with his fingers, or move entirely away from her pussy to play with her sensitive breasts. It was about to drive her mad. "Please — I need to — oh, God."

Erick stopped touching her altogether and she cried out. "Sorry, kitten. You don't get come until my dick is buried in your ass. Until Owen is deep inside your pussy."

Just the idea of it was enough to push her need to higher levels. Desperate and so turned on she couldn't think of anything, couldn't do anything, but writhe against Owen.

"I think she's ready," Owen said from behind her. He pulled his fingers out of her ass, and her need turned to rage.

She threw herself at Erick, clawing and biting and doing her very best to hurt him. He caught her easily, holding her hands at her sides. She growled at him, bit at him. He controlled her easily, which made her scream in wordless frustration.

"Fuck. Her tiger's right at the surface. She's going to be able shift soon." Owen's words didn't penetrate — not the meaning — even though something in her brain was shouting that what he was saying was important.

Owen lay down on the rug, and with an ease that angered her, Erick and Owen positioned her over on top of him. His cock stood proudly, jutting at her like a temptation, like a challenge. She stopped fighting and reached for Owen's cock. Touching him calmed her, and gently, she rubbed him, jerking him off with her hand. Beneath her, he groaned loudly.

"Better hurry up. Not going to last long if she keeps doing this."

From somewhere behind her, Erick grunted. She heard the click of a bottle closing. Then Erick's hands gripped her hips. He positioned her so her ass was in the air, accessible to him.

"Beautiful," he murmured.

Pressure again, on her tight — and now slightly sore — asshole. She arched her back, and the tip of Erick's cock penetrated her.

A long groan behind her, then a curse as he pushed his way in just a little farther.

She stilled, stunned at the new sensation. Ever so slowly, he worked his way in. Using shallow strokes, he penetrated her inch by inch. It was pain. It was pleasure. It was beyond words.

Owen watched below her, a savage expression of lust on his face.

Finally, Erick worked his way all the way inside of her. She could feel his balls brushing her bottom, his cock filling her like she'd never been filled before.

It was almost too much. Too much of everything. And when Owen started working his way into her pussy, while Erick filled her ass, she was sure she couldn't take it.

But she couldn't object. Couldn't voice her fear. All she could do was moan.

Gently, Owen slid his way into her like it was their first time making love. And when he settled all the way to his hilt, she thought she might die from it. From the insane pleasure.

"So fucking tight." Erick brushed a sheaf of hair behind her ear. "Do you know how good you feel? How perfect?"

Owen nodded in agreement, gritting his teeth.

She thought she couldn't take anymore, couldn't feel anything more pleasurable than this. Then they started to move.

Slow at first, they found a rhythm together. Thrusting in and out of her so that she was never empty, they moved together. She panted, unable to move, unable to do anything but take them. Accept what they gave her. How they gave it to her. Their pace quickened. Stars hit her vision, and the orgasm hit her unexpectedly.

A scream wrenched from her lips. The sound turned to a low moan as wave after wave of pleasure rolled through her. Her body shook with the intensity of it, and the men cursed as her pussy and ass clamped down on them with the force of her orgasm.

Their movements became erratic, desperate. Erick cursed and Owen was strangely silent as they pistoned in and out of her body.

Erick thrust into her hard and stiffened. Deep inside of her, she could feel him finding his release. Beneath her, Owen's thrusts grew even more frantic. Erick groaned out her name. Seconds later, Owen let out a long moan and spent himself inside of her sex.

A long moment passed before anyone moved. A moment of such bliss, she couldn't manage to do anything but feel. Then, ever so gently, the men pulled themselves from her body. Erick plucked her up into his arms. And together, they took her to the bathroom. Owen drew a bath while the prime held her close. No one spoke. No one needed to say anything.

They all knew that nothing was every going to be the same.

Erick woke to the sound of his cell phone. Even from the living room, the sound cut through the air.

Careful not to disturb the others, he got up from the bed. Beside him, Daniella murmured. On the other side of her, Owen's eyes flickered open.

Erick pressed his index finger against his lips, and Owen nodded. He pulled Daniella closer, spooning her. Trusting his second to keep her warm, he headed for the living room.

The call had dropped, but Grayson's name flashed to life on the screen as it started ringing again.

This late, it had to be important.

He touched the screen and brought the phone to his ear. "What is it?"

"We've got trouble," the wolves' alpha said on the other end of the line.

Movement caught his attention, and his gaze shifted to a sleepy-eyed Daniella, and Owen behind her. His second was right — her first shift was close. Her hearing had certainly improved if his hushed tones had woken her.

"Is that Grayson?" she mumbled. "What's wrong?"

Refusing to help the wolves was no longer an option. Not only because he knew Daniella would battle him every step of the way. Not only because the stalker could be a real threat to Owen.

Because for some reason, he gave a damn. There was only one thing he could do.

Fight for his clan.

Fight for his mate.

PART FOUR

Chapter One

For some reason, Daniella had expected a weretiger funeral to be different. To be somehow foreign and strange and thus less painful. But the day they laid Glenn to rest was much like any funeral. A woman cried—his mate, she was told. His friends were somber and stoic. And his prime—as well as his people—were angry. A chill breeze that was always only a blink away in the Colorado mountains whipped over the attendees.

Worst of all, she could barely concentrate on the funeral given the news Grayson had called with the day before. The stalker had struck again. This time, not taking someone Daniella knew and loved, but it was almost worse. The stalker had taken the werewolves' equivalent of a civilian.

A shifter so weak that she could barely be called one.

The service itself was similar to what she might've expected for a standard human affair. Erick stood, poised like the king he was, at the dais. He spoke of Glenn's bravery, of his commitment to his people. Even going so far as to mention the man's dislike of Erick, personally—drawing a low murmur of laughter from the crowd.

"But Glenn wasn't the type of tiger to allow such minor differences of personality to dissuade him. He was a warrior. A man of his people. And he died to protect them." Erick finished his speech and stepped down. A woman replaced him. Glenn's sister, if Daniella had to guess.

After the brief service, Glenn wasn't buried. Instead, he was burned over a pyre. That part of the service should have struck her as odd. Instead, it felt old. Ancient.

It felt right.

After the fire was lit, and silence reigned over the gathering for several long minutes, the weretigers moved to the main house—the large building that housed everything from a cafeteria to the library to offices. Again, very much like the humans they appeared to be. The tigers met for food and drink. Congregated to share memories of their fallen comrade.

Daniella quickly found herself alone among the many shifters. Erick had a duty to see to Glenn's widow, and Owen was busy as well—greeting and speaking with his people. Daniella suppressed the urge to stick closely by Owen's side. It was uncomfortable to be alone—she barely knew anyone here—but she had to stand on her own two feet. How could she ever expect Erick to trust her with more serious things if she couldn't even manage a social gathering without one of them by her side?

So she wandered. Around her, the weretigers alternated between somberness and laughter—between moments of grief, and moments of sharing happy memories they had with Glenn. She felt bad that she hadn't gotten a chance to know him. He had seemed the most stoic of the weretigers, the most distant. But from the bits of conversation that reached her ears, it was obvious many of his people cared for him.

The faces around her weren't unwelcoming, but they weren't exactly welcoming, either. She was a stranger here, and she felt almost like she was intruding on a very private moment. She barely knew Glenn, and it felt wrong to try to insert herself into conversations with his friends and family. So she did what anyone would in an uncomfortable social gathering — she went straight to the food table.

Her stomach roiled; she wasn't entirely sure she could eat anything. But she grabbed a couple of cookies and a few of pieces of finger food. Small plate in hand, she turned and scanned the room. Erick was still nowhere to be seen, and Owen stood with four people around him, tigers who were raptly listening to whatever was he was saying. She frowned and glanced down at her food.

It didn't help her comfort level that they hadn't had a chance to talk about what happened, what it might mean. The night with Owen and Erick had been amazing — beyond anything she could have imagined. The pleasure, yes — holy cow, the things they'd done to her body were beyond words — but it was more than that. She'd never felt such a strong connection before. When they were together, it was unadulterated bliss. Like she'd finally found a puzzle that her oddly shaped piece fit.

And she was terrified.

She picked at one of the cookies and tried to think of anything else when someone touched her shoulder. Startled, she gave a little jump and almost lost the food on her plate.

Cat grinned at her, managing to stifle a chuckle with her hand. "Jumpy much?"

She resisted returning Cat's smile—just barely. "I have no idea what you're talking about," she deadpanned.

Cat rolled her eyes. A taller form stepped beside her librarian friend, and Cat looked up to smile at him. Chris. The young man Daniella had threatened to sleep with when Erick threatened to leave her behind. He still had a year or two before he grew into his gangly limbs and big feet, but he was already handsome. She put him at around twenty.

"Hey, Chris," she said, giving him an apologetic grin. "I never got a chance to say I was sorry about—you know, the whole thing…" Her cheeks heated, and Chris smiled.

"No problem." He glanced around, then added, "It was worth it, just to see Erick's expression."

Cat looked back and forth between them, clearly not getting the joke, and Daniella made a mental note to tell her the story at a more appropriate time.

"So how's *everything* going?" Cat asked, stressing the words in such a way that Daniella knew exactly what she was asking.

Her face warmed again, and Cat's grin widened.

"Later." She mouthed the word, and Cat nodded eagerly. Chris was suddenly very interested in what his feet were doing.

"Hey, can we talk after this? About something important?" Daniella asked.

Cat quirked an eyebrow at her. "We can sneak out now if you want."

She glanced around. Owen was still occupied, and Erick still nowhere to be seen. She stomped out the bit of irritation that spiked in her. Today wasn't about her, it was about Glenn. "Do you think that would be rude?"

Cat shook her head. "People will be in and out now. I doubt anybody will notice that we're not here."

"Meet you in the library?"

"Sure." Cat headed toward the exit. Surprisingly, Chris followed at her heels. Huh.

She tried to catch Owen's eye, but he was pretty engrossed in a conversation with someone who looked more than a little upset about Glenn's passing. Not wanting to interrupt, she edged her way into his peripheral vision and pointed subtly at the door. His eyes flickered to meet hers for half a second. Figuring he got the message, she headed to the exit.

Before she passed through the doorway, a voice on the other side caught her attention. A familiar voice belonging to a person she'd hoped to avoid—Leann.

"…I mean, it's not as if she's shifted yet. For all we know, she's a dud."

Daniella's stomach swirled and she swallowed hard. They were talking about her—Leann and her cronies. What did she mean, a dud?

"Odds are ten to one that she'll never shift. Just another inbred royal who'll turn out to be a good breeder—if she can even do that right." Leann snickered, not even bothering to keep her voice down. Did she know Daniella was listening?

The thought turned some of her mortification into anger, and she strode through the open doorway, shot Leann and the small group of women around her what she hoped was an unaffected stare, then turned and walked directly to the library.

Her hands shook when she pushed open the door, and she clenched her hands into fists. Dumb. Here they were with real problems, and she was letting some jealous twit get her worked up.

But doubt lingered, and the second Cat glanced up from the table where she stood overlooking a stack of books, Daniella asked, "What's a dud?"

Cat blinked, eyes wide behind her dark-framed glasses. "Context, please."

"As in, a tiger who isn't able to shift." She swallowed hard and clarified. "A *royal* tiger."

Clearing his throat, Chris stepped out of one of the stacks with a book in hand and set it down by Cat.

Whatever. If those losers were talking about it out in the open, the rumors were likely something Chris knew about anyway, or would soon enough.

"I'm still not sure…" Cat began.

"It's a weretiger who's stuck in human form," Chris said.

"Oh, that." Cat's face twisted like she'd tasted something sour. "That's a terrible way to put it. It's really called dormancy. A were of any kind who can't shift is called dormant."

He gave the librarian an apologetic glance, as if just knowing the term was an endorsement.

Cat ignored his look, her gaze never moving from Daniella. "Where did you hear the term?"

"Is it real?" Her heart raced in her chest. "I mean, does that actually happen?"

The librarian's mouth twisted and sympathy touched her expression, telling Daniella everything she needed to know before she actually spoke. "Yes. But, it's incredibly rare." Her eyes widened. "Did Erick or Owen—"

"No. Just something I heard." Complaining about Leann and the others felt petty, so she didn't elaborate. "What can you tell me about this…dormancy?"

"Not much." Cat shrugged and grimaced. "It's

something that affects a small number of shifters. No one really knows why. There just haven't been enough of them to study…errr, you know what I mean." She shot Chris a glance, and the man shifted on his feet, obviously wishing he could melt into the floor as much as Daniella did. Despite his presence, Cat added, "*You* have nothing to worry about."

"I'm not worried." Lie. But she was done talking about this. For now. "Anyway, we have more important stuff to talk about."

Cat didn't miss a beat. "What's up?"

"I think you could really help us with this stalker situation."

She pushed up her glasses, not covering her surprise one bit. "Of course. I'll help however I can."

Chris crossed his arms and frowned, but didn't object. Likely, he realized that neither of the women would be swayed by his words. Smart man. Or was he hoping that Daniella might bring a little excitement back into his life if he kept his mouth shut? Since the fight at the house—the site of Owen's rescue and Glenn's demise—Erick had kept Chris stationed safely at home.

"Nothing too exciting," she clarified, just in case that's what Chris was hoping for. "Just some research." She watched for Chris's reaction, but his eyes were locked on Cat. He didn't seem to be going anywhere. Interesting. "I'm not sure how much you've heard, but Erick is working with the wolves in Denver to track down the stalker."

"I'd heard about that." She didn't look at Chris, but it was pretty apparent who she'd heard it from by how hard she was *not* looking at him. "I think it's a good idea. Checking on the stalker, I mean. But I can't say I'm sure about trusting the wolves."

Daniella bit back a sharp retort at that. Cat didn't know the wolves, had never met any of them. There was no reason for her to think of them as trustworthy. The tigers seemed to have an innate distrust for other creatures. It bothered her, but maybe she was just being naïve. After all, she'd only barely been introduced to this world, and already things were trying to kill her or capture her. Living in this world, growing up in it, she could see how that would be enough to make a person paranoid.

"I think we can trust the wolves," she said. "The problem is—and maybe it's just me—it doesn't seem like anybody has a good idea, a good strategy, for finding and killing this…vampire." She almost said creature, but managed to stop herself just in time. To her—practically a human—vampires were very much creatures of legends. But to weretigers, they might be people. Shitty, slave-dealing people, but people nonetheless.

"It's not just you," Chris interjected. "Stalkers are rare. Granted, our people don't spend a lot of time in cities—not our clan, anyway. But even in more populated areas, stalkers are almost unheard of. It's likely been decades since even Grayson's pack has had to deal with one."

She had gotten the feeling the wolves' alpha—despite the aura of competence that he exuded—had never dealt with a stalker before. Granted, she guessed the man couldn't be a day over thirty, but he didn't act like he'd inherited the leadership of his pack recently. "If that's true, maybe there's some way to fight this thing, or at least some way to track it, that we aren't thinking of." She looked at Cat expectantly.

Her eyes widened. "And you want my help?"

She quirked a brow. "Can you think of anyone better to help research something?"

"I can't," Chris said, giving Cat an encouraging grin.

Cat's face flushed pink, but she didn't look down. "I'd love to help."

Her obvious shock at being asked to help bothered Daniella. The young woman was wicked smart—Daniella had been able tell that within two seconds of meeting her. Maybe book research wasn't the way tigers found information historically, but it was the twenty-first century, dammit, and she would bet that if a person dug deep enough, there was a lot of good information on the Internet—even about this hidden world. Erick wasn't exactly modern in his way of thinking about things, but maybe she could help him see a new path. Heck, it was worth a try.

Not that she didn't plan on working with Cat to research it anyway. But it would be nice to have the prime's backing. More, it would be heartwarming to have Erick's support.

"Thanks, Cat," she said.

Her smile widened. "No, thank *you*. This will give me a good excuse to go through the histories—old journals that prior primes and librarians have left behind."

"Journals?" Chris asked.

"I stumbled across them when I was going through Old Dale's office last year." She gestured behind her. To Daniella, she added, "He was the last librarian—he died before he could really pass on much information to me."

Chris snorted. "Like you didn't have to pry every bit of knowledge out of him while he was alive."

"He wasn't exactly *evolved* in his thinking." Cat shrugged. "Not terribly happy a woman was going to replace him."

Daniella gave her a sympathetic smile. But what Cat said had piqued her interest. "So you've read the journals?"

"I've skimmed them." She tapped her chin. "I remember a few actually referring to vampires that would be good to go through first. To be honest, I suspect half of them or better will be useless. You wouldn't believe the idea some of those old primes had about what was important to record. One was a list of…" she leaned toward Daniella and lowered her voice, "…conquests."

Daniella snorted.

Across from her, Chris blushed, then tried to cover it by glancing down at a stack of books on the table. Cat didn't seem to notice, but Daniella had to fight the urge to tease him.

"Well, sounds like a good place to start," Daniella said. "Maybe not with the conquests one."

"It was
 a list," Cat said, matter-of-factly.

She fought a grin. "Don't forget to try Google, too. I wouldn't be surprised if there was good information out there. You might just be knowledgeable enough to separate the useful from the crazy."

Cat gripped her chest, a forlorn expression on her face. "You wouldn't ask such a thing if you knew how slow our Internet is out here."

Daniella laughed, and almost promised to talk to Erick about it. But another thought hit her. "Owen said something when he first mentioned vampires to me. I haven't had a chance to follow up with them about it, but maybe you'll know what he meant. He mentioned that there were *worse* things out there than vampires. Ring any bells?"

Chris and Cat exchanged worried glances, but

it was the librarian who spoke. "Worse things? Not that anyone's actually *seen* around here—thankfully. Anything worse would probably be demonic—not even of this world. Not exactly something you want to mess with. Or…"

Hope surged. "Or?"

"He may have been talking about the keepers," Chris said, looked anything but hopeful.

"The keepers?"

"They're not a different species, exactly. They're a group of nonhumans—a mix of shifters and vamps and witches, among other things. Supposedly, insanely tough ones. They give their lives to keep the order."

Her brows scrunched together. The way Cat had said the word, *order,* it sounded like an official term, not a generic word. "The order?"

"They keep the boundary between nonhumans and humans. They punish nonhumans who either purposefully or accidentally reveal our world to humans." Cat shook her head. "I'm not explaining this very well, but suffice it to say, if a keeper shows up at your doorstep, you did something to bring them there." She looked up, and the fear in her gaze was palpable. "And if they come to you, you don't live to tell the tale to anyone else."

Chris waved nonchalantly in an obvious attempt to break the tension. "It's not *that* cut and dry. It's not like a random shifter taking up with human is going to get their attention. The bigger stuff will bring them in—or so they say." He shrugged. "But they don't intercede to save one set of nonhumans from another. We can't expect any help from them."

The librarian laughed nervously. "From what I understand, most of what they do isn't anything so nefarious. But they do somehow manage to keep the real stuff—werewolves shifting, vampires flashing fang, stuff like that—from appearing on YouTube. They're the good guys. Kind of."

Chris snorted, but didn't contradict her.

Given all the insanity she'd dealt with since finding out about this new world, Daniella hadn't taken a moment to consider why she'd never heard any credible rumors of it before. But now that they mentioned it, it was rather amazing. Given the fact that nearly everyone could record videos and take pictures on their phones, it seemed almost impossible that credible evidence of this world had remained undiscovered. Especially given the public's interest in all things supernatural.

"We are lucky to have them," Cat added, addressing Chris. Her gaze shifted to Daniella and she grinned. "I'm sure there are a lot of nonhumans that you've probably never heard of yet. Probably even some that *I've* never heard of."

"For such a small world, there seems to be a lot of crazy stuff in it." A fact that she might find interesting, if not for the fact that everything in this world seemed so dangerous.

"Just wish I got to see more of it," Cat said, wistfully.

Daniella smiled, but worry spiked through her. Cat might be better off here—staying in the safe shell her people kept her in. Because what was out there seemed far worse than the boring life Cat feared.

Owen scanned the room, but Daniella never reappeared. He'd been aware of her, looking a little lost in the crowd. The desire inside of him to go to her, to reassure her, to simply to be at her side among his people, had been fierce. However, reaffirming his place as Erick's second was also important. And comforting Glenn's relatives wasn't a duty he could skirt. Not to mention reassuring them that retribution would be sought.

So he left her alone.

Part of him knew that if he stuck by her side, he would be showing her that he didn't trust her to make her own way among their people. He didn't want to set that example. Neither for her nor for the other tigers. They also had to see the new royal in their midst as a strong, courageous woman.

If Daniella had been the type to simply act as — well, what Daniella would have called a broodmare for Erick's children — their people's perception of her wouldn't have been so important. But Daniella could never simply be the mother of the prime's children. Could never be the woman who stood idly by while decisions were being made, when she felt she could be helpful. Could never be less than a full partner to Erick and Owen.

So she had to stand on her own two feet.

But he was keenly aware of her, of her nervous movements around the room. When Cat and Chris approached her, he was tempted to pull away from the people around him. And when she followed the librarian and her shadow from the room, he barely kept himself from following. He managed to hold his place — for a good fifteen minutes.

Then his stomach began to twist with worry.

It took some wrangling, and some excuses, but a few minutes later he was walking down the hallway where she'd disappeared.

She'd been following Cat, so there was little doubt

in Owen's mind where they had gone. Sure enough, her scent grew stronger as he approached Cat's oasis. Low laughter touched his ears from inside the large room designated as the pack library. When he entered, some of the tension left his body.

Daniella was fine.

Chatting easily with Cat and Chris, his mate looked almost at home. Hope surged in his chest. Unlike Erick, who seemed to assume that he could make the pack accept Daniella through the force of his will alone, Owen knew it wouldn't be such an easy fight.

Her background made her odds of being accepted among the tigers doubly hard. She had two black marks against her. Being raised among humans wasn't a cardinal sin, but it was almost unheard of. It almost made her an outsider. And to the tigers, outsiders were not to be trusted.

If that wasn't bad enough, a female royal joining the pack put everyone's rank, the pack hierarchy, into question. They would be lucky if they managed to get through Daniella's first year among them without bloodshed.

Daniella laughed at something Owen missed, and touched Chris on the shoulder. The other man grinned at her, and a bubble of rage rose inside Owen.

He gritted his teeth against the emotion, his human mind knowing that Daniella was simply acting as a friend. But the tiger inside of him wanted to protect, claim his new mate. Make sure no other male touched her.

The tiger was more than a little possessive.

Owen cleared his throat, managing to stay put and not cross the room to get between Daniella and Chris—a feat that had him almost shaking with the effort. Daniella turned to face him fully, and when her eyes met his, her smile widened.

Warmth touched his chest, expanding from his heart into his limbs. God, the woman's smile was like nothing else.

"Hey, there," Daniella said, closing the distance between them. She took his hands in her own, and he smiled at her before turning his attention back to the others.

"What are you three doing in here? Hatching plans and schemes, no doubt." He'd meant to joke, but the words came out with a bit of an edge.

Daniella raised her eyebrows at him. "It seems like a plan would be a good thing right about now, wouldn't you say?"

Her words had just a tiny bit of bite, too, and he grinned. "I suppose it is."

"Heck, I'd pay good money for an actual scheme." She turned to glance at Cat. "So let me know if you think of anything."

Cat offered her a small smile, but avoided Owen's gaze. He didn't have Erick's reputation for being a hard-ass, but he was second in command. Chances were, the little librarian wasn't totally sure of Daniella's authority. Yet…she was still willing to follow her lead.

That boded well.

"I've just got Cat looking into some things." She blinked. "And Chris is assisting."

Owen glanced at Chris and the man looked away. The day that Chris—a soldier through and through—was into research was a day that Owen would eat his own shoe. He was either trying to impress Daniella or Cat.

The thought forced Owen to suppress a growl.

Seeming to sense his change in mood, Daniella

squeezed his hands in hers. The little minx was no doubt trying to distract him. "When are we heading back to the city?"

"Soon." Not exactly a lie, but an exaggeration. Erick probably wouldn't get away for another hour. But Owen needed her out of here—needed to get her alone. If only to hold her. Smell her.

He wrapped an arm around her. Her eyes widened, but she didn't object. If anything, she snuggled a little closer. Then she tilted her face up and took a long breath—scenting his neck. He clutched her tighter.

"Well, then—" he began, nuzzling her hair.

"Owen." Erick stepped into the room, startling Daniella. Owen held her tighter, and turned to face his prime. New tension rode Erick's shoulders, and Owen's stomach sank.

"What is it?" he asked.

Erick's gaze flickered to Daniella, but he ignored Cat and Chris. "We have to go. Grayson called. They've taken another wolf."

Chapter Two

"**I** don't care what we have to do. I don't care how dangerous it is. We're taking this fucker out." Grayson slammed his hand on the table, and Daniella flinched.

"Calm yourself." Erick took a step closer to her, and she touched his arm reassuringly.

His concern was understandable, but she didn't feel threatened by Grayson. She just wasn't used to the man showing such a temper. An hour before, when she was driving down the mountain with Owen and Erick to return to the werewolves' warehouse in Denver, she wouldn't have thought the normally easygoing man capable of it. But apparently, even the alpha of the werewolves could be shaken.

"Two people. Two people who had zero chance of defending themselves. Don't you get it?" Grayson glared at Erick, as if this was somehow his fault. "She's not picking off my lieutenants. She's not going after our warriors. She's taking civilians. Wolves that will get her almost nothing on the market. Hell, Alicia can't even shift so much as a pinky finger. It's only through bloodlines that you'd know she was a werewolf. What the hell kind of sense does that make?"

"She's making a statement," Daniella said, realization hitting her. It was the only thing that made sense.

Grayson nodded. "Exactly. This isn't about survival for the stalker. This isn't only about getting us to leave her alone. This a very clear statement that she can do whatever the fuck she wants in my territory. *My* territory." He said the last with resolve, as if by saying it, it would make a difference. That it would somehow prevent the stalker from plucking his people from their homes.

If only.

"The vampires don't have a great sense of smell. How did she find these werewolves?" Daniella asked. "I mean, before my…things changed, they watched me with Owen and didn't seem to pick up on what I was until after they'd attacked him." Her cheeks flushed. Bringing up her heat felt personal, intimate.

Grayson shook his head. "We don't know for sure. Hell, she could've seen them at one of our gatherings."

"I have a hard time believing that a stalker could get anywhere near your stronger wolves without one of them scenting her." Erick crossed his arms.

"How she found them doesn't matter. What matters is getting them back. What matters is taking her out before she can do it again."

Daniella opened her mouth, then closed it. That the alpha was more interested in getting his people back than the details of how they'd been plucked out of the crowd was understandable. But figuring out the how and the why of it could be just as vital. But now didn't seem the right time for logic. Grayson was obviously more interested in action. Changing his mind wasn't likely until he calmed down.

"I'm ready to bring in a few more men," Erick said. "But I need somewhere to point them."

Grayson growled with frustration. "We're working on that. But drawing this fucker out isn't easy."

"It might get easier with me here." Owen didn't look happy about it, but he had a point.

Daniella's stomach twisted and she swallowed a growl of her own. The idea of Owen in that kind of danger again—the still too-vivid memory of how she'd felt when he was taken before so fresh in her mind—made something inside of her want to rage and slash and burn.

It scared the shit out of her.

One of Owen's hands gripped the base of her neck, and he massaged her softly. She glanced at him and he gave her a reassuring smile. Maybe she wasn't hiding her unease as well as she'd hoped.

"We go out tonight," Grayson said. He pointed to the map that was spread across the table. "Most of the scent hits that we've had have been in this area." He indicated part of the grid that appeared to be north of Denver proper. "We'll concentrate our hunt there tonight." His gaze moved to Owen. "You'll come with us. Maybe you'll be enough to draw her out."

Owen tensed, but didn't drop his hand from her neck.

"That isn't much of a plan," she muttered, more to herself than to any of them.

"If you have a better idea, I'm happy to hear it." Grayson quirked an eyebrow at her. Some of the happy-go-lucky man was peeking through to tease.

"Not yet, but—"

"Then we go with the plan we've got."

The stars were hidden by the city's bright glow even

miles from the center of town. The bright lights of Denver not only blotted out any sign of the natural sky, but the strange mix of scents and sounds from far too many people living closely together made discerning any useable information difficult. Erick didn't care for it. It made it far too easy for enemies to attack unnoticed until it was too late.

Through the darkness, he stalked. The neighborhood wasn't what he'd expected. Not the type of place Erick figured vampires would prefer. As a whole, they tended to be old creatures. Wealthy. He'd thought to find the stalker in one of Denver's older neighborhoods, or at least in a home that offered some privacy—like the one they'd smoked her out of when they found Owen. But the homes that dotted this area, while nice and not overly small, were new. And they offered little privacy.

The signal came across his earpiece and he trotted forward. The wolves would be more likely to actually find something, given their keen sense of smell. But it wasn't outside the realm of possibility that Erick, or one of his tigers, might catch sight of one of the suckers first. With a quick thought, he shifted his vision. The night's darkness would cover the evidence of his eyes if a human happened by. And he could shift back quickly if needed.

With his vision changed, the night shifted. Details became clearer, even as other details faded.

He'd been loath to leave Daniella behind, even in the werewolves' care. Trust for Grayson grew with each day they cooperated. And he'd earned a lot of Erick's goodwill when he came through and helped him save Owen.

Yet still, the idea of someone else protecting his mate rankled him. Particularly since Owen was out here with him as well. His second was the only one he trusted to keep her safe, and even that wasn't as good as protecting her himself.

The distinct lack of resolution in his relationship with Daniella also didn't help. Taking her together had been unforgettable. She was the most incredible thing that had ever come into his life. Erick wasn't given to romantic notions, but the things he'd felt that night—well, he'd fight for all he was worth to hold on to that kind of happiness.

But as to how to make sure she knew that, he had no idea. Owen would scoff at him, tell him to simply say how he felt. But that wasn't easy. More, words weren't good enough. Trouble of it was, he wasn't sure what would be.

And he had yet to claim her with his bite.

Time hadn't been on his side. The middle of the night phone call from Grayson to tell them that the stalker had moved on to civilian prey hadn't exactly set the mood. Then they'd had to head back to the den for Glenn's funeral.

A car passed him on the road, headlights flashing. He averted his gaze so they wouldn't see the reflection of his nonhuman eyes. He trotted through the similar-looking buildings and tried to focus on the task at hand. The time they needed to resolve their situation wasn't likely to arise until they took down this stalker.

Erick had claimed Daniella's body, and, he thought, a little bit of her heart. Hell, he hoped so. But what they had was still unofficial. The fact that she'd grown up with humans made her position in the pack all that more tenuous. They needed resolution, not just for his, Owen's, and Daniella sake. But for the pack.

Tigers didn't group well. And the slightest hint of

uncertainty among leadership and he could begin to see his clan unravel.

The darkly spiced scent hit him halfway through one of the many small parks dotting the area.

Vampire.

He halted and scanned the area, holding still in an effort not to scare away his prey. A wolf howled, somewhere close. Then, movement.

He sprinted for the running shape. But as he closed in, the shape took form. Kara, Grayson's sister. The young woman smelled of panic and fear, and she moved so quickly he didn't think any other tiger could have caught her. If he hadn't been so close, hadn't seen her out of the corner of his eye, he may not of caught her, either.

"Heading west with Kara. She's got something." His voice was low over the earpiece, and he felt strange about the use of such technology while hunting. He couldn't be sure their exact location, but he gave his best guess. "One of the parks in the southwest grid."

Damned houses all looked the same.

"What is it?" he demanded when the woman didn't even slow to acknowledge him. But she didn't respond. Instead she just stopped.

They hadn't gone far, but now stood in a different park. No, not a park. Yes, there was plant life, but large rocks covered the ground beneath their feet. A wash?

The smell hit him, and his thoughts were torn away by a new scent.

Blood.

His eyes found what his nose had discovered seconds earlier. Dimly, he heard Kara next to him, echoing over his earpiece — telling her brother to hurry.

Owen didn't have a weak stomach, but the image of what Erick and Kara had discovered stuck in his head far beyond the lights of Denver. It remained in his mind clear up to the cabin he—and he thought Daniella and Erick—had come to think of as an oasis. One of Grayson's people—the woman Aiko—had taken Daniella back up to their cabin earlier in the night and stayed with her. But when he and Erick arrived, Aiko disappeared into her little Jeep with barely a wave.

No doubt she needed to get back to her people.

What they'd discovered had been grisly, but it hadn't put a stop to the hunt. If anything, it added a bit of hustle to their step. Desperation-fueled, at least on the part of the wolves. Yet even after searching the neighborhood and surrounding areas, they hadn't found anything else of note. Kara had managed to catch vampire scent in a few spots, but none of it had led them any closer to a lair.

Erick glanced at him and turned the key in the ignition, cutting the noise. The night fell eerily silent, and both of them seemed loath to break it. But when they got into the cabin, Erick muttered, "I need a shower."

A shower would be nice, but it didn't draw Owen in the way his mate did. He needed Daniella. Needed to see her, hold her, touch her—needed to make sure she was okay. She was a brightness in an otherwise dark time. Leaving her was painful. The stalker knew of her existence, and that made him itch to be at her side, to protect her. The idea that vampires could slip in and take her when she wasn't under his watchful gaze—or Erick's—was maddening.

He shook off the uncomfortable thought, and entered the bedroom. Daniella was half-covered by a sheet, and her blankets had been shoved to the far corner. Her sleep looked to be anything but restful. And the sun peeked over the horizon; yet another exhausting day lay ahead.

But they had a few hours yet. A few hours he and Erick would need to recharge. But first…

He crawled up the bed, and pulled her against his body. A little ball of warmth, she mumbled in her sleep, but her arms settled over his when he pulled her close. God, she smelled amazing. Like love and sex and home.

Damn. He was already hard, and the temptation to slip a hand between her legs—get her ready for him—was intense. Just barely, he resisted. She needed to rest. They all did.

A moment later, she let out a small sigh, but her eyes remained closed. "Anything?"

"Nothing good."

At that, her eyes did open—but only halfway, and the sleepiness lingered in her expression when she looked up at him. "Are they…"

He didn't want to tell her what they'd found, but it was unwise to let her wonder—no doubt the horrors she'd imagine would be worse. "We found a hand." He took a deep breath. "Two of them. One from each of Grayson's people."

That wiped the sleepiness off her face immediately. "I —" She shook her head, eyes wide.

"Gruesome, but it's something they could live through." Small comfort, but the best he could offer. He pulled her closer and took in a deep breath of her sweet, sultry scent. "But I don't want to talk about it tonight. Don't want to think about it. Believe me, there will be plenty of talk tomorrow at Grayson's."

She wriggled around and buried her face in his chest.

With his mate resting safely in his arms, he slept.

Daniella felt far more comfortable during the drive back to the city than she had in days. Something about Owen curling into her arms after their very rough night had soothed her. And when Erick joined them a few minutes later, wrapping himself around her other side, she felt a sense of completeness—a sense of peace—she couldn't remember ever feeling before.

They'd woken a few hours later. And now, just before noon, they were almost back at the werewolf's warehouse.

Owen hadn't added any details after the brief bit he'd told her the night before. And over their late breakfast, she hadn't asked for any. Instead, they kept the conversation light. She teased the men, and they teased her in return. Well, Owen teased her. Erick had mostly grunted and given her *the look.* The one that said jokes were inappropriate while hunting. But she'd managed to draw a hint of a smile from him twice. She counted that as a win.

They hadn't had sex—not since the first night the three of them had been together. They'd all been running around so much since that amazing night that they barely had time to eat or sleep.

And her heat had been almost dormant. The why of it wasn't something she cared to think about too closely. But Leann's words haunted her. What if she was a dormant tiger?

The wolves waited in the warehouse. Grayson looked up from the long wooden table when they entered, where a map of the city lay. His sister and one of his lieutenants—a man whose name Daniella had yet to catch—stood next to him. Grayson looked like he still hadn't slept. Dark rings circled the man's eyes, and several days' growth of hair covered his face. It certainly didn't detract from his handsomeness, but it looked odd on the normally lighthearted man's face.

"Morning," Grayson said, though it was a few minutes into the afternoon.

"You been here all night?" Erick asked

Grayson shrugged. "Not like I'm going to be able to sleep right now."

In her pocket, Daniella's cell buzzed quietly. She pulled the phone out and turned away from the gathering as the men began discussing the events of the night before.

She fought a grin at the message and typed a quick reply, hoping Erick wouldn't explode when he found out what she was doing.

He would understand—he had to. There were only so many ways she could help. Running around in the night, looking for vampires, searching the area for missing werewolves, wasn't exactly in her skillset. So she had to help in her own way.

Owen shot her a curious glance when she returned to the group, but she just only gave him a small smile in response. Chances were, he wouldn't approve of her meddling, either—although she expected he'd be a lot more supportive than Erick.

Luckily, no one seemed worried about her text message, and Owen and Erick joined Grayson and the other wolves around the table. For several minutes, they debated strategies, trying to hammer out their approach for the coming night.

The main door slammed shut, and Daniella flinched at the sound. The men didn't look up. The warehouse was well-protected by werewolves patrolling outside, and vampires were an unlikely threat during the day.

"What I don't understand is the why." Owen tapped the table, staring at the map as if it would give him answers. "Why leave gruesome presents? Why take werewolves who will bring the slavers nothing?"

"I think I can answer that," a perky voice said from behind Daniella.

Erick cursed loudly.

Chapter Three

"And who is this?" Grayson asked as he managed to wrestle up one of his killer smiles for Cat.

Erick gave him a withering look—the man didn't seem to notice—and Daniella turned to greet Cat before the look could be directed her way.

The librarian's head tilted, as if she was unsure how to take the werewolf's attention. Grayson's smile widened, and Chris moved closer to Cat, a deep frown cutting into his lips.

Daniella avoided Erick's gaze.

Okay, it wasn't very tough of her. Happy to scheme, but less than happy to be called out on it. He'd likely make her pay for it later.

A thrill ran up her spine at the thought.

"Two of my tigers," Erick said, as if Grayson's nose hadn't already told him that. "Two of my tigers who are *not* supposed to be here right now."

"Oh, I remember the boy. But I'm sure I haven't met this tiger yet."

Cat blushed at his flirtatious tone and glanced away. Chris moved even closer to her, territorial in his stance and expression. Daniella wondered if the librarian had any clue that Chris had feelings for her. Cat might only

245

be two or three years older than him, but it was an important two or three years. He was still a young man, still growing into his gangly long limbs. And Cat…

Well, she might not have experienced her first heat yet—something that she seemed to find almost shameful for some reason—but she was already a young woman. And Daniella couldn't see her holding out for Chris to grow up. She might not have had her first heat, but it couldn't be long now. At twenty-three, she was already beyond the age most tigers experienced it. Not unlike Daniella.

The reminder brought Leann's biting rumor-mongering back to the forefront of her mind, and Daniella swallowed hard. No. She wasn't going to let that worry her. Not now.

"This is our librarian, Cat," Owen said, gaze sharp. Maybe Chris wasn't the only one feeling overly protective of their Catnip. Daniella knew that Owen's interest was in keeping the young tiger safe. Tigers didn't trust outsiders—not even the wolves—not really.

Daniella shot him an annoyed glance, but he didn't seem to notice.

"Yes, our librarian." Erick crossed his arms and turned his hard gaze to focus on Daniella. "What I can't figure out is why she's here."

Daniella felt her neck heat under his scrutiny. But she squared her shoulders, and forced a nonchalant shrug. "I invited her."

Erick arched an eyebrow at her challenging tone, but she saw the slightest quirk of his lips before his expression flattened. "And *why* did you invite her?"

She almost sighed in relief. A week ago, Erick would've reacted immediately to the challenge of his authority. And his reaction would have been angry, leaving no room for negotiation. Now, at least he was willing to listen to her. Was it just the change in their relationship, or was Erick actually loosening his tight grip on his command?

"I've had Cat looking into vampire lore. Stuff she's been able to dig up on the Internet. And from some old books she found in your library — our library." The tigers were her people, too, but she was still getting used to that fact.

"Journals left by previous primes, actually," Cat added. "Well, mostly. Some histories from prior librarians, too."

Erick's eyebrows rose that that, but he didn't comment. She wondered if he'd even known that the primes of his clan had once kept journals of important events. Until his father, that was. Did he know that librarians had been responsible for acting as historians?

Cat had been enthusiastic about the idea of reading through the journals and had texted Daniella the night before to let her know she'd found something. After Daniella had let her know about the dismembered hands this morning, Cat's excitement had been palpable, even through text messages.

That had struck her as more than a little weird, but possibly a very good sign.

She didn't fully understand just yet how useful what Cat had come up with would be, but she'd known it was important to bring her here. Relaying information secondhand would be inefficient and time-consuming. Cat needed to be here to answer questions and to explain her findings. And they didn't have time to waste.

Silence filled the air for a long moment, as Erick watched her. His expression was unreadable, and she could practically hear the gears working in his mind as he thought through how to react to this undermining of his authority.

"So…do you guys want to know why the stalker is doing this, or not?" Cat asked. Daniella could hear a quaver in her voice, but she did a pretty darn good job sounding confident.

"Yes," Grayson said, the flirtatious tone gone.

Cat took a deep breath. "I think the stalker is trying to become the master of the city."

No one so much as breathed for half a second. Then chaos exploded.

Daniella had expected the reaction—from what she understood, city masters were powerful, rare, and pretty much a big deal in the nonhuman community. Unfortunately, that was about all the information she'd had a chance to get out of Cat thus far.

The librarian's big eyes widened at the barrage of questions and angry exclamations around her. Only when Grayson addressed her, his voice rising above the others, did she respond.

"I'd be happy to go over the reasons. If you guys will be quiet for a minute." Cat opened the binder she'd been carrying, consulting her notes.

Daniella almost smiled at the sight of the diminutive woman scanning the pages as werewolves and weretigers glowered at her. For Cat to be intimidated, she'd have to notice them all first. Not likely when she had any sort of reading material in front of her.

"I didn't put it all together until Daniella texted me this morning about the…" Cat pushed her glasses up, obviously looking for a better phrase than dismembered hands. "…About what you found last night. That behavior didn't fit with the idea that this stalker is a simple slaver."

"You're right. It doesn't make sense for a slaver to kidnap weak wolves—especially if she's trying to hide from us." Grayson scratched at his new beard.

"Exactly," Cat said. "If this was about money—or only about money—that would make no sense. But what this stalker is doing right now is very similar to what I've read about other master vampires taking cities."

"There are multiple accounts in our histories of master vampires claiming cities?" Disbelief was apparent in Owen's tone, and Daniella flinched for her friend.

But Cat didn't seem intimidated. "Only one where the prime had personal experience—he was in Atlanta when it was claimed." Her confident expression faltered. "The rest I've had to piece together from stories mentioned secondhand in the journals." She hesitated. "And the Internet."

Someone snorted, but Grayson's gaze remained locked on her. "Go on."

Her gaze held his for a moment, before she turned back to her notebook. "As you all probably know, it's pretty rare for a vampire to take over a city—at least a large city like Denver. Some cities, especially older ones, already have master vampires ruling them—likely all powerful stalkers. But in most of those places, leadership hasn't changed in our lifetime."

"What do weak werewolves have to do with vampire politics?" Erick ground out, apparently losing patience with the history lesson.

Cat glanced at him before returning her gaze to her work. "It's a show of strength. A show of power. A vampire rising to the position of master of the city—or of a territory—doesn't only have other vampires to worry about. They also have to either control or work with local nonhumans of other races." She looked up from her notebook and frowned. "It's pretty rare for vampires to choose to try to work with others. They tend to either drive them out—like in New York City—or they simply keep the local populations cowed enough so that they aren't a problem. I think that's what the vampire's doing here."

"*Trying* to do," Grayson said, voice firm. "No way in hell are we laying down for this fucker."

Cat blinked, seemingly surprised by the anger and Grayson's tone. "I don't expect we will," she said pertly, and it was Grayson's turn to look surprised.

"So, what? That's all this is about? Taking Owen, injuring the wolves?" Erick asked.

"I'm not saying that selling Owen to slavers might not have been part of this vampire's plan—I'm sure funding whatever she's going for here isn't cheap—but I don't think that was her endgame." Cat shrugged. "I could be wrong on this, but it's the only thing that fits."

Silence reigned for a moment while the group digested that.

"So…there are places where vampires and other nonhumans live in harmony?" Daniella asked, her brain sticking on that bit of information.

Cat gave her an apologetic grin. "Probably not *harmony*, but the master vampire of Chicago is said to live in something like that with the other nonhumans in his area."

Erick snorted. "Would have to see that to believe it." The rest of the room murmured their agreement.

She would have to see that to believe it, too. What she'd seen of the vampires thus far didn't lead her to believe that they were very cooperative with anyone— she imagined they rarely got along with each other.

"I'm not downplaying the importance of this

information," Grayson said. "But I don't see how this changes our endgame. We need to find my people and get them out." He shot Cat a small smile. "But this is good information to have—I just don't think it changes our plan of finding and killing this fucker."

Now for the hard part. "I'd like to work with Cat to try to come up with a different plan. Maybe look into research—look into those journals—see if we can figure out another way to fight this thing. Or at the very least, a way to find her."

Erick looked like he was about to go into his canned response about her staying as uninvolved and far away from danger as possible, but it was Owen who spoke. "You and Cat are welcome to research all you want. As long as you stay out of the field."

She frowned at him. Sure, she expected to immediately be shut down by Erick, but Owen had always seemed to trust her judgment by default.

"You could be doing this kind of research back home. It might be easier in our library, where Cat has access to all of her books." Erick reached out, and slid the back of his fingers against her cheekbone. His expression was serious, yet tender.

She wasn't fooled.

Oh, he might be feeling warm thoughts about her, but she wasn't about to let him send her back to the tigers' territory. She'd have to claw and plot her way back here if she allowed that.

"No freaking way." She smiled sweetly. "But, nice try."

He flashed an almost-grin back at her, before his serious expression returned. "Fair enough."

The lack of argument almost startled her. He was trying to be more open to her fully participating in this.

More open to her being a full partner to him—him and Owen. The man couldn't change fully overnight—heck, she didn't expect him to do a full one-eighty ever when it came to her safety, let alone one within a week. But she did appreciate that he was trying.

Her eyes found Cat's and they shared a long look. Who knew things would actually go according to plan?

Suddenly the world seemed a whole lot brighter.

Daniella felt invigorated. Part of her realized that she shouldn't get her hopes up so quickly. What Cat's research had revealed…well, it wasn't a solution, was it? Yet, Daniella couldn't help but feel like they were on the right track.

Maybe it was unfounded optimism, but she felt like with Cat's brains, Owen and Eric's brawn, and her own can-do attitude, there was nothing they couldn't accomplish. Including taking out a stalker plotting to become master of the city.

With that in mind, she remained behind at Grayson's, along with Cat and Chris, until Owen and Erick returned from the field. Together, they researched—Cat reading old journals and Daniella clicking through sites on the computer. Chris bounced between hovering mostly unhelpfully, and bringing them snacks.

When Chris went out to grab them dinner with one of the wolves, Daniella decided to take advantage of their relative privacy. She scooted her chair closer to Cat's, the loud squeak of the metal sliding against concrete drawing an annoyed glance from their current bodyguard. Luckily, he was across the room and,

Daniella figured, most uninterested in the topic of conversation she had in mind.

"Are you aware of the ginormous crush that guy has on you?" she said when Cat looked up.

Her mouth dropped open and she glanced to their bodyguard.

"Not *him*," Daniella clarified, blushing at the long glare the grizzled, older wolf gave them from across the room. Maybe he could hear them more clearly than she'd hoped.

"Of course not." She shrugged in an awkward attempt to look unaffected, but her eyes widened when she leaned closer and asked, "Who are you talking about?"

For someone who was trying to play it cool, Cat was listening awfully hard. Daniella fought a grin. "Chris."

Cat choked—on her own spit, apparently, since she wasn't drinking anything—and flew into a coughing fit. Their guard folded his newspaper to his lap to watch them, but didn't so much as drop his feet from where he'd propped them on another chair. Daniella slapped her on the back a few times until Cat caught her breath.

"That's insane! Chris is like…" She waved her hands around, struggling to come up with a word that explained how she thought of the younger tiger. "He's like my little brother or something. A friend. I've known him since we were in diapers and—you're wrong." Cat shook her head so vigorously, Daniella almost cautioned her to be careful.

"I could be wrong." No way was she wrong.

Cat stared at her suspiciously. "Why do you think— you know what? Never mind."

Daniella turned back to her computer. Should she have kept her mouth shut? Probably. But she'd wanted to think about something lighter than vampires for a few minutes, and Chris's open adoration was plain for all to see. She hadn't expected Cat to be surprised.

Less than a minute later, she saw Cat turn to her in the corner of her eye. She opened her mouth, then closed it. Not wanting to make things worse, Daniella pretended to be engrossed in her latest Google results — most of which seemed to be Buffy the Vampire Slayer fan sites and a few devoted to The Vampire Diaries.

"You really think —"

"Definitely," she said, without looking away from her search results.

"He's almost two years younger than me." Cat took off her glasses and cleaned them vigorously with her shirt. "Okay, that's not much in the grand scheme of things, but I've never thought of him like that."

"Something to think about." She gave Cat a grin, one that the other woman halfheartedly returned.

"I guess…"

"He won't be young forever." She winked.

Cat laughed and shook her head. Another long, silent moment passed, then, voice soft, she asked, "What's it like — I mean…"

She knew exactly what the little librarian was asking. Problem was, she didn't know how to put into words the way being with Owen and Erick had tilted her whole world. "It's…indescribable. They've made my life so different that it's hard to put into words."

"Better?"

"The best." She glanced at the grizzled wolf who was watching over them to see if he was listening. If anything, he seemed to have his face buried even farther into his newspaper than he had before. Maybe too far to read anything. She bit her lip to keep from laughing.

Owen and Erick returned to the warehouse early —

by eleven o'clock. Grayson and Kara came with them — all looking exhausted.

Grayson's people were rotating in to give the tigers a chance to rest — a chance Daniella was grateful for. It twisted her up inside to see them so obviously exhausted. The men, on the other hand, didn't look terribly happy about turning in early.

"Exhausted alphas — and primes — are useless. What will you do if we find the stalker in a few hours? Fall asleep on her shoulder and attempt to defeat her with large quantities of drool?" Kara asked when Grayson got snippy about her order to get a few hours of shut-eye on a cot in one of the warehouse's offices. After that, she practically shoved Daniella and her mates out the door.

Daniella almost asked if they should stay in town — find a hotel or something — so they were closer in case Grayson's people found the stalker. But she knew neither Owen nor Erick would feel comfortable with her that close to the stalker. The men wouldn't get a wink of sleep. Besides, she felt optimistic for the first time in days — she felt good. Chipper even.

And for what she had planned, she needed privacy.

Happily, Cat decided to stay at Grayson's warehouse. His sister had found something similar to the prime's journals in the wolves' belongings. Cat wouldn't be given total access to the old journals, even though Grayson had seemed to think it wasn't a big deal. Kara, on the other hand, disagreed. So she stayed behind as well, to peruse the journals before she allowed Cat to look through them. Unsurprisingly, Chris decided to stay at Cat's side.

More tired than she'd thought, Daniella found herself nodding off during the drive to the cabin. And when the SUVs engine cut out, she snapped awake.

Owen shot her a grin from the passenger's seat. "Honey, we're home."

She laughed at his singsong comment. "Didn't realize I was so tired."

Erick frowned as he looked at her through the rearview mirror. "We should've sent you back here hours ago. Chris could have brought you."

"As if you could pry him away from Cat…" she muttered.

Erick's expression didn't change, but there was no doubt her voice had carried, because Owen shot her a curious glance. An angelic smile—or as near as she could manage—was her only reply to his unspoken question. He snorted and opened the door.

They walked into the dark cabin, and Owen hit the light. "Are you hungry?"

She waited for Erick to complete his quick search of the cabin and return to the living room before she replied.

"Starving." She waggled her eyebrows at Erick across the room, and then going to her tiptoes, faced Owen for a kiss. Obligingly, Owen leaned down so she could press her lips against his.

A rush of desire rolled over her, immediate and powerful, the second she touched him. It wasn't her heat; that felt different. This was just a woman needing her men. A tiger needing her mates.

After a split-second of hesitation, Owen was kissing her back. Tender and warm, his lips caressed hers. His tongue dipped softly into her mouth, tasting her gently. She didn't mind the tenderness. The softness. But she wanted some wildness, too.

She broke the kiss and smiled up at him. Owen grinned back, and for a moment there was a perfect understanding between them. She could've stared into his eyes forever. Have kissed and touched and caressed him until her last day. But she wasn't about to exclude Erick.

Pulling away from his warmth was tough to do. For one, she always felt so safe in his arms, and she hadn't gotten a lot of that lately. For another, he didn't seem to want to let her go, either. His arms offered just a bit of resistance, but he relented after a moment and she turned to Erick.

There was a hunger in the prime's gaze that she hadn't really seen—hadn't more than glimpsed—in days. That open need filled her with confidence. She hadn't been with him—hadn't been with Owen, either—since they took her together the first time. Days had passed. Days that had felt like a lifetime. Enough time to build doubt in a woman's mind. Particularly when the woman was in a very new kind of relationship, one that was different from anything else she'd ever experienced.

But the fire in his eyes was a welcome reassurance. She crossed the three paces between them and wrapped her arms around his neck. Like Owen, he didn't resist the kiss she offered. And just as she'd hoped, though he tried to be gentle, some of his wildness peeked through in the kiss. His lips were neither soft nor pliant, and half a second after pressing his lips against hers, he took control. His tongue slipped between her lips, taking rather than asking. If Owen's kiss had been a sweet question, Erick's was a spicy demand.

She broke the kiss, breath already coming in short gasps, before she could get fully swept away in him. But Erick's gaze didn't show the understanding that Owen's had. Their relationship was different, new, and not on the same footing as her relationship with Owen.

If there hadn't been a question in his kiss, there was one in his eyes.

"The heat?" Erick asked, a frown touching his lips.

She stepped back out of his arms, her feet moving of their own volition, as she tried to keep the shock from her face.

"No." Did he not want her if she wasn't under the influence of the heat? Had she been that stupid?

She wrapped her arms around herself. Though she still wore all of her clothing, she suddenly felt very exposed.

"What's wrong?" Erick said, confusion quickly replaced by his normal flat expression.

She shook her head. "Is that—I mean..." She swallowed hard, squared her shoulders, and faced the prime. This was a discussion they needed to have. One she was scared to death of. But dammit, if she could help these people face down vampires, she could face the *what are we* question about her relationship with the man.

Owen moved in behind her, and his hand touched the small of her back. The show of support bolstered her confidence. "Is that important to you?"

Realization seemed to hit him, and his eyes widened, before narrowing. "Are you asking me if I'm only interested in you—being with you—when you're in heat?" He closed the short distance she'd created between them and took hold of her upper arms, almost painfully. "I know we've known each other only a short time. But do you really think this time with you has meant nothing to me?"

She shook her head and forced a deep breath "I didn't—but, we've never talked about it."

Erick looked as though he just suddenly sucked on something sour. "Must everything be *discussed?*"

Owen made a sound behind her — one that sounded suspiciously like a laugh. She didn't turn around — it was bad enough she had to deal with Erick right now. If she saw Owen laughing at her current situation, she might just throttle him.

Erick's gaze shifted to the other man, and it looked like he might have the same thought on his mind. But when he spoke again, he spoke to her. "I care for you. I don't know how to show that to you more plainly. I worried that we'd been ignoring your needs while hunting for the stalker."

Heat crawled up her neck. "Oh."

Chapter Four

"Do not doubt what I say now. We are mated. You, me, and Owen. This is not a temporary thing. I will not stop wanting you simply because you are not in heat." He stepped closer, overwhelming her with his size and the conviction in his gaze. "I may not ever be able to explain my feelings with pretty words, but I would kill for you." His jaw ticked. "I would die for you."

Erick cradled Daniella's face, hands shaking with emotions he couldn't voice properly. Saying how he felt wasn't something that came naturally to him, but he was doing his damnedest to *show* her how important she was, even when it required suppressing all of his instinct to do so. How could Daniella not understand what she meant to him?

He must have failed. Perhaps because he was still growing to understand his feelings—what they meant. Owen was the one who was good with this sort of thing. But Erick would have to be better. His lack of care had hurt her. Something inside of him shifted painfully at that thought. Failing Daniella was not an option. He would do better.

He had to.

Worry still creased Daniella's brow, but before Erick could inquire further, she kissed him again. And with the soft touch of her lips, the world around them disappeared.

There was only her. The sweet scent of her filling his lungs and the perfect feel of her filling his arms.

Mine.

He'd never kissed another woman, so he had no direct knowledge that it wasn't always this good. But somehow he knew that kissing another would never be like this.

Fire raged through him and he pulled her closer, needing to have every inch of his skin touching hers. Needing to brand her with his kiss. Brand her with his scent. He would've gone on kissing her all night if she'd allowed it, but she broke away. Cheeks flushed, lips swollen, and desire in her gaze.

She glanced at Owen, but she didn't pull away from Erick. "Did you guys realize that I've never been in a two-person shower?"

Owen, who had stayed close as they kissed, had desire plain to see on his face as well. But at Daniella's words he flashed a grin. "That's a damn shame."

Erick picked her up, eliciting a squeak of surprise from his mate. "Our mate should be deprived nothing."

Before Daniella could respond to that, Erick was headed for the bathroom, with Owen right behind him.

Once there, he regretfully set Daniella down. Not touching her had become painful. Especially now that he needed her so much, now that he'd accidentally caused her pain.

He and Owen made quick work of their own clothing as Daniella watched with hooded eyes. She didn't reach for her own, but when they began plucking clothes from her, she didn't object. Erick could smell her desire in the air, almost taste it. The heat might not be upon her, but her need for them was still plain.

Something in his chest twisted.

He'd half wondered if she would want him once her heat had passed. She had a relationship with Owen, a history. They had nothing of the sort. He hadn't worried about losing her, exactly — he would not allow that, no matter what. Letting her go was not an option. But an annoying sliver of doubt had nagged him. Would she still want him with the same fire?

But when she looked at him now, desire so plain in her gaze, his doubts evaporated. Weight he hadn't fully realized he'd carried lifted from his shoulders. And he couldn't get her into the shower fast enough.

Erick switched on the spray, and stepped beneath it without waiting for the water to heat. The cold did nothing to dissuade his erection. Owen stepped in under the other spray, grimacing at the cold. His cock jutted from his body as well. Erick wasn't the only one who needed his mate.

As one, they turned to look at Daniella.

A little shy under the bright bathroom lights, she offered them an unsure smile. One of her hands came up halfheartedly to cover her breasts, and Erick reached for her, tugging down the arm and pulling her into the shower with them.

"I wish there were three showerheads in here," Daniella muttered when she stepped inside. Without a word, Erick stepped left, taking her closer to him so she would be fully under the hot water. Luckily, there was enough room for more than three people — even if there weren't quite enough shower nozzles. Once things settled down, he was going to make sure his cabin — their cabin—was equipped with three showerheads. One never knew when a quiet getaway would be in order.

Owen reached for the soap and grinned at Daniella. "Someone looks a little dirty." He waggled his eyebrows

Daniella laughed outright, and even Erick couldn't manage to swallow a small snort. She tried to grab the soap from Owen, and the bar flew through the air. Erick caught it, and she turned to grin at him.

Laughing at their own awkwardness—at their own silly jokes—the three of them managed to get somewhat clean. Hands slick with soap, Erick half-pretended to clean Daniella's breasts, but before he could fully enjoy the sensation of the weight in his hands, Owen slipped a soapy hand between her legs.

Daniella threw her head back and moaned, obviously enjoying their ministrations. But before the men could react, *she* had the soap. Even as they worked her body, she reached for their cocks with slick hands.

Erick bit back a groan, and went still as Daniella gripped his dick and began working it.

On the other side of her, Owen let out a low moan. With one of them in each hand, she jacked them off, her grip strong but her movements achingly slow.

"Fuck," Erick ground out, as her pace increased.

Daniella shot him a naughty grin, and began working him harder. Eyes going back and forth between them, she bit her lip as she worked. Adorable and sexy as hell.

Unable to take it anymore, Erick shot Owen a look. Understanding the unspoken message, Owen nodded, offering him a grin. "Prime first?"

"Sounds good to me," Erick said, so worked up he wasn't about to argue.

Daniella shot Owen a curious glance.

Before she knew what was happening, Owen had picked her up from behind, startling her into releasing them from her torturously good ministrations. Erick missed the sensation for about half a second, before Owen was turning her to face him.

Erick reached down to cup her ass and pulled her against him, and Daniella's naked legs wrapped around his waist automatically. Without waiting to check if she was ready — he knew, without a doubt, that she was very, very ready — he slid into her waiting heat.

Heaven.

Daniella almost came as Erick slid home. She'd been enjoying teasing the men, but nothing could compare to this. His big, hard cock filled her easily — her pussy was already so wet, so ready. Teasing them had done that. Their desire for her had been so obvious in their expressions it had made her weak in the knees. Who was she to make these two strong, sexy, powerful men so aroused?

She didn't know how she'd gotten so lucky, but she was more than willing to enjoy it.

Erick cursed under his breath, but remained still. He filled her completely, and Owen moved in closer behind her back.

"Lean against me, kitten." Owen secured her, holding her weight against his chest. His face nuzzled her neck, and he nibbled her ear. He reached around to tease her breasts, and she moaned at the sensation.

Trusting Owen to hold her, Erick began to move. With her legs wrapped around his waist, he slid in and out of her heat, and a slow and steady motion.

She wrapped her arms around Owen's neck, and he began playing with her breasts in earnest. He felt their weight in his hands, before squeezing them gently. He pinched softly at her nipples, sending a shock of need straight to her pussy.

"You're so fucking beautiful—so amazing," Owen said, voice a guttural growl in her ear.

"So fucking tight, too," Erick said, always the romantic. She couldn't help but smile at that, but then he began driving into her harder. Her body was getting used to the size of the men, but it felt wonderful, almost brand-new, as he drove himself into her. He was so big, and thick, it pushed her body to the edge of pain as he drove in harder and harder, faster and faster.

Owen began massaging her breasts more roughly, tweaking her nipples. The words he murmured in her ear turned from sweet to dirty as they urged her closer and closer to orgasm. Finally, one of Owen's hands reached between her legs.

Erick's eyes locked on her. "Come for us, wildcat. Come for us now."

Owen pinched her clit hard. The tension in her belly broke, sending waves of pleasure through her whole body, and a long cry from her lips.

Erick's fingers dug harder into her hips as his pace became erratic. Only a few seconds after her, her name escaped his lips, more a guttural groan than a real word. Inside of her, she could feel his cock jerking over and over, sending his seed into her womb.

Utter bliss hit her for a moment, before she realized that only she and Erick had found release in the moment. Guilt hit her, but before she could wallow in it, she found herself being turned around. Before her sluggish, satisfied brain grasped what they were doing, their positions had reversed. And she suddenly realized what they intended to do.

Before, they had enjoyed her together — they'd taken her in a way she'd never experienced. This time they intended to take their pleasure from her one after the other. She'd counted on the fact that they would all end the night satisfied, but she hadn't expected this.

Owen slid into her waiting heat, even more easily than Erick had. A cry escaped her. It was too soon. She'd only just come. Surely it was too soon.

But Owen gave her a look of pure male satisfaction. "God, you feel amazing."

"I can't — it's too much —"

"You can take it, kitten," Owen slid in and out of her slowly, drawing a low moan from her lips.

"Our fierce little wildcat can take anything we can give her. Can't you, wildcat?" Erick nuzzled her neck, and Owen moved slowly in and out of her — not giving her time to recover, but waking her body nonetheless.

As they'd done before, one man was at her back, holding her and teasing her body, while the other drove into her sensitive pussy. The overwhelming sensation never faded, but her body quickly became flushed with renewed need. Her belly tightened and her breasts ached to be touched.

But with Erick at her neck, she suddenly had another thought. Would he finally bite her? God, she hoped so. Tears burned her eyes at the thought. It felt like the one thing they needed to solidify this. She turned her head slightly, giving him better access to her neck. He nuzzled her, but he didn't bite.

And soon she couldn't think well enough to worry about it.

Owen's pace increased, and his hips moved almost

frantically. Touching her, teasing her, watching Erick take her, had gotten him worked up. But he was gentle as he held her hips, and the tender expression never left his face as he drove himself into her over and over, harder and harder. Erick was rough with her breasts, but by then, that was exactly what she needed. Her body tightened, on the brink of another orgasm.

This time, Erick reached for her clit. He rubbed her hard, over and over, as Owen drove himself into her. The sensation was too much, and her pussy contracted hard around Owen's thick, long cock. Barely a sound escaped her, a small scream as her body convulsed and shook. Owen drove himself into her, and only Erick at her back, with his strength, kept her in place so Owen could fuck her as hard as he needed to. Owen came with a low grunt, and his thrusts slowed.

With great care, the men helped her back to her feet. But they didn't release her. Not right away.

They held her close. The three of them stayed that way, under the warm spray, until the water heater finally gave out.

Chapter Five

*D*aniella should've felt like she was on top of the world after her tender night with Owen and Erick. Her body still buzzed with excitement, with satisfaction. And it was true that she'd never felt closer to her mates. So why wasn't she skipping around for joy, instead of doing everything she could to keep her head held high as she followed Erick and Owen into Grayson's warehouse?

It was stupid. Erick hadn't bitten her, and for some reason that made her feel restless. Was she insane? A couple of weeks before, she would've found the idea of someone biting her during sex—or anywhere else—to be more than just a little bit horrifying. But knowing, as Owen had told her, that it was part of cementing their mating bond, she felt incomplete without it.

She shook herself, and Owen gave her a curious glance as he held open the door. She couldn't see Erick's expression behind her, but she offered Owen a reassuring smile.

"You okay? Owen murmured as she passed

"I'm fine. Just tired."

It wasn't a lie. Not really. She just had to get the

primitive tiger part of her brain that insisted things weren't finished until Erick bit her to shut the hell up.

Cat sat at Grayson's conference room table, hunched over an old journal. Daniella couldn't tell if it was one of the tigers' books she'd brought with her, or if it belonged to the wolves. Whatever its source, Cat seemed engrossed in its contents. With one hand, she held the leather-bound journal open, and jotted notes on a legal pad with the other.

To her right, Chris was doing an unconvincing job of looking interested. Heavy eyelids and a blank stare gave him away. Until Erick entered the room. Then he stood, and faced his prime as they approached.

The blonde wolf on Cat's other side didn't rise, either. Instead, Kara leaned back in one of the chairs with her feet stretched out to rest on the table. Much more relaxed than she had been the night before, the wolf was no longer hovering over Cat. Perhaps she had already finished going over the wolves' journals and had discovered no secrets that needed to be kept from the tigers.

"How goes it?" Daniella sat across from Cat. The librarian looked up and blinked, as if she hadn't noticed their arrival until Daniella spoke. Maybe she hadn't.

"It's coming together, I think. No eureka moments yet, but that might be the lack of sleep."

She grimaced. Cat had started researching days ago. How many that night said she'd denied her friend sleep by now? "Maybe you should up to the cabin. Get some rest. You'll probably think a lot better after getting some Z's."

"The vamps are unlikely to strike during the daytime," Owen offered. Daniella shot him a smile of gratitude, and he winked at her, warmth radiating from his eyes.

Before Cat could respond, the door slammed.

Seconds later, Grayson and one of his warriors, Aiko, strode in from the back.

"We lost her again," Grayson said without preamble.

Erick cursed. "What do you mean *lost* her?"

"I mean exactly what I said," Grayson snapped. Cat looked tired, but the wolves' alpha looked positively exhausted. "We got reports last night from another clan. A small group of werecoyotes. One of theirs was taken." He hesitated, scowl deepening. "A child. Not more than ten."

Daniella's stomach dropped to the floor. A long string of expletives flew from Owen's mouth. Erick, on the other hand, went quiet.

The man was at his scariest when he was quiet.

Grayson took off his jacket and tossed it on an empty chair. "We managed to follow the vampire to a shopping center—not far from where we've caught her scent before. But she was gone by the time we closed in. No fucking scent to follow"

"A car?" Owen said, voice deceptively mild.

Grayson gave him a dark look. "No shit. But day was breaking—they have to have a specially rigged car for her not to be toast. Vampires don't typically keep competent humans in their employ that long—they get hungry, and the humans get weak or dead."

"Why weren't we called?" Erick asked, voice low.

"There wasn't time—" Grayson started.

"Of course!" Cat jumped to her feet and smacked the table, far too much joy in her voice given the conversation at hand. "That makes sense."

The room went quiet and all eyes turned to her. Oblivious to the attention, Cat stared down at her notes.

"Maybe you should expand a little bit on that, Catnip," Daniella said, nervously.

The tension in the room was so thick she could physically feel it pressing against her skin. Cat's exclamation hadn't deadened the feeling; it had only pushed it up a notch. The whole place felt rigged to explode in violence at any second.

"Sorry. I was thinking." She blinked and glanced around, as if surprised to be the center of attention. Had she been listening to the conversation at all?

"Think faster," Grayson growled.

Cat flinched at the anger in his tone, but she didn't back away. Instead, she gave Grayson a not-so-kind glare for his attitude. "The vampire wants to take over the area. Rule as a master of the city. We can assume she's probably been here for a few months, at least. Long enough to have gathered some support."

"That makes sense. That she's been in the area a while, I mean. There was evidence that at least one vampire had been watching Owen for who knows how long." Daniella's eyes found Owen, as if she needed to reassure herself he was still there. The time he'd been gone—no, she wasn't going to dwell on it right now. She didn't need to rustle up any more fear. She had more than enough to give her nightmares.

Cat nodded. "Right. She would have been watching him, but not only him. The wolves, too. Probably other communities of nonhumans in the area. She needed information to properly plan this takeover."

"Get to the point, Cat," Erick insisted.

She pushed up her eyeglasses. "During that time, she would have figured out there was no way that she would be able to turn Erick to support her. Tigers don't work well with others in general. And…" She shot her prime an apologetic smile. "Erick is, in particular, not known for working well with others."

Erick grunted.

Her gaze flickered to Grayson. "I suspect she thinks the same of you, for whatever reason. Given she's never approached you, never tried to gain your support through other means."

Grayson's expression went cold and Daniella glimpsed the strength of a man powerful enough to rule a pack of wolves. But it was Kara who spoke. "Vampires killed our parents. Gray would die first."

Cat started, and sympathy soaked her expression when she looked back at the werewolf alpha, but his cold stare didn't crack. No denial of what his sister said, but he didn't seem willing to add any details, either.

"My point is," Cat said in a rush of words, "that just because she didn't think you guys would support her in this, doesn't mean that nobody else would."

That sunk in for a moment. "Someone is helping her." Owen's hand fisted at his side. "Why the fuck—"

"Power." Grayson's hard expression didn't shift, but Daniella had the sudden urge to step back from the alpha.

"I'm not sure I—" Daniella began.

"Grayson promotes a certain amount of…getting along with humans. And each other," Kara explained. "Most nonhumans in the area look to him as a leader among leaders in the region. He's stepped in more than once to ensure peace. To make sure that one group doesn't stomp all over a weaker one. And a lot of people don't like to be told what to do—especially by someone not of their species. An outsider."

Eesh. There was no shortage of distrust among the groups. Apparently, the tigers weren't the only suspicious ones around.

"What my sister is trying to say is there is no short

supply of people who'd love to see someone stronger than me take hold of the area."

"Are we sure it isn't just humans helping her?" Daniella asked, for some reason finding that idea less despicable than someone in their own community turning against them.

Cat shrugged. "Possible. But the way she's plucking people off the street after you eliminated several of her vampires, I'd guess more than humans are helping her. Like Kara said, it might be another group that wants power they can't get with Grayson controlling the area."

"It would have to be someone who can hide her during the day," Owen noted. "Not that that eliminates much more than vampires."

"Someone capable of tracking down wolves who can't even shift," Erick added.

"Likely some group who really doesn't like you very much, given how focused they've been on taking the wolves." Cat frowned at Grayson. "They haven't snagged any other tigers yet, and we're trying to help take her down, too. Granted, we're smaller in number and tougher to get to, but still. The way she's going after wolves who can't even fight back…"

Grayson and Kara shared a long look — a hard stare that appeared to be a battle of wills more than a simple communication. Kara looked down, and Grayson spoke. "The witches."

Not long after Grayson's declaration, most of the wolves headed out. And Erick got on the phone, bringing in more tigers to help. As many as the clan could spare.

Unsure of how to help, Daniella wracked her brain

and thumbed through journals while Cat took a quick nap on a cot in one of the warehouse's offices.

After dropping the bombshell of who he suspected was helping the stalker, Grayson refused to explain why he thought they were responsible, dismissing the information as irrelevant.

The alpha did say that he couldn't be entirely sure where the witches might be hiding the vampire during the day, but he had a few ideas. They hoped, between Grayson's local knowledge, his sister's first-class nose—along with a little investigation and no small amount of bullying—they might be able to pinpoint the most likely places to check. It was imperative that they did.

Before he left, Grayson circulated a picture of the little boy that was missing. As if any child found among vampires wouldn't become first priority. But the knowledge that a child had been taken, not to mention the picture of that smiling face, had certainly lit a fire under everyone's butt.

Early afternoon turned to evening, and Cat awoke from her far-too-short nap to continue researching. Despite the dark circles under the librarian's eyes, the thought of a child in the stalker's hands seemed to offer her all the adrenaline she needed to continue. Daniella distracted her with various plans, none of which had a chance in hell of working.

But she had to try.

Daniella rubbed her throbbing temples and resisted the urge to throw the journal in front of her across the room. Her attention kept wandering as she read through the old, dusty tomes, and she was certain she'd read the current page at least five times.

What would a vampire do with a child like that?

Surely she wouldn't just kill him. But any alternatives seemed almost worse.

After a quick, late lunch delivered by one of the wolves, Daniella picked up another journal off the pile. The scrawled handwriting was difficult to read, but she managed to get the gist of the story.

"I thought vampires had a terrible sense of smell?"

Cat didn't look up from what she was reading. "Not terrible compared to humans, but pretty far down on the totem pole compared to any other…nonhuman, I guess you'd say."

She frowned at the journal. Was it possible she was misunderstanding the text, or perhaps—like many stories—this one was exaggerated in the telling? "According to this, the vampire tracked an alpha's mate miles by scent."

"I think I read that one. Didn't it say she was bleeding pretty profusely? That the vampire had already injured her?"

It did indeed. "Is that important?"

Cat made a grossed-out face. "There's only one thing vampires can track by scent better than a wolf. Blood."

Gross. "Makes sense—in a really disgusting way."

"Yeah, wouldn't want their prey to get away." She snorted.

Daniella grimaced, but her mind was working overtime. An idea niggled at her brain. An almost certainly terrible one. One that the guys would hate.

"Oh, boy, I know that look." Cat stretched. "On a scale of one to ten, how risky is whatever you're concocting over there?"

She wondered if Cat was a movie fan. "Let's just say the scale now goes up to eleven."

Chapter Six

"No." Erick's tone brooked no argument.

Good thing she was used to that.

"This could work. It's low-risk." Daniella wrapped her arms around herself, wishing she'd brought a heavier jacket to the warehouse. Of course, she hadn't counted on standing outside arguing with Erick and Owen as the sun disappeared behind the mountains.

"Low risk? In what universe?" Owen leaned against the warehouse wall, arms crossed. He didn't hover over her, intimidating her with his size, like Erick did. She appreciated that, but she would have appreciated a little less attitude even more.

"I'm not totally defenseless," she said. Erick snorted, and she seriously considered kicking him in the shin. "I'm light years ahead of a *child*."

That sobered them. Hard fact to argue, but she still felt like a jerk for bringing it up.

"Your plan has...some good points," Erick conceded. "But putting you at risk isn't acceptable."

She glanced at Owen, but he only offered her a grim smile. "Sorry, kitten. No way."

The lack of even a hint of support twisted something painfully in her chest. Sure, she hadn't expected enthusiasm—or, really, even a quick agreement—but their immediate dismissal left a sour taste in her mouth.

"Excuse me, but when did I start giving you two the impression that I'm open to taking orders? You're welcome to skip the plan, but I can damn well do whatever I want to." She stopped short of adding *You're not the boss of me*—just barely. It would be tougher to get them to take her seriously if she sounded twelve years old.

Owen ran his hand through his hair. "You aren't going to drag us into danger unwillingly. And you know that if you're in danger, we'll be right there with you."

Crap. The man knew her too well. "Fine. But let's get one thing straight—if you want this thing with us to work, you will not treat me like a defenseless child."

Owen pushed away from the wall. "Then stop acting like one—"

"Enough." Erick raised a hand, cutting off Owen's retort. Then he turned to her, his eyes a bright green—too bright. "You bring out our protective instincts. You know this."

Daniella swallowed a flippant reply. "I get that. Mostly. But this plan is good. It's workable. Moreover, it's the only one we have."

"Grayson's plan is workable." The prime wasn't forbidding her; that was a start.

"Grayson's plan makes assumptions—ones I don't think we can rely on."

"Explain."

"First, he assumes the hostages, or whatever you want to call them, will be safe until morning. Given the fact she left…pieces of two of them for us already, I don't think that's a safe thing to assume."

Erick frowned, brows creasing. He was thinking about what she said. Good.

"Guessing there's a number two?" Owen still looked unhappy, but at least he wasn't sniping at her.

"Yes. I think it's silly to assume you'll be any safer attacking that hideaway during the day." She paused, waiting for the arguments, but none came. Instead, Owen and Erick exchanged a long look. Damn. They weren't arguing because they knew she was right.

"You could be right," Erick said, echoing her thoughts. "But I still don't see why we need to take such unnecessary risks. There are others who could serve in that capacity just as well."

He didn't look at Owen, but his meaning was clear. Owen's jaw was tense, his shoulders set. It looked like she wasn't the only one who was ready to risk herself to take the stalker down.

She took a deep breath. Explaining this the right way was important. She'd only get one shot at it—she could see that in the way they watched her, the way they both appeared to be on the edge of movement. One way or another, that stalker was going down tonight.

Her way made the most sense. But she had to make them see that.

"I understand why you'd want to send in Owen." She waved at her neighbor turned friend turned mate. "Look at him. An excellent example of a ferocious weretiger, if I do say so myself."

Some of Owen's anger cracked, and the slightest hint of a grin touched his lips. Erick looked like he was making every effort not to roll his eyes. "Indeed. Ferocious being the key word here. He can defend himself in ways you cannot."

It wasn't a crack about her lack of shifting, she knew that. She hadn't even brought up the question of dormancy to them yet. But the words still stung.

"Exactly. And that's why he'd make terrible bait." She gestured to herself. "This? This is prime bait material right here. All scrumptious and obviously lacking in fighting prowess. If I were a stalker on the hunt—one who had lately been showing a predilection for taking weak creatures—I'd snag me over him."

"She grabbed me before," Owen countered.

Daniella nodded and crossed her arms. "Sure she did. Before Erick and the others took out most of her vampy helpers. If she were as confident of those she has left, or her witchy friends, she'd be going for bigger game."

Snap. Argue that one.

Her elation was short-lived.

"No," Erick said, finality in his tone. Behind him, Owen looked grim, but he nodded.

Something inside of her cracked at that immediate refusal. "You'd consider it if I could shift, wouldn't you?"

Erick shrugged. Answer enough.

"Is this why you haven't bitten me?" She didn't mean to ask the question, but she didn't wish it back, either. "Because you're afraid I'm a dormant tiger?"

Erick flinched like he'd been struck.

"That's it, isn't it? You're afraid that I won't be able to shift, so you don't want to lock me down, right? Got to keep your options open." Her voice had risen, and the wolves inside the warehouse could likely hear her. But she didn't care.

"What are you talking about?" Owen asked.

"You think some fear about your shifting is why I haven't bitten you?" Erick said, incredulously, at the same time.

"Isn't it?" She glanced at Owen. "You said it yourself that the prime must mate with a royal. What if I'm not really a royal?"

"You think that I would let you go simply because you might not be able to shift?" Erick shook with anger, and her foot slid back, her body automatically reacting to the heat in his gaze. He took a deep breath, and some of the tension faded from his expression. "I'm not angry with you. Please don't look at me like that."

How was she looking at him? Like a scared rabbit, no doubt. She schooled her own expression. Erick wasn't going to hurt her—she knew that.

"I'm not angry with you," Erick said. "But the idea that you thought..." He shook his head.

"The chances of you being dormant are miniscule." Owen closed the distance between them and hugged her. "God, what made you think of such a thing?"

She shook her head, not willing to rat out Leann, no matter how big of an ass she was. Some things she needed to handle on her own.

Owen stepped back, and she turned to Erick. But he wasn't looking at her. Jaw tense and hands fisted at his sides, he looked like he was fighting a battle inside of his own head.

She walked up to him and took his clenched fists into her own hands. "I just worried that's why you hadn't—"

"No. I didn't bite you because I wanted to give you time. Make sure you were ready." His hands closed around hers, and he tugged her closer. Anger still touched his expression when he looked down at her, but there was something else there, too. Sadness?

Her chest constricted, and she squeezed his hands. "I'm sorry."

"I should be the one to apologize, for not making myself clear," he said. Fiercely intense, his gaze should have scared her, but she found she couldn't look away.

"Even if such a thing happened. Even if by some strange twist of fate, you were never able to shift, it wouldn't matter. You. Are. Mine."

A warm body pressed against her back, and Owen took a deep breath, nuzzling her hair. "Ours."

"I love you," she murmured. "I love you both so much."

Erick kissed her softly, and Owen pressed a soft kiss on her neck. A peck, from both of them, but so sweet her heart hurt.

"But that doesn't mean I don't need you guys to trust me."

She saw the acceptance in Erick's eyes before he spoke, and it meant she was actually going to have to go through with her crazy plan.

"After this is over, I will be biting you, wildcat. And thinking of many other ways to make sure you understand how I feel about you. Tell us your plan again," Erick said. Behind her, Owen muttered a curse.

The alley was dark and dirty. Small bits of trash littered the area, but the smell was the worst part. Rotten food, and other things she didn't want to think about. Her hand moved to touch the whistle tucked under her shirt, but she dropped it to her side.

"Did we have to start in the dirtiest place in the suburbs?" Daniella muttered. Of course, that had been pretty important—and part of her plan. But it was still unpleasant.

Cat grimaced. And Daniella wondered if it was even worse for her. Sure, her senses had seemed to get sharper in the past couple of weeks, but she had nothing on a tiger who'd had the benefit of training to hone her senses her whole life.

"You ready?" Cat asked. The way she held the knife, knuckles white from her tight grip, Daniella was almost afraid she would hurt herself.

"As ready as I'll ever be to get stabbed." she joked.

Cat looked like she was about ready to throw up. Daniella held out her arm, but Cat just stared at her skin.

Maybe asking a friend to cut you was more of a one year minimum of friendship kind of thing. Gently, she took the knife from Cat's rigid fingers.

"I'll do it," Daniella said. "Gimme."

Cat cleared her throat, but she didn't fight her for the knife. "Sorry. I didn't think I'd be so squeamish."

She snorted. "You not wanting to stab me is totally okay with me."

Cat laughed, but the sound was more than a little hysterical.

"Tigers heal faster than humans, right?" she asked, voice a little too high to sound as joking as she'd hoped. Silly. There was a vampire out there who'd love to get her hands on her—one she was presently trying to lure in with her own blood—and she was worried about a little wound?

Her hand shook as she pressed the sharp blade against her tender skin. Before she could lose her nerve, she struck.

A series of expletives escaped her lips at the sharp pain, but she gritted her teeth and forced the knife all the way down her forearm.

Cat's eyes widened, and she didn't seem able to look away from the blood pooling on Daniella's skin.

"Sorry," she muttered. "I don't usually curse like a sailor."

Cat managed a grin. "Don't be. If I had some paper, I'd be taking notes."

She chuckled nervously. Then she did her best to spread the blood around the area. Her stomach twisted, and bile crawled up her throat at the sight of her blood being splashed around the alley. It wasn't that much blood, not really. But the sight was unnerving.

"Good enough, you think?"

Cat nodded, and pushed up her glasses. Her throat contracted in a hard swallow.

"Don't throw up," Daniella said, only half-kidding. "You'll cover up the scent of the blood."

Cat's eyes widened as if she hadn't even considered that, and she nodded.

"Good. Time to go, then."

They didn't move at a leisurely pace, but they didn't run, either. The point wasn't to get away—just to get far enough away. To get to the nice open space they'd planned on so the vampire would be able to see that they were truly alone.

Heart pounding in her chest at the thought, she tried to keep her fear off her face.

"I still think you should have stayed with the wolves." Daniella left her wound open and uncovered—letting droplets of blood make their trail on the asphalt.

Beside her, Cat's gaze danced across her path—watching for danger they had little hope of stopping even if they did see it before the danger saw them. "And let you have all the fun?"

Daniella was nervous—more than nervous. She'd never been so scared in her life. But she trusted Erick and Owen. She trusted Grayson. She knew that they were doing what needed to be done. The fact of the matter was, no one could guarantee anyone's safety—

not in this. But the lives of the innocents were worth the risk. Making sure that the stalker didn't get her claws into the city of Denver—thus making the lives of all the nonhumans in the area miserable for the foreseeable future—was worth it.

Too bad that knowledge didn't make her heart stop trying to thump its way out of her chest.

She couldn't wimp out now. Not after she'd convinced Erick and Owen that she could handle this. That kind of trust—she knew it didn't come easy for either of them. They hated it. Her risking her life. But they knew her idea was the best one they had, and they trusted her to do her part. Like an equal partner.

The gift was precious—every instinct inside of them must have fought against them agreeing to this plan. She couldn't even express how that made her feel in her own thoughts—she certainly hadn't expressed it well to the men before they'd gone their separate ways.

She only hoped she got a chance to tell them before all this was over.

Tears pricked against her eyes at the thought, and she started to walk faster. She forced herself to take a deep breath and let it out slowly—easier to do now that they'd put a little distance between themselves and the stinky alley. This wasn't the time to get emotional—she needed to stay aware of her surroundings.

They had to be ready.

After less than a minute of walking, Daniella stopped. The parking lot was wide open and free of places for anyone—or anything—to hide. It would make the fact that they were alone obvious.

Minutes passed. She resisted the urge to chatter nervously at Cat—it would be too easy to slip and give something away.

Fear crept up her spine, leaving goosebumps in its trail. And from the darkness she heard a soft thump. Slowly, she turned.

Moonlight bathed the empty parking lot. Just enough light to illuminate a shapely woman's form.

Daniella's first thought was that this couldn't be the stalker that pursued them. That perhaps they'd happened upon some poor human in the wrong place at the wrong time. But the woman's head tilted, as if she were listening. Her movements were slightly off—too precise for a human. Too strange.

She stepped closer, close enough that Daniella could make out delicate, pretty features in the moonlight. Then she smiled, revealing tiny, sharp teeth. Despite the teeth, she was pretty. Beautiful, even. Not at all what Daniella had expected—not that she really had a clear expectation in mind.

Next to her, Cat inhaled sharply.

The stalker's lips curled into a wider smile. "What delicious bait for such a terrible trap."

Chapter Seven

"But terrible trap or no, I'm happy to take the bait with me," the stalker said, voice mocking. Her head tilted again, her expression quizzical. "Did you really hope to take me by yourselves, or that you might be able to escape me by running?"

She could hear Cat's panicked breathing next to her, but she ignored it. She had to focus. "Splashing around the blood was too obvious, huh?"

The stalker's eyes narrowed. "Just a bit."

"Next time I go vampire hunting, I'll try to be more subtle." Daniella went for laid-back and uncaring in her tone, but it sounded false, even to her own ears.

The stalker's eyes narrowed. "Next time? How optimistic of you."

"This isn't a trap, exactly—as you can probably tell." Daniella gestured to the empty parking lot. "It's a negotiation."

"Exactly what do you have to negotiate with?"

The stalker was playing with her, moving closer even as Daniella fought the urge to run away. To her side, Cat edged away. This would be easier if the stalker couldn't see what the librarian was doing.

"Myself, of course." Daniella turned and walked

a couple feet away from Cat, trying to appear casual. Turning her back on the stalker made her stomach twist with tension, but she didn't have a choice. But the stalker didn't take the opportunity to jump her—likely because she knew Daniella would be just as easy to take down even if she was facing her. "I'm sure a royal tiger is worth more than a few innocents to you."

The stalker raised a perfect brow. "A royal, you say?"

"So I'm told."

"And why would a *royal* offer herself in place of a few useless wolves?"

Huh. Did she not realize that the werecoyotes had come to Grayson after the stalker took one of their children? They'd been told not to, but surely she suspected they would ignore that edict. Or, perhaps she did know, and was just messing with Daniella.

It didn't matter. All that mattered was keeping her distracted long enough for Cat to get the signal out.

"What can I say? I've got a hero complex." Daniella tapped her chin. "I'd say a heroine complex, but that sounds way too druggy."

Just out of the stalker's peripheral vision, Cat raised her own whistle to her mouth. Hope surged in Daniella's chest.

Back in the necessarily stinky alley, Erick waited. Huddled inside of the dumpster, dealing with smells Daniella couldn't even begin to imagine, he listened intently for that whistle. The man had had to arrive a couple of hours before Daniella and Cat—so that there would be no danger of the vampire scenting him—so he had to be more than ready to escape that stinky box. But he would stay put until the whistle sounded. It was a risk, Daniella knew that, but tigers had very good ears.

The stalker was on Cat the second the whistle

touched her lips, and so quickly that Daniella didn't even see her move. One second, Cat was inhaling to blow, the next, she was flying across the parking lot.

The vampire turned to face Daniella.

Shit.

Struggling to pull the whistle out of her clothes, she knew she'd be too late. Sure enough, the stalker was on her before she could even find the string that held it around her neck. She braced herself, but the stalker didn't touch her, save the barest brush of her skin against Daniella's neck when she tore the whistle off.

"Nice try—how far away is your backup hidden? Too far, I think." The stalker sounded like she didn't particularly care either way.

"Not worried?"

The stalker moved in close—she was a couple of inches shorter than Daniella, but she had to fight the urge to shrink away.

"No. You are a prize worthy of a small risk."

"If you say so. I can't even shift." She struggled to keep her eyes on the stalker instead of trying to see if Cat was okay. If either of them were going to get through this, she had to find an opening—any opening.

It wasn't the best idea to confide in the stalker her weakness, but the words had just come out. Keeping her busy was more important than keeping secrets, anyway.

Something moved at the edge at Daniella's vision, too far away in the darkness for her to make out anything. Her pulse jumped. Of course the stalker wouldn't come alone.

She had to get that whistle. Cat was still crumpled on the ground. God, she hoped she was okay.

"Enough talk. Time for you to come with me."

"Isn't that going to be tough if your new home

is overrun with werewolves?" Daniella asked. She managed to keep her gaze from darting down the street, looking for rescue. It would be pointless, anyway. Rescue wasn't coming until she blew that whistle.

The vampire lunged without warning. Daniella dropped to the ground to avoid the stalker, but the woman caught one of her arms in a painful grip. As quickly as she could, Daniella reached into her pocket and pulled out the small defense she'd brought. Closing her eyes, she held her breath and sprayed.

The stalker dropped her, falling back into a fit of coughing. Daniella crab-walked backwards, coughing despite the fact that she'd held her breath.

Pepper spray worked on vampires. Good to know.

She turned to run, but the vampire grabbed her hair, halting her movement and pulling out no small amount of her ponytail.

"You bitch!" The vampire's voice was garbled and hoarse.

She opened her mouth to scream, but the sound was cut off when the stalker tossed her several feet. She rolled into a ball, a pitiful defense against the assault she knew would come.

The temptation to get up and at least try to run was fierce. But she couldn't do that—not when she didn't know if Cat was okay. No way was she running and leaving someone she cared about in danger again.

Seconds later, the choice was taken out of her hands. The stalker grabbed her, plucking her from the ground with a single hand. Mouth wide, she struck.

She prepared herself for pain, but none came.

The stalker was gone.

Daniella fell to the ground again, landing hard on

her butt. Eyes bleary from her close proximity to the pepper spray, she wiped at them with her sleeve.

Erick stood over the stalker, his eyes a blaze of light. Then, his form twisted, shifting strangely and so quickly she could barely track the movement.

He was no longer Erick.

Where the man had stood, a gigantic tiger crouched. Keeping himself between her and the stalker, he didn't turn to look at her; his eyes were locked on his enemy.

The stalker went to her feet, any semblance of humanity lost in the very inhuman movement.

They sparred. Her tiger and the stalker. Daniella fumbled for her phone, hoping that Owen was close. Hoping that he'd brought backup. He hadn't been able to stay with Erick because the stalker might sense him close by and not take the bait Daniella offered. And the wolves had—rightly so—been focused on getting the innocents out. But one of the wolves, along with Owen, were ready to close in if needed.

From the shadows, more forms moved, approaching quickly. Not Owen.

Vampires.

The stalker hadn't come alone.

Erick would have a hard enough time with her, let alone fighting others. She jumped to her feet, phone pressed against her ear. No one answered. The other vampires closed in, grappling with Erick.

Shit.

They held him, wrestled him to the ground. The stalker wiped blood from her mouth and bared her fangs.

She was going to bite Erick.

"No!" Daniella screamed.

The world narrowed, twisted. A sharp pain radiated

from her chest into her limbs. She couldn't breathe. Blackness descended. She shook it off. Tried to.

She blinked rapidly, taking in a huge breath of air. The world looked off. There was something wrong with her eyes.

The stalker sucked at Erick's neck. And Daniella lunged.

She might not be able to save Erick, but she'd be damned if she didn't try.

But her balance was off. Instead of grabbing the stalker, she flew too far, too fast, and hit her with the full force of her body. The two vampires that held Erick flew, and the stalker rolled out from under Daniella's claws and hopped back to her feet.

Claws.

Daniella stared down at her hands. No—her feet. Her furry, clawed feet.

Someone cried out her name. Owen, she thought, still unable to look away from her paws. The pavement seemed to be spinning beneath them.

The world went dark.

Epilogue

Daniella set a hand on her stomach, rocking in her comfortable new chair, and watched the drama unfold.

"It goes in like this," Owen insisted, waving the instructions at Erick.

Erick crossed his arms. "Are you questioning your prime?"

"Damn straight, I am. If you look here," Owen pointed at the page, "you'll see that—"

She lost the fight, bursting into laughter. The men turned to look at her. Neither seemed to see the humor in the moment.

"Is this funny to you, mate?" Erick deadpanned.

"I find this hilarious." She grinned. "Take out a stalker and save the city—no problem. Share a mate—easy peasy. Have to work together to build a crib—the claws come out. Thank goodness I haven't brought any Ikea furniture up here, yet."

The men glared at her, the twinkle in their eyes and the grins tugging at their lips belying their glares.

She pushed up from the chair. "Fine, fine. Don't let me interject any logic here. Please, continue squabbling without me." As one, they moved to help her up, and she batted them away. "Stop that. I'm barely showing. I don't need help to get up." *Yet,* her mind added, most annoyingly.

The men returned to the crib, and she walked out to the living room and grabbed her cell phone. Then she typed in a text message.

Save me.

A moment later, Cat's reply came through.

Oh, dear. What now?

Daniella grinned. Now that things had settled down, she didn't mind being stuck for the foreseeable future at the clan's stronghold. But there were times when she needed to escape with her new friend slash co-conspirator.

Three months had passed since she'd helped take down the stalker seeking to take over Denver. Three months of unadulterated bliss.

Luckily, no one had been killed during the skirmish with the vampires or the witches. A couple of Grayson's people had been badly injured, and few of the people fighting the vamps had come away with a new scar or two, but everyone had survived.

It was a better result than she'd dared hope.

Cat had been the most gravely injured of the tigers—her and Erick. But tigers, Daniella discovered, healed quickly. Thankfully, so did wolves. The two civilians bore the worst of it after the stalker had maimed them, but they were alive, and that was something.

Best of all, they'd saved the werecoyote child before the stalker had done anything more than frighten him.

And to Daniella's surprise, things were settling down among the tigers, as well. Apparently saving their prime with her last second surprise shift—not to mention proving she could shift into a full tiger—made her outsider origins far less of an issue. Sure, the shifting thing was still…well, she was working on it. She'd get it down with enough practice. Or so her mates insisted.

And she was pregnant.

Not exactly something she'd planned on so soon, but she was ridiculously happy about it. They weren't sure whose it was, but she couldn't have cared less. Best of all, neither of her mates seemed to care either.

A buzz from the counter pulled her from her thoughts.

"Erick, phone," she called.

Something clunked to the floor, and Owen cursed. She covered a grin as Erick strode out and grabbed his cell phone off the counter.

"What?" he said.

Ah, the man had a way with words. It probably shouldn't strike her as adorable, but it did.

He went still, attentive. And the hairs on the back of Daniella's arms stood at attention. She watched him for any sign of what was happening on the other end of the line, but despite her improved hearing, she couldn't make out much other than the fact that he was speaking to a man. And Erick, like usual, revealed nothing of his emotions.

"Yes," Erick said. Then he hesitated. "It is…good to hear from you."

"Who was that?" she said, after he hung up.

Erick frowned, and worry creased his brows. "My brother, Nicolas. He's in trouble."

Sneak Peek of
Broken Prime

Read the prequel to Evie and Nicolas's story today!

When Evie loses her way in the woods during a terrible storm, she is determined not to die. But snow and darkness close in and all seems lost—until a stranger finds her. Warm and safe at his cabin, she can't help notice how sexy her rescuer is, and things go from warm to scorching hot.

But Nicolas lives alone on the mountain for a reason. And his secrets may be more dangerous to Evie than the cold.

Broken Prime is currently available on Amazon, or continue reading for an excerpt.

vie Lane refused to die at twenty-one.

Panic pushed her pace to a jog, but though the whited-out landscape flew by faster, nothing looked familiar. Snow continued to fall, and she cursed loudly, blinking back tears that threatened to burn their way down her cheeks.

So stupid to tell the others to go ahead on their snowshoe trek. The sun had been out, the cabin smoke clearly visible in the sky, and she hadn't realized there was zero cell service to be found. If she'd done what she'd said, taken a few pictures and caught up with her friends a little ways down the trail, things would have been fine. But she'd gotten distracted. Found a few shots she couldn't resist. Decided to wait a little longer until the sun was perfect in the sky, providing just the right angle to the light.

And then the sun disappeared.

The storm rolled in so quickly, she'd barely noticed the first cloud on the horizon before the entire sky blotted out. She'd trudged on, even as snow started to fall, in the same direction the other girls had gone. When it got too dark to really see where she was going, she'd relied on their trail in the snow. Then the fresh snow piled high so fast that the trail disappeared, and she wasn't even sure she was headed the right direction.

She forced a deep breath, then shivered violently. The air was cold, and her feet colder. She'd lost a glove at some point when she was still taking pictures, and her pocket didn't seem to do much to keep out the chill.

Exhaustion seeped into her as she slowed to a walk.

"Help!" she yelled — or tried to. Her voice was wispy and thin after hours of calling out for her friends.

She crumpled in front of a tree and leaned against the solid wood, putting her face between her knees.

So tired.

The angry howl of the wind around her seemed to insulate her from the world, and for a while, time stood still. Regret filled her. She should have listened to her parents, gone with them to Europe. Might have been stressful, watching them try not to fight in front of her the whole time, but it would have been safe. Heck, she could have stayed at the dorm, used her break to study.

She'd wanted an adventure.

"Hey. Hey?"

Someone shook her, dragging her back into reality. She opened her eyes. The area around her was almost as dark as the one behind her eyelids. But she could make out a form, large and human-shaped, kneeling in front of her.

"I'm going to pick you up. Take you somewhere warm."

Her mind moved slowly, and it took a few moments before she comprehended his words. But before she could nod in reply, the man had swept her into his arms and was moving. And either her perception was really messed up because of the cold and her freezing state, or the man moved *fast*.

Acknowledgments

Thank you so much to my readers. Your amazing support humbles me, and I am so thankful for each and every one of you. You're all awesome. :)

And I'm sending a big thanks to my editor, Cindy, for her fantastic work and going above and beyond for me with this series. You rock!

Also by Andie Devaux

Royals
Claiming Their Royal Mate: Part One
Claiming Their Royal Mate: Part Two
Claiming Their Royal Mate: Part Three
Claiming Their Royal Mate: Part Four
Broken Prime

Office Party
The Interview
Customer Satisfaction
Pushing the Limits
The Punishment
Long Term Deal
Office Party: The Bundle

Other Titles
Snowed In
Against the Wall
Office Heat
Sweet Ride

About the Author

Andie writes sexy erotic romance and erotica stories that push boundaries. When she's not writing (or reading!), she can usually be found daydreaming or attempting a new recipe. She thinks that life should require happily ever afters. And since she doesn't make the rules of life, she instead applies this philosophy to the worlds she can control–the ones in her books.

Website:
http://andiedevaux.com/

Newsletter:
http://eepurl.com/MkT1X

Twitter:
@AndieDevaux

Facebook:
https://www.facebook.com/authorandiedevaux

20118128R00183

Printed in Great Britain
by Amazon